MIND THIEF

MINDJACKER SERIES, BOOK TWO

C.A. HARTMAN

5280 PRESS

CHAPTER 1

QUINN RAN AS HARD as she could.

Her lungs ached, her heart pounded, and her legs buckled a little as the deep sand slowed her pace. She trudged up the dune, sweat pouring from her as the midday desert sun scorched her scalp and blistered her skin.

Nobody should brave the open desert in midday. In today's world, it was suicide.

She let out a frustrated grunt at her slowed pace. For every two steps forward, she lost one to the shifting terrain, and her boots grew heavier and heavier as they filled with sand. The endlessly tall dune got so steep that it was easier to get on all fours and scramble up the thing like an animal.

Finally, she crested the hill and flopped down on the other side, along the slope. She lay there catching her breath while she peeked her head over the top of the dune. Nothing but a sea of dunes just like the one she'd climbed, golden and glistening in the heat as far as the eye could see. Then, she saw them.

Four of them—in all black, bodies as fit as athletes—heading her way. Gaining on her.

Fuck.

Quinn got up, her throat dry as she began running again. She kept to the ridge so she could get some distance from them, looking for a place to hide. But there was nowhere to hide in the desert. No trees, no shrubs, no rocks or houses or sheds. And no winds that day to erase her obvious footprints. Only the burning inferno of a sun, and her enemies.

There had to be a way out.

But there wasn't, and within minutes the four Black Jays caught up to her and grabbed her, taking her down to the sand that burned her backside.

"Fuck you," she seethed at them. "You're not getting shit from me."

"We'll see about that," said the one with the leering smile. Another placed nodes on her head while the two others held her down, making her struggle pointless. Then the desert faded to nothing.

Now she was somewhere Downtown. In an alley, between brick buildings, the stench of stale beer and rotting garbage permeating her nostrils. When she turned around, she found she wasn't alone. A guy—big, muscular, tattooed—stood there, staring at her, hatred in his pale eyes.

He came after her, getting closer and closer. She deployed the usual defenses and tools, including her brass knuckles, but he saw them all coming and blocked them until he was millimeters from her.

He yanked her by the hair. "Do as I say, bitch, or I'll kill you."

Quinn ignored the threat. No way would she give in without a fight.

Die with your boots on, as Wyatt used to say.

She elbowed him in the gut, getting ready to go for the nuts next. But he was too quick for her and blocked her attack, then punched her. Then again. Pain radiated through her head as he knocked her around and swore at her... until he began yanking at her clothing. Panic struck along with revulsion, and Quinn began screaming and thrashing like a wild animal, scratching at him and trying to gouge, bite, or kick anything she could.

No!

But he would not stop.

He warned her again, and she refused to quit fighting. Then she felt it, the pain that took her breath away, from the knife he'd gutted her with. And everything went black.

When Quinn opened her eyes, her heart was pounding like crazy. But she wasn't in the alleyway, or the sand dunes. She was inside a white room. Maybe a hospital.

Then she remembered the stabbing. She reached down to feel her gut, wondering just how torn up it was. But she felt only smooth skin.

"You're fine, Hartley. Nobody stabbed you."

She blinked a couple of times and looked over to find a pair of intelligent, piercing blue eyes watching her. A mixture of sympathy and amusement danced in them.

Remi.

She looked around at the now-familiar room with no windows and nothing but an open cabinet filled with technical equipment. She was at the Protectorate's headquarters, and the nightmare she'd just lived was nothing more than a simulation.

"Damn," she muttered. "That was the mindfuck of mind-fucks. What the hell, man?"

"That's what you need to be prepared for." Remi removed the nodes from the base of her skull.

She sat up on the cot, the air conditioning cooling her sweat and reassuring her she was safe. "But going down two layers like that? Getting assaulted and stabbed? It wasn't like the others, Remi. It was so real I forgot I was in training."

"That's the point. With the Black Jay threat, you need to be prepared. For clients with top-notch training to prevent mind invasion... even for being jacked yourself. You started to drown and I had to pull you out."

"But... how do I even fight something that powerful, something that hijacks my own fear centers?"

"Same as always. You find a way to combat the fear."

"Go to my happy place?"

Remi took a swig of water before gathering the equipment. "That, among other forms of mental control. All of which you're capable of."

"I never even got that far."

"You will next week."

Next week. Ugh. "You sure about that?"

Remi gave her a look. "The mind is nothing but neurons conducting electrical impulses. It's your slave, not your master."

"But—"

"It's no different, Quinn. It's just the next step."

Quinn said nothing, skeptical. Almost drowning in a flood of thoughts and images was one thing, as were the other tricks targets used to prevent being mindjacked by people like her. But to target *her* limbic system? *Her* amygdala? "Come on, Remi. We've never seen anything of this nature in all these years. Our data from Borelli and Gary Linden showed no signs of this kind of thing."

"You need to be prepared for the worst."

Then she had an even darker thought. "But what if it doesn't work? What if no matter how much we train, there's always a level that will crush us? What if the control they get is so good... so real... so right in your amygdala centers that you can't fight it? What if no happy place is happy enough?"

Remi eyed her. "Then stop fighting it."

Quinn gaped at him. "You can't be serious! There isn't a protocol for that situation?"

"No. No one's ever been in that situation. No one with our training, anyway." He paused, a crease in his forehead, one that didn't make Quinn feel any better. "We're still figuring out how to deal with this new threat. But, my view is... stop fighting what you can't fight. At this level, it's about control over your own mind. When you were being attacked in that simulation—"

"By you."

"—by me, it was nothing but your mind playing tricks on you. No one stabbed you. I never touched you. You have control. You can choose to stop fighting, if you want to."

Quinn squelched a scoff. Stop fighting? Right. Like she would ever do that. Like she would ever give in and let some assailant control her, even if only in her mind. It went against everything she'd ever been taught. Because she knew. If you gave in once, if you stopped fighting, then they had you.

Remi motioned toward the door. "Time's up. I've got another agent to torture at eight." He gave her an inscrutable smile.

Quinn gathered her things and headed toward the door.

"See you in a week," Remi called after her.

"And not a moment sooner, Remi."

Quinn emerged from the back door of Protectorate headquarters, relieved to get away from Remi and the rest of them and take in her familiar city—the heat emanating off the tall glass buildings and asphalt roads, the sounds of traffic, the smell of dust in the air. As she headed deep underground to catch the train, images from her training session still haunted her.

Being chased, jacked, stabbed. Feeling every sensation—the heat, the anger, and most of all, the fear. It was nothing like she'd ever experienced, in training or in the field. If the Black Jays could conjure up anything remotely close to that, the Protectorate had its work cut out for it. And so did she.

The Protectorate needed to train Quinn and the rest of the agents to deal with what had become a menacing threat: the Black Jays. Tier One jackers in particular had to undergo grueling simulations that made any previous training seem like nothing but fun. She'd expected difficulty, even drowning, but wasn't remotely prepared for the shit show that went on today.

Weeks had passed since that terrible night at the Lindens' home, when they'd discovered the Black Jays were behind the Borelli job. They'd been the men in black who'd tried to kill Quinn and Jones and who'd murdered Gary Linden, his wife, and restauranteur Tony Borelli. The Protectorate had cancelled all jobs to focus on training their agents to deal with this new enemy. It had also deployed its special ops agents to conduct field research on the Jays, and information was trickling in now.

The Protectorate, and everybody who worked for them, still had no idea who this enemy was, where they were headquartered, or what their mission was. So far, it appeared that their mission was nothing but mayhem and violence. But Quinn knew they must have some goal driving them. They were too well-organized and well-trained to be nothing but thugs looking to hurt people.

Quinn's phone rang, interrupting her obsessive thoughts. Yolanda.

"Good evening," she greeted her boss.

"Quinn," Yolanda said, her voice neutral as usual, making it tough to determine whether the call would bring good news or bad. With Yolanda, either was possible.

"What's up?"

"Remi briefed me on your training."

"And?" Quinn held her breath.

"You have more work to do."

Quinn sighed. She didn't need Yolanda to tell her that. "And?"

"And I need you to do that work."

"I plan to—"

"Starting tomorrow."

Quinn's stomach roiled at the thought of going back there so soon. "I need more recovery time, Yolanda. It was... intense."

"We don't have more time."

"Why not?"

A pause. "We've got an important job coming down the pipe now. It's an extremely high-profile client, and it may offer us some intel on the Black Jays. I want you and Jones to take the lead on the job."

Excitement coursed through her. A high-profile client. And they wanted her and Jones, despite her being the newest Tier One agent. "That's great! I'm—"

"I won't authorize it unless I know you're ready."

Quinn's excitement waned. "Tell me more about the job."

"Not yet. Keep working with Remi and wait to hear from me."

Quinn nodded. "Will do. And... thank you. For the opportunity."

"Don't thank me yet. Show me you're ready."

Yolanda hung up.

CHAPTER 2

QUINN GRABBED the serpent-shaped handle of Sidewinder's giant wooden door and gave it a tug. The air conditioning felt like a relief, despite it being well into October, when El Diablo's temperatures had simmered down to the low one-hundreds. Which felt downright comfy after another summer from hell in Devil's Town.

In the center of the room sat a square bar, surrounded by tables. The walls were covered in murals of giant painted snakes with scales that gleamed and sparkled with plastic jewels. The dive was unpretentious enough for Jones, served diablos with real lime for Quinn, and was roughly equidistant between their two homes.

Quinn looked for Jones, expecting that his large, heavily-tattooed form would be easy to spot this far north in Downtown. But the place was packed and she had to weave through a crowd until she finally found him at a small table in the corner, nursing a freshly brewed root beer. He sat hunched over his beverage, deep in thought. She sank down into the other chair.

"You alright?" she asked.

He nodded.

"Why is it so busy tonight?"

"Demons game. Went into overtime."

She looked around, searching for a server. "I need a drink."

"That bad?"

"Worse."

Jones raised an eyebrow, his shaven head and arms glistening just slightly from the heat. A server wearing skintight snakeskin-printed pants came over to take Quinn's order. When she walked away, Jones's eyes followed her, taking her in.

She could hardly blame him. Lately, her own eyes lingered on certain men for longer than probably necessary. After everything that happened with Noah, she'd given up on meeting anyone, even for short-term company.

"They use them new simulations on you?" Jones asked.

"Oh yeah."

Quinn told Jones about her mental adventure. Jones grimaced at the stabbing part, his hand going to his gut, probably remembering his own very real and recent injury, the one that almost killed him. When the server brought her a diablo so large it took two hands to hold, Jones showed no sign of disapproval.

"New world," he said, "with these assholes in black to contend with."

Quinn took a drink of her diablo. She closed her eyes just for a moment, enjoying the taste of the real thing, now that she could afford it.

"How's the fancy new joint?" Jones said with a quirk of his mouth.

"It's nice... but my neighbors aren't friendly. At all."

Jones scoffed. He didn't seem surprised by that, but Quinn was. She'd figured by getting out of Downtown, she'd leave the attitudes and untrusting looks behind. But, at least so far, the other tenants hadn't taken any interest in her.

"How's Jeffrey?" she asked.

Jones's expression softened. "He's good. But, now that I'm

makin' a little money, I'm lookin' into some of them programs designed for... people like him. My mom could use a break, you know?"

Quinn nodded. "Sounds like a good plan."

"It will be, but we need another job. Soon."

"Looks like one's coming. A good one."

His eyes lit up. "How good?"

"Super high-profile client, I'm told."

"When?"

"Soon."

After she proved herself, apparently. Dread hit her at the prospect of facing Remi again.

Jones eyed her. "Why ain't you excited? The fact that Yolanda's givin' this to us means we're high on their list right now. And we should be, after everything that went down at Linden's place."

After Quinn and Jones saw the Borelli job through to its bitter, violent end at Gary Linden's home, they not only managed to stay alive after being blindsided by two highly-trained mind thieves, they conquered the two attackers and uncovered a conspiracy led by the Black Jays to breach the Protectorate's carefully constructed walls and steal its well-kept secrets.

"Agreed," Quinn said. "We're their favorite pet lizards, and we'll get the good food and terrariums for a while. But..."

"But what?"

"I have to go back tomorrow and do another sim. To prove to Queen Yolanda we can do this."

Jones rolled his eyes. Then his worried expression returned.

"What's bugging you?" she pressed.

"All of it. We still don't know shit about these fucken Jays or what their endgame is. All we know is they're dangerous and they got tech no one else has. Like that night at the Lindens'—my proximity detector was workin' just fine and I didn't get any warning those goons were comin'. Which means they got some kind of blocker that even the jacker cops don't have."

"I'm told we're working on that," she said, taking another swig of her diablo, finally feeling relaxation set in.

"And what about them breakin' into your old place?" Jones went on. "That means they got past that system you rigged."

"It wasn't exactly a top-of-the-line system."

"So? How'd they get around it without you gettin' notified? Assuming it was them..."

Right. Assuming it was them and not Noah, the just-for-fun guy who'd turned into something much more, only to find out he was jacker police. Just when they'd thought the Borelli job nightmare was over, someone had snuck into her old apartment and left two things: a blackbird figurine and her stolen Blue Banner butterfly art, the latter sporting a bullet hole through its center. Had the Jays broken into her old place twice? Noah didn't seem a likely culprit. Yet, the art—and the bullet hole in particular— seemed far too personal for the Black Jays.

"Whoever it was probably knows security systems. Like we do."

Jones sat there for a moment, like he had more to say. "Why'd that cop let us go that night?"

Quinn sighed. That question. She'd hoped it wouldn't come up again, that Jones would just buy her story that everything would be okay. Noah had a weapon trained on them in the alley that night, then let them go. The police report had no mention of two mindjackers at the scene. Maybe Noah's reasons were noble... maybe they weren't. She only knew she didn't want to worry Jones needlessly.

"It doesn't matter."

"He's a fucken cop, Quinn. He could end everything for us, take away our livelihood and throw us into the clink for ten years. Rule number one—don't get dimed."

"Jones, if there were going to be repercussions from that night, we'd have seen them by now."

His eyes narrowed. He knew she was hiding something. "You ain't workin' with the cops, are you?"

"No!"

Jones looked relieved. Collaborating with the police in any way was even worse than getting dimed. It meant not only immediate termination from the Protectorate, but that they would take further measures to punish the traitor. Quinn didn't know the extent of those measures; as far as she knew, no one had made that mistake.

"What if he's waiting?" Jones went on. "Holdin' his cards until he can take the whole pot? You know how them guys work. They're sneaky."

"Stop worrying," she insisted. "The case is closed. They can't trace the weapons to us. They have nothing to put in that pot. Besides, I've moved to a new place under a fake identity. Lots of Tier Ones do that, especially after a dicey job or a brush with the cops. In other words, whoever broke in can't find me and neither can the cops. And no one's bothered me since then."

Jones still frowned.

"Even if the cops try anything, which they won't, I've got an ace in the hole. A really good one. So just trust me, okay?"

Jones said nothing more. Soon, they shifted to less troublesome topics, finished their drinks, and left Sidewinder. Outside, he took a long, vigilant glance around the busy street, like their previous conversation still haunted him.

"Before you go," Quinn said, "I have something for you."

"What's that?"

She reached into her pocket, then eyed his. Once getting tacit permission, she removed the item from her pocket and lowered it into his. Jones furrowed his brow and stuck his hand in. Then, his eyebrows went up. He peeked down to make sure it was what he'd suspected.

An energy weapon. Very difficult to obtain, illegal as hell.

"Holy shit," he said, chuckling. "Where the hell—" Then he figured it out. "You stole it that night at Linden's. I wondered why the police report said they only found one, when I know them assholes each had one."

Quinn smiled. "Mystery solved."

Jones shook his head. "You a wily one, girl."

"Like I said, you have nothing to worry about." She grinned, then waved and jumped into a waiting taxi.

As she watched the city go by, Quinn reflected on their conversation and Jones's concerns. Unlike him, Quinn wasn't concerned about Noah. She had much bigger things to worry about.

Like the Jays. The next training session with Remi. The fact that when it came to this new enemy, they had tons of questions and very few answers. Even more, when that black-clad Jay jacked her that night at the Lindens', she couldn't get anything on him. It was the best blocking she'd ever seen. Better than hers. She'd tried to keep him out, but felt herself losing the battle and beginning to drown, until Jones pulled her out.

That scared her. Especially when the Protectorate had ramped up their simulations to a terrifying level, which told her only one thing: they'd finally encountered an enemy they couldn't beat.

And it was only a matter of time before Quinn would have to face them again.

CHAPTER 3

WHEN THE TAXI turned onto Hillcrest Avenue in Mayfair, Quinn paid the driver and got out. She was struck by how quiet it was compared to Downtown, a quiet she'd never had in her entire life until now. She'd always wanted that kind of calm—an escape from El Diablo's frenzy and furor—but now that she had it, she realized it would take some getting used to.

Still refusing to let any taxi driver know where she lived, she walked several blocks past buildings of glass and stone, the side-walks smooth and the small yards filled with decorative rock and sculpture. Soon, she arrived at the stone apartment building she'd had her eye on for ages. She still couldn't believe she lived here. For so long, she'd admired the building and hoped it would become her home. But despite her never-ending ambition to leave the tribulations of the world she'd come from, part of her never quite believed it would happen.

She punched in her code and entered the lobby, comfortable cool and lined with clean white tile. As she headed to her mail-box, out of the corner of her eye she saw something scurry across the tile. Quinn froze for a moment, her heart pounding. She wasn't used to seeing wild creatures. Not anymore. But when she realized what it was, she smiled.

An iguana. Big, probably twelve inches long, not including its tail. Green with yellow spots, and a spiny ridged back. The reptile ran up to her like it wanted something.

"Lucifer!" came a stern male voice.

Quinn looked up to find a man about her age. He was dressed like a Midtowner, in light-colored slacks and a plain t-shirt, a few inches taller than her at most.

He gave a half-smile. "Don't mind him. I don't usually put him on his leash until we go outside. No one's usually around at this hour on a weeknight."

To sidestep any questions about the strange hours she kept, Quinn kneeled down to get a closer look at the iguana. "That's okay. I love animals."

And she did. She'd never had pets growing up; they were too expensive for most Downtownies. Dogs and cats had fallen out of favor once the climate got too inhospitable for them, and only Uptowners had them. But iguanas, at least some of them, could handle El Diablo's harsh conditions. However, they were very expensive, more expensive than the average Midtowner could afford. She wanted to pet the creature, but knew from experience that he would probably bite her.

She stood up again. "Lucifer, huh?"

He shrugged. "He's a little devil. The name fits." He kneeled down and put on Lucifer's leash. Lucifer immediately went back to Quinn again, as if sniffing her out.

"He likes you."

Quinn grinned. "Then he can be my first friend. I'm new in the neighborhood."

He studied her face. "I didn't think I'd seen you before. I'm Devin." He offered his hand.

Quinn shook it, surprised at what was perhaps her first real conversation with any of the building residents. "Quinn. Good to meet you both."

Devin glanced outside. "I need to get Lucifer outside so he can burn off some energy. Isn't that right, you little bastard?" He turned back to Quinn. "Good to meet you, Quinn."

He made eye contact with her for just a moment, his dark eyes locked with hers in a way that made her blink a couple of times. A guy hadn't looked at her like that in a long time. Like he was studying her, assessing if she was his type.

Quinn shrugged. Didn't matter. It seemed her type was trouble, so it was better to avoid them all.

Devin and Lucifer headed outside, and Quinn noticed that Devin walked with a limp, although briskly enough that it was clear he'd lived with it a long time. No matter how high-tech medicine got, it couldn't solve all problems.

Quinn went to get her mail. She rarely got physical mail anymore and only checked the slot about once a week. Sure enough, the box had a manila envelope, addressed to her and with standard postage, but without a return address. Curious, Quinn tucked it under her arm and headed to the elevator.

Inside her apartment, she set down her mail and removed her two best friends—her brass knuckles and her energy weapon—from her jacket pockets, stowing them in their special hiding place, small locked compartments she'd mounted on the inside of her bed frame. She took off her denim jacket with the El Diablo lettering before stripping down to her undies, waiting for her AC to kick in. More money or not, she wasn't going to waste her hard-earned cash running the AC all day just to put more money in Saguaro Energy's pockets.

Her place was only about six hundred square feet, but that was a mansion compared to the micro-apartment she'd lived in before. The floor tiles were good quality, the apartment was quiet, and, best of all, her window afforded her a view. Rather than the brick wall she used to stare at through the whirring of her fan, now she enjoyed a view of the street, the building across the way, and the sky beyond that.

She poured herself a glass of chilled water and sat down to open her manila envelope, wondering what it could be. The computer-printed label on the front gave nothing away, but a weird part of her hoped it was something from Noah. Something good, like a peace offering. But she shook off that thought, knowing that he had no idea where she lived now, and even if he did he would never send her anything after what happened. She opened the envelope and pulled out its contents.

There were only two items. One was a piece of heavy-gauge cream paper, eight by ten inches. She turned it over; it was a print of a butterfly, artistically rendered and matte black. She couldn't decide if the print was beautiful or frightening. Was it from Noah, sending her a message?

The other item was a note, folded neatly in half on cream card stock. She opened it to find a handwritten message:

Quinn,
I know how much you love butterflies. Here's one just for you.

Why the move? Was your previous Downtown home not secure enough? Or did you think I wouldn't find you?

No matter where you go, I will always find you.

Quinn stared at the note, her blood turning cold and a shiver running through her. She read it again.

The printing was angular and masculine, reminding her of Noah's writing. But it couldn't be.

Could it?

Suddenly feeling underdressed, she put on a t-shirt and dug into the one small box of treasures she saved and brought with her wherever she lived. The contents held no real value, except to her. She pulled out the note Noah had sent her, along with the Blue Banner art, now with a hole right through its center. She compared the two notes.

The handwriting was identical. Even down to the strange little details, like the letter "E" comprised of four different limbs that never quite attached.

What the fuck??

Quinn shook her head, another round of chills running down her arms and out to her fingers.

It couldn't be. Noah had no way of knowing where she lived. Even jacker cops didn't have the means to dig that deep and find her. If they did, they would have dimed and arrested a host of mindjackers by now.

Besides, Noah wouldn't do this. He wouldn't threaten her, stalk her, try to scare her.

Would he?

Quinn took out her energy weapon and set it by her bed. That night she had fitful dreams.

The next morning, Quinn woke up and threw on clothes to run out and get some coffee. She needed a jolt of caffeine if she was going to get through a few hours of reading the endless reports Yolanda had sent her. Everything spec ops had found on the Black Jays so far, in excruciating detail.

As she entered the lobby, she spotted a young woman unscrewing one of the air-conditioning vents. Merritt, one of the maintenance workers who kept the common areas clean and the building in working order.

"Hey Quinn!" Merritt called out, standing up and eagerly walking over to her, like she hadn't seen a soul in days. Her braided red hair tumbled over her desert-brown overalls.

Quinn stopped reluctantly, wanting coffee more than she wanted conversation. "Hey Merritt. More dust in the vents?"

"It never ends." She gestured at the vacuum nearby. "You would think a fancy place like this would have a self-cleaning system, you know what I mean?" She winked.

Quinn smiled. Just then, a pretty woman in a sundress walked past.

"Hey Patricia!" Merritt called out.

Patricia gave a tight smile and a small wave, never stopping before she disappeared out the door. It seemed Quinn wasn't the only one getting the chilly shoulder in the building.

Merritt, unfazed, turned back to Quinn. "By the way, who's the hot guy?"

"What hot guy?" Quinn wondered if Merritt had seen her talking to Devin last night. It had been late, but Merritt seemed to work strange hours.

Merritt gave a knowing smile. "There was some cutie-pie here yesterday, looking for you."

"What did he look like?"

"Tallish. Dark hair, dark eyes. Midtown," she added wryly.

A bad feeling creeped over Quinn. She pulled out her phone, did a quick search on the El Diablo PD site, and downloaded an image. "Is this him?"

Merritt's face lit up. "Yes! That's right, his name was Noah. Who is—"

Quinn put her hands on Merritt's shoulders. "Merritt, did you tell him I live here?"

Her smiled disappeared. "He already knew you lived here—"

"Did you tell him anything?"

"No. I... I just said I didn't know where you were."

Quinn let out a painful sigh, her mind swirling with too many thoughts.

"I'm sorry," Merritt went on. "He was polite. He said he was an old friend and to tell you he stopped by. Is he dangerous? Is he an abuser? I've heard a lot of abusers are cops because they can get away with it—"

"He's... not a good guy. If he ever comes by again, tell him I moved away. And let me know right away, okay?"

Merritt nodded.

Quinn went back upstairs, her coffee forgotten. She studied the note and art again. The more she did, she more she had to face the truth she hadn't wanted to face.

Jones might have been right. It was beginning to look like Noah had sent the threatening message, that he was more dangerous than she'd feared.

And now he knew where she lived.

CHAPTER 4

"GOD DAMN IT."

Jones's face reddened as he heaved the t-shirt he'd been folding at his pillows. Quinn flinched, having momentarily feared he would throw the shirt at her. Jones shook his head, ignoring the rest of the clean laundry pile on his bed.

He turned to her, his eyes dark with anger. "You were involved with that cop? Are you outta your mind?"

"I didn't know he was a cop—"

"Not a cop, Quinn. Fucken jacker police."

"I didn't know, not until that night we got up close and personal with the dumpster."

"And you hid it from me!" He glanced down at the laundry pile, almost as if looking for something else to throw.

"Keep your voice down!" Quinn hissed. "You don't want to upset Jeffrey."

Jones glared at her. "That's why you wanted to talk here, ain't it? 'Cause you knew I'd have to keep a lid on it."

Quinn said nothing. It was partly true. But she also didn't think he would react this badly.

"Why didn't you tell me about this before?" He folded a pair of cargo pants and slapped them on the bed.

"I was planning to. But I thought..." She trailed off, recalling how she'd thought Noah had been gaming her the whole time. "I ended things with him. It was just bad luck—or good luck, depending on how you look at it—that he was the one who broke away from his unit to apprehend us in the alley. When he didn't arrest us, I assumed he was willing to let it go."

"Right," Jones scoffed. "'Cause jacker police are known for forgiving and forgetting." He shook his head, slapping another pair of cargoes on top of the others before he moved on to the t-shirts. "I knew it. I knew it was too good to be true that we got away. I knew that shit would bite us in the ass. Didn't I say that in the hospital?"

"He wouldn't have seen us if I'd done what you told me and left your ass at Linden's. I would've missed him and been long gone, and he would've called you an ambulance right before arresting you and sending you to the clink."

Jones hesitated at that, then dropped his half-folded t-shirt and sat down on the bed. He leaned forward and rested his head in his hands. "I know, okay? I know you risked your ass tryin' to save mine. I just... I got a family dependin' on me. It's gonna be a while till I got shit set up for them... you know, in case anything happens to me. I can't risk gettin' canned or going to prison right now—"

"I know you can't." Quinn sat down next to Jones. "The same job that pushed us forward has also raised the stakes for us. And I'm sorry. If I'd known, I would never have gotten involved with him." She paused. "He can't dime you anyway. He saw you, but he doesn't know who you are. I'll take the fall if it comes to that."

Jones shook his head. "I don't want that. I want you to nail that fucker to the wall. He let us go, and he can't be stalkin' you and messin' with you now that he's had a chance to stew about it all."

Quinn sighed. She stood up, took a t-shirt from the pile, and began folding it. She understood Jones's anger, and his fears. They did have more to lose now. She'd finally reached Tier One and brought Jones along with her, and they'd finally started to enjoy the comfort and safety that came with the higher pay and better jobs. Jones and his family hadn't moved out of White Sands yet—they wanted to choose a location that fit their needs, and Jeffrey's.

The one thing that had brought Quinn comfort was seeing that Noah wasn't crooked, that he hadn't been gaming her and was genuinely surprised to find out she was a mindjacker. So his most recent behavior was unsettling. Having an enemy was one thing, but an enemy with power, whose behavior you couldn't predict, was quite another.

But then again, should she be surprised that Noah hunted her down? After all, like Jones said, he'd had time to stew, to reflect on who Quinn was and what she'd done. To him, she was the enemy, one of the lawless cretins who'd partly crippled his father, and one he'd let go in a moment of weakness. Noah was someone who needed, more than anything, to win. And now, he no longer had a reason to let her get away with being the thing he hated most.

So he would mess with her. And he would do so because he could.

Jones stood up again, and they folded the rest of the laundry in silence. Finally, Jones turned to her.

"You gotta nip this shit in the bud. One way or the other. If he finds you, if he apprehends you... we're both done for and I can't have that."

Quinn nodded. "I know."

Jones grasped the door handle, but hesitated. "You said you got leverage, an ace in the hole. Use it, girl."

He opened the door, and they emerged from the bedroom. Jones's mother Christa sat on the couch with Jeffrey, watching the Demons game. Christa looked over, her face round and soft while being wary and hard at the same time, a combination Quinn often saw in Downtown women over forty. She smiled and came over to shake Quinn's hand.

"It was good to meet you, Quinn. Jones has said nice things about you."

Quinn smiled back, knowing that Jones wasn't feeling any of those things at the moment. "You've raised one hell of a guy, ma'am," she said, grasping her hand.

"His father was one hell of a guy," she replied. "But I guess you know all about losin' a parent too young, don't you?"

Quinn nodded, but said nothing. She didn't let herself think about her mother that often. She looked over at Jeffrey, who was basically a doppleganger for Jones, but without the tats or swagger.

She waved. "Bye Jeffrey! It was great to meet you!"

Jeffrey looked at her for a moment before looking down and away, bringing his fingers to his mouth to chew on his nails.

"It takes a while before he feels comfortable around new people," Christa added.

"I understand. He's a cutie, much cuter than his thuggish brother." She poked Jones, who rolled his eyes.

Christa snickered at that.

Quinn waved goodbye, giving Jones a reassuring nod before she left and started making her way back home.

She thought about her situation. The easiest thing to do was find another partner and release Jones from any liability that came with partnering with her. But then she would only transfer that liability to a new partner, and there was no guarantee Jones would get picked up by another Tier One jacker. Besides, she'd grown fond of Jones. More importantly, she trusted him.

Instead, she would do what it took to keep Jones and his family safe. They hadn't come this far to let some angry jacker cop take away their livelihood. She needed to make it clear to Noah that harassing her had consequences.

And she already had an idea.

CHAPTER 5

Quinn looked around again, her eye on the nearby stair-well. That was her escape if a neighbor happened to emerge from an apartment or the elevator. She tinkered with the security system on the door, hoping it wouldn't take her long to disable.

Fortunately, there wasn't much activity in the building. It was late on a weeknight in Corazon, the "heart" of El Diablo, so-named because the neighborhood was roughly in the center of the city, not because it was particularly warm or caring. Corazon was just another decent Midtown neighborhood, filled with Midtown apartment buildings that housed Midtown people.

People like Sergeant Noah Martinez: jacker police, good lay, and, apparently, harasser of women he believed would cave to his fear-mongering tactics.

Well, fuck him. She grew up Downtown, for crying out loud. She could handle him.

Or so she told herself from the moment she came up with this crazy plan.

Quinn fiddled with the security system for several more minutes, realizing how dependent she'd become on her tech partner for disabling the stubborn things. She wouldn't need to break in at all if Noah hadn't changed the damned entry code since she was last there.

Yeah, she'd surreptitiously watched as Noah entered his code when he brought her home on those three nights. Just in case. Back then, she had no idea who she was dealing with. Neither did he.

Suddenly, she heard voices, then the fatal click of a door handle. Quinn quickly darted around the corner and into the stairwell. It was hot and stifling inside, reminding her of her former home and its sweltering, stuffy hallways.

After hearing the ding of the elevator, the voices disappeared. Quinn tiptoed out and resumed what she was doing. Finally, the security console lights went dark. She looked up and down the hallway one last time before she opened the door and entered Noah's place, reengaging the security system before she closed the door quietly.

It looked like she remembered. Neat, nice but unpretentious furniture, a single piece of art—a painting of a baseball glove with a ball inside—hanging next to a bookshelf. It smelled clean and masculine. Like Noah.

She tiptoed around, making sure he wasn't there. She'd staked the place out earlier and waited for him to leave, knowing he headed to work and wouldn't return home until evening.

Being there brought back a flood of vivid memories, every one of which she batted away like a persistent fly.

She went to the bookshelf, expecting a collection of crime fiction or books on baseball lore. But instead she found a series of textbooks, the kind educated people kept, with titles like *Essentials of Criminal Justice* and *Justice in Today's World* and *The Politics of Water Rights*. Quinn sighed. It was just one of many things she'd liked about Noah. Until she learned what kind of guy he really was.

She sat down on Noah's comfortable couch and planned her next steps.

Under no circumstances would she let Noah terrorize her or threaten what she and Jones had spent most of their twenty-eight years working their asses off to achieve... merely because he liked to "win." Yeah, he had dirt on her. He knew she was a mindjacker and had pretty much caught her and Jones redhanded that night after the debacle at the Linden home. That wasn't good.

But she had dirt on him, too. He let them go, for one thing, something she was sure his superiors wouldn't enjoy hearing. Especially after finding out Noah had engaged in a romantic little affair with her. For which she had proof, including the butterfly art and the handwritten note, both covered in his fingerprints.

Or, if that didn't impress them, maybe the more recent art and note filled with threats would, showing that Noah wasn't the justice-seeker he pretended to be. And even if EDPD's Division of Mind Invasion was crooked and didn't care about her procured evidence, she felt pretty confident the media would gobble it up, which meant taking down Noah's entire department and its reputation with it.

"Dumbass," she muttered. "All you had to do was leave it alone. I was willing to. But no... you have to *win*."

All she had to do now was wait for Noah to come home from work, let her weapons and the element of surprise work in her favor, and kindly explain to Noah that threatening or otherwise bothering her in any way was not in his best interests.

He would have little option but to agree. Pissed off at her or not, needing to win or not, Noah would make the choice that meant preserving his job and the reputation of his unit. That, she knew.

As the evening wore on and the sun disappeared, Quinn sat there, growing more and more restless as the time she expected him home grew near, then passed. She'd prepared for this, knowing that someone like Noah wasn't a homebody and wouldn't spend an evening sitting around his apartment drinking beer and watching baseball. She'd wanted to be there in case he did, though. But as time wore on, past dinnertime and well into evening, she grew more and more antsy. Sitting around wasn't her thing either.

Especially when she needed something to get her mind off that day's training session with Remi, which was nearly as terrifying as the first. She'd been more aware of what was happening this time, but the attack on her fear centers was as real as before... and just as crippling.

Maybe this was a mistake. Noah was powerful, and here she was breaking the law and trespassing on the property of someone who could easily take her all the way down for at least a decade. She was powerful too, but Noah had the city and the law on his side.

She paced, wondering if she shouldn't leave, shouldn't go with a more conventional plan, like cornering him somewhere in the city, where he couldn't do anything about it. Just as she began gathering her things, she heard the elevator ding. It sounded close, like it was on this floor. Then footsteps and the light swishing of fabric growing closer.

When Quinn heard beeping as Noah entered the security code on his door, a rush of adrenaline ran through her. It was on.

Quinn secured her brass knuckles on her left hand and her energy weapon in her right. She knew Noah would challenge her, would probably test her to see how serious she was about using it. Oh, she would use it alright. She knew just where to aim that thing, and how hard to press, to ensure the injuries were bad enough to temporarily hobble him.

The door opened and she heard footsteps on the tile. Quinn raised her weapon and got ready to recite her greeting. A figure entered the apartment. Long, dark hair. Red dress.

A woman.

Quinn quickly ducked behind the chair before the woman could turn around and spot her. She heard the clicking of heels, followed closely by the louder, heavier sound of a man's footsteps.

"Oh, my goodness," a feminine voice said in a flattering tone. "What a nice place."

"Thanks," Noah said.

Quinn muttered a silent curse as she heard the door close. She couldn't do anything now. She couldn't have some witness seeing her face, ruining her plans. Ruining her life.

Fuck. She'd never considered that Noah would bring someone home. As if she were the only one he'd ever brought there.

Quinn remained squatted down and perfectly still. Her legs burned from kneeling in the same spot, not wanting to budge even a millimeter, knowing that Noah would hear and the jig would be up.

"Can I get you something?" Noah asked.

There was no answer. Only the sound of two people embracing, breaths heavy and followed by the sound of more swishing clothing, the pop of buttons, the thuds that followed after shoes were kicked off.

When the sounds began to fade, Quinn guessed they'd ventured into Noah's bedroom. This was the one and only chance she would have of escaping her ill-considered plan and getting the fuck out of there. And she had to do it quietly.

Quinn waited for the bedroom sounds to grow more energetic. It had to be now. She finally peeked her head around the chair and eyed the door. Crouched low, she made a beeline for it, opening it quickly and tiptoeing into the hallway. She pulled it closed with all the patience and finesse she could muster, then sprinted into the stairwell and barreled down the steps to the lobby.

When she arrived, she peeked out the door again, in the tiny chance that Noah had pursued her and managed to arrive by elevator already. No sign of him.

She exited the door and emerged into the hot night, and began to run.

CHAPTER 6

WHEN QUINN STEPPED off the train in Westgate station, she made a face at the unique blend of body odor, garbage, and cannabis she was long-familiar with but had never grown used to, made even more pungent by the weak air conditioning the Downtown train stations were known for. The odor seemed more noticeable now, flooding her with reminders of everything she'd grown up with, and left behind.

As she walked down the street in her sundress and sunshades, people stared at her and she suddenly felt out of place in her Midtown duds. She liked the new clothes, but more than that she liked that they made her look less like her old self, the one that Noah or some other enemy would immediately recognize.

The glutted traffic, the smell of grilled meat, and the constant rattle of cheap AC units welcomed her back to the place where she'd grown up. To her surprise, it felt strangely comforting.

Out of nowhere, a memory popped into her mind of Noah guessing where she'd grow up. Guessing correctly.

Then a more recent memory surfaced: last night's debacle at Noah's, where she listened to Noah pleasure some other woman while she watched her carefully-considered plan evaporate before her eyes like a puddle of water on the desert floor. She groaned as a feeling of stupidity washed over her.

Even worse, a flash of jealousy hit her for a moment, before she remembered that this was the guy who'd decided to take this game to the next level.

Don't think about that. Think about Plan B, how the hell you're going to get your hands on that wily coyote of a cop and make sure he stops harassing you.

She turned the corner and waited at the intersection. Soon, a little black taxi arrived, and a vaguely familiar face glanced out the window at her. Instead of getting inside, she walked over to the driver's side. He opened his window, looking annoyed.

Quinn held out a wad of cash. He frowned and looked at it for a moment.

"What's the story, lady?" he said. "You said you was lookin' for a ride."

"You gave me one once, from Midtown. I skipped out on you for the lot of it, and this is what I owe you, plus a little extra."

He stared at Quinn for a moment, chomping on his gum. Then his face changed, like he finally remembered driving her to Coyote after she'd spent the night in a Midtown alley after dropping a near-dead Jones at Midtown General. He took the wad, quickly thumbing through it to see how much was there. Quinn gave the car a couple of quick raps before she turned and left.

A few blocks later, she arrived on a familiar street. Women with bright-colored hair and men with bright tattoos loitered around, eyeing her like she didn't belong.

"Midtown princess," one quipped as she walked by.

Quinn reined in any temptation to give them some Downtown attitude, unsure whether to feel contemptuous of their judgment or annoyed at being called a moniker she'd used in that same tone during her younger years. She didn't know whether to feel disgust at their pettiness, or impressed that they showed pride in themselves the only way they knew how.

When she arrived at an industrial-looking building, she pressed the buzzer for 112.

"Yeah," came the flat, gruff voice.

"It's Quinn."

At her dad's place, the baseball game played on TV as Joe Hartley stood up from his favorite chair. He muted the sound as she handed him the bag—burritos from Chubby's and a six-pack of Snakebite orange soda. When he looked in the bag, his frown turned into a slight smile.

"I knew there was somethin' I liked about you," he said.

He set the bag down on the counter and pulled out two sodas. They sat down to eat their burritos, and when her dad took his first swig of the premium soda, he paused for a moment, eyebrows raised. Quinn couldn't help but smile.

"How's the illegal job?" her dad asked as he unwrapped his burrito.

"Not bad. How's dealing?"

He shrugged. "Same old."

Quinn sighed. She was done lecturing her dad on the ills of dealing sand and other drugs, but it didn't mean she had to like it.

"How's Midtown?" he said between bites, wiping a dribble of green chili from his stubbled chin. Quinn could hear the mild sarcasm in his tone.

"Safe," she said.

"Quiet too, I imagine."

"Almost too quiet sometimes."

"Yeah. Them rare days we get a sprinkle of rain and there's a game on... and it gets real quiet around here..." He shook his head. "I don't like it. Ain't natural."

Quinn nodded. She knew the feeling.

"So who's the fella?

Quinn stopped chewing. "What fella?"

"Ran into Daria the other day, comin' to check on her mama. Said you got a fella."

Quinn had told Daria about Noah, just before she'd discovered he was a cop. "Not anymore."

Her dad eyed her. "Daria said you was talkin' like you had somethin' there."

"It all went to shit. Like it always does." She took another big bite of her burrito, the taste of the gooey cheese and spicy chilis making her feel better.

Her dad scoffed. "Ain't that the fucken truth." He paused for a moment, his burrito just sitting there. "He a cop or somethin'?"

Quinn felt her face heat up. "What makes you think that?"

He shrugged. "What else could it be? You ain't had anyone worth mentioning since that troublemaker you were so tight with years ago. And I figure with you doin' whatever it is you do, he's gotta be a lawman for shit to go sideways, 'cause you ain't the type to make the same mistake twice."

It was true. For all the dumb things she'd done, each time she always found a new way to screw up.

He took another swig of soda. "Don't let it get you down."

"Who said I'm down?" she said, maybe a little too defensively.

"Your face. And 'cause it gets everyone down, bein' alone."

Quinn sighed. "Yes, he was a cop. It would never have worked."

"Did you love him?"

She shrugged. "What difference does it make?"

"Tell me about him."

Quinn hesitated, surprised by her dad's curiosity. "He was smart. Generous. He cared about what mattered, about making things better. He was from Sunnyside, got out when he was a kid." Joe nodded at that. "He was everything Wyatt couldn't be, even if things hadn't happened the way they did..."

For some reason, it all hit her at once. The disappointment, the regret. For how everything turned out. For how Noah had turned out. Her burrito sat on the coffee table, only partly eaten.

"So that's it? He's such a do-gooder he can't deal with whatever you do?"

"No. But it doesn't matter. He turned out to be an asshole."

Her dad chuckled a little. "You sure know how to pick 'em."

Quinn laughed. But it was a bitter laugh, carved out of the knowledge that she would probably wind up alone like her father, with little to comfort her but her work and her favorite beverage. She could now afford the real diablos with lime... but she'd enjoy them all alone.

"You know I'm just messin' with you, right? 'Cause if there's anyone who gets what it's like to lose the one you love, it's me. Your mother was the only one who got me, you know? And then she was gone, leavin' me with a daughter to raise and a giant fucken hole in my heart." He looked away, grasping his soda bottle tightly. "Drinkin' was the only way I didn't put a big fucken bullet in my head and leave you to fend for yourself in the foster care system."

Quinn stared at her dad. It was the first time in the eighteen years since her mother died that he'd even mentioned her, much less shared what losing her did to him. It had never occurred to her that his drinking, the thing that ruined him, had been a crutch he needed, at least for a while.

"You ever think about meeting someone new?" she asked.

"Nope. I'm good where I'm at." He finished the empty bottle and tossed it into the recycling bin before opening a second. "But you... you'll find a way. You don't wanna end up alone."

"Want to or not, I made a choice to do what I do. And that's more important to me."

"More power to ya, kid." He unmuted the TV and sat back to watch.

Quinn wrapped up her burrito, put it in the mini-fridge, and sat back to watch the game. She ended up staying to watch the entire thing, and it was the first time she'd done so in longer than she could remember.

After saying goodbye, she put on her El Diablo jacket and ventured into the warm evening air. There was a light layer of clouds in the sky, muting the moonlight and making it seem even darker with the burned out streetlights. She kept her weapons close, just in case, as she headed to the train station.

Then she saw movement from the corner of her eye. Suddenly, someone grabbed her and covered her mouth before she could scream, bear-hugging her so tight that she had no chance of reaching for her weaponry. Before she could engage her fists and elbows, everything went blurry... then faded to nothing.

CHAPTER 7

WHEN QUINN CAME TO, she tried to move and found that she couldn't. She was bound, and her arms strapped to her sides. She panicked and tried harder, pulling against her restraints, knowing full well that it would do no good.

What the hell?

Then it started coming back to her. Hanging out with her dad, leaving his place, then... nothing. Someone had grabbed her and drugged her.

She blinked, and her eyes began to clear. The first thing she saw was a pair of pendant lamps hanging from the ceiling, their orange glass casting a warm glow throughout the room. There was something familiar about them, about that glow. Her stomach jolted when it hit her.

Noah. Noah had lamps like that, hanging in his bedroom. What the—

"Recognize the lamps, do you?" came an amused voice. "You spent plenty of time in this very bed, after all, eyes facing that very ceiling."

Quinn looked over, and there stood Noah, leaning against the wall in slacks and a t-shirt, his shoulder holster still on. The holster itself was empty, and Quinn soon realized Noah held his

service weapon in his hand, not pointing it at her but there none-
theless, reminding her she was powerless.

"Too much time, apparently," she snapped. "And I did a lot
more than stare at that ceiling." She didn't know why she added
that second thing, but for some reason it bugged her to have him
even suggest she didn't get as much out of those encounters has
he had.

"Oh, I'm sure," Noah said, his tone heavy with sarcasm. "I'm
sure screwing a jacker cop is a fucked-up sort of turn-on for you."

Quinn scoffed. Was he serious, thinking *she'd* gamed *him?*
"Right. Like stalking me, drugging me, and kidnapping me is
probably a turn-on for you."

*Not to mention sending me ominous art and nasty-grams
filled with threats, asshole.*

And then it hit her. She was at Noah's place, bound on his
bed. A gut-level, stinking fear permeated her, knowing that right
now she was at his mercy... and that Noah could do whatever he
wanted to her. And nobody would ever know.

She couldn't let him see her fear.

"Untie me, asshole," she snarled at him. "And if you do
anything to hurt me, don't think I don't have safeguards in place
that will fuck you right in the ass later."

Noah's eyebrows went up. Amusement, but also genuine
surprise at her threat. "You can take the girl out of Downtown
and stick her in a cute sundress, but she'll always be a Downtownie at heart."

Quinn's panic waned a little. Something told her that whatever Noah's intentions, they didn't include torture, murder, or
even arresting her. If he'd wanted those things, he'd have done so
by now.

Instead, he only leaned against the wall, looking almost irri-
tatingly handsome with those dark eyes and dimples. Fortunately,
his smug look of winning erased all that, leaving her only with the

desire to punch him. And... even if he wasn't going to hurt or kill her, he had plans for her and they couldn't be good ones.

"Why am I here, Noah? If you really wanted another round with the Downtown trash, you could have called."

His dark eyes flashed with anger. "I appreciate the offer, but I'm sticking with my Midtown options these days. I used to prefer Downtown women because they were less spoiled and understood what was important, but it turns out they're trouble, just like I was warned."

Humiliation washed over Quinn. As much as she wished otherwise, the comment cut her. Because she saw the truth in it, and always had. No amount of her living in Midtown would change that.

"But you already know that, don't you? That I'm courting Midtown ladies these days, even bringing them to my place?"

Fuck. He knew she'd been in his place the other night.

"It seems mindjacking isn't the only lawbreaking you enjoy," he added.

"Don't get all high-and-mighty, Noah. The fact that I'm bound and waking up from being drugged proves that Sergeant Martinez isn't so pure either. So you can cut the shit."

He came closer to her. "Tell me about these men in black, with the blackbird tattoos. The ones you flattened with your illegal energy weapon that night at Linden's."

"I'm not telling you shit."

He shook his head. "Protecting your own kind, huh?"

"They're not my kind."

"Oh yeah? Why's that?"

She couldn't tell him anything. "You wouldn't understand."

Noah's jaw tightened. "You sure about that? You know my father has never been the same after one of you fucking mindjackers got through with him. You know that and you sit there and—"

"No mindjacker would ever do what happened to your father, Noah!" she cried as she tried to sit up, only to be reminded once more that she was bound. She cursed and gritted her teeth. "Your father was attacked by a mind thief. They have lesser skills and no respect for the target—"

"Spare me your we-do-it-for-the-right-reasons crap, Quinn," Noah barked at her, slamming his service weapon down on his dresser. "You have no business rooting around in other people's minds. And if you think you do, you're even more disturbed than I thought."

"You think I do this for kicks?" she shot back. "You think the people I target aren't sleazy pieces of shit, like Gary Linden was?"

"It's not your job to distribute justice. That's what law enforcement and the legal system are for."

Quinn rolled her eyes. "Because those work so well."

As she argued with Noah, Quinn began considering ways to break free of her restraints. Her arms were bound, but her hands had some play, possibly enough to reach the tiny holster on her thigh. She began inching her hand over to find out.

"Looking for this?" Noah held up her energy weapon.

Of course he'd checked her pockets. But a routine pat-down would miss the other thing.

Noah set her weapon down and crossed his arms. "The justice system isn't perfect, but it works. And I can prove it to you."

"How's that?"

"You become my confidential informant, and I won't arrest you and put you away for ten years." He smiled, as if offering her the world.

Quinn stared. "You've got to be kidding me."

"I'm not." His expression changed to something almost genuine. "With your help, I can nail the people who killed the

Lindens and attacked you and your partner that night. We can nail all kinds of them. And you can avoid jail time..."

She could probably reach her groin, she decided. But she couldn't do it without Noah noticing. Then she had an idea.

She forced herself to cough. Then again. She was thirsty as it was, and played off that. "I need some water. Do you mind?"

Noah stood there a moment, eyeing her like he didn't want to leave her. Soon, he left the room, and Quinn quickly yanked her hand over and scrambled her fingers until her dress was up at her hips. Hearing the fridge open, she yanked the blade from its tiny hiding place and sliced at the twine that bound her. With a snap, she felt the release of the tension, then cut the rest until she was free.

By the time Noah returned with a glass of water, Quinn had her energy weapon in hand, aimed at him. He didn't react, other than to glance at the weapon, and then at her, his dark eyes smoldering with a new round of anger.

She walked toward him, pointing the weapon at his chest until he set down the water glass and backed out of the room. She headed toward his front door, keeping the weapon trained on him. Then she paused.

"You can take your stupid offer and shove it, *Sergeant*," she sneered at him. "I'm nobody's CI. I may have gotten under you in that bedroom, but I'll never be under your thumb. That's one *win* you'll never get."

"Don't be so sure about that," he said coldly. "You can run all you want, Quinn. But I know who you are and I know where you live. It's only a matter of time before I find you again... and I promise that next time my offer won't be so generous."

"Is that right? Because I wonder what your colleagues at the EDPD will think about your having screwed around with someone like me, taking me out and sending me notes and art covered in your fingerprints. I also wonder what the media will think when I show them those little artifacts, and the log of all those times you called and messaged me."

Noah's face hardened, his eyes dark balls of fire.

"And I'm sure they'd love to know that El Diablo's finest is stalking and harassing a woman, showing up to her apartment building—yes, I have witnesses—and even leaving her threatening notes to scare and intimidate her."

Noah's angry expression shifted, like he hadn't expected that last thing. "What the—"

"Stay the hell away from me," she warned. "We both have something to lose here, but the difference between you and me is that I can always find a way to do what I do. But you, once you get pinched, can never be a cop again. Remember that. And remember that you're dealing with a Downtownie—you fuck with us one too many times, we will resort to desperate measures."

And with that, Quinn opened the door and left, closing it behind her.

As a taxi took her to Mayfair, Quinn wondered which side of Noah would prevail—his need to win, or his love for the job. For her, the choice was easy. The job always came first. Time would tell whether Noah was the same way.

Deep down, Quinn hoped he was.

CHAPTER 8

Quinn lounged in bed the next morning, sipping her iced coffee and enjoying a little cool morning air from her open window before it got too warm. She searched through the news headlines, but her mind kept returning to what happened a couple nights ago at Noah's place.

He hadn't contacted or bothered her since. Yet, the whole thing still got under her skin. She'd hoped not only that Noah would leave her alone, but that he would do so because some part of him still cared for her and didn't want to see her locked up. Because the truth was, not a day had gone by that she didn't wish things had gone down differently, that Noah was any damned thing but a jacker cop.

Now she saw how foolish that was. It was bad enough that they turned out to live on opposite sides of the fence. But now she had to contend with the reality of Noah... the hunting her down, the threats, the leaning on her.

Her dad was right. She really did know how to pick 'em.

When her phone rang, she jumped, wondering if Noah was calling to offer up a few more threats. But it was Yolanda.

"Good morning, Yolanda."

"Quinn," Yolanda said, as warm and welcoming as always. "It's time for us to have a chat."

Quinn held her breath.

"Remi says you're still struggling with the simulations. However, so are my other Tier Ones... and we can't wait any longer."

A flash of excitement ran through her. "I'm listening."

"The job I spoke of before—the important one with the high-profile client? The client is George Hatch."

Quinn raised her eyebrows. "As in George Hatch of Scorpio Cooling Systems?"

"The very one."

Holy shit.

Scorpio Cooling Systems had cornered the market on air conditioning systems and repair, and deregulation had made it so the company had little competition even before the drought. Now it had none at all, which meant one of the most important commodities in El Diablo was expensive, prohibitively so for many Downtownies. Hatch, Scorpio's illustrious CEO, was a pillar of success—raised Downtown, managed to educate himself before the drought hit, climbed the ladder to success. He and his wife were good-looking, likable society types who donated to lots of charities.

"So what's the story? And how does it involve the Jays?"

"Mr. Hatch himself is being targeted by mind thieves. He reported a jacking attempt in the parking garage at his office, which was sparsely populated that late in the evening. The thieves subdued Hatch's guards, but their attempt was thwarted by a silent alarm that drew his private backup security quickly, before the thieves could extract anything. The attackers escaped. Hatch admitted to being quite rattled by the attack."

"How do we know he's not baiting us, like Linden did?"

"Mr. Hatch gave us permission to conduct a limited mindjacking. It wasn't difficult to locate memories of the attack, which corroborate his story."

"Was it the usual men in black?"

"We believe so. Given their skill level and Hatch's status, it's likely. However, Hatch and his security detail were blindsided, and Hatch was injected quickly, before he saw much. Which is why we need you."

"You want us to target the backup security guys," Quinn surmised. "To see what they saw and hopefully get some information on the attackers." Now that was a challenge indeed, worthy of a Tier One. Security guards at that level had military training and would not go down easy.

"No. Not the security guards."

Quinn hesitated, then her jaw dropped. "You want us to jack Hatch himself. You don't trust him, and you want us to see if he's hiding anything."

"We can't afford to trust anyone now, not after the Borelli job."

Quinn was speechless for a moment. Powerful people were always difficult targets. But someone of Hatch's status was a whole new level of difficult because people like him knew they were targets and therefore made sure they were well-protected at all times.

"This is high-risk job, Quinn. It may draw the Jays out of the woodwork. That's why the compensation is high."

"I understand."

"Can I count on you?"

"Of course. Hatch will never know we were there. And I'm more than happy to go after those black-clad assholes."

"This isn't a search-and-destroy mission, Quinn. This is recon only—get in, extract as much data from Mr. Hatch as you can, and get out."

"Send me the info sheet, and Jones and I will start planning."

"You'll have it by the end of the day."

Later, after doing some research on George Hatch, Quinn checked her watch. The mail had probably arrived by now. She'd gotten into the habit of checking it more often, just in case it contained any more special messages from Sergeant Asshole.

She took the elevator to the lobby. When it stopped on the third floor, the doors opened and Merritt stepped in. Her red hair was in braids and her hands awkwardly gripping her tool-box, like she wasn't used to carrying one. That seemed odd to Quinn, but it was entirely possible this was a new job for Merritt.

"Hi Quinn!"

"Hey Merritt. Which floor?"

"Lobby." She glanced at Quinn and smiled. "You'll be happy to know that no more weird hot guys have come sniffing around for you."

"That's good news."

"But I saw you talking to those two cuties, though..." Merritt added archly, a gleam in her brown eyes.

"Which cuties?"

"The guys... Devin and Lucifer." She grinned at her own cleverness.

Quinn chuckled. "You like iguanas?"

"I love them! I love all animals, including the human kind. Wish I could afford one," she added wistfully.

"A guy or an iguana?"

Merritt laughed a little too hard, like she was trying to flatter Quinn. "Either. But I meant an iguana. Also, I think Devin might be gay."

Quinn raised her eyebrows. "Really? I didn't get that vibe from him."

"I could be wrong. I've just never seen him with a girl, and he's cute. And I'd never care about the limp, you know?"

Quinn would never care about a limp either. But this was El Diablo, where a limp could hurt your chances in the cutthroat dating pool.

When they got to the lobby, Merritt lingered, as if hoping to talk more. "What are you up to?"

"Oh, just checking the mail. Good talking to you." She went off to her mailbox and left Merritt to her duties, a little glad to leave Merritt's orbit. Merritt was nice enough, and friendlier than most in that building, but there was something about her that seemed... off.

When Quinn opened her mailbox, dread came over her when she saw a large envelope inside, the same size as the previous one. Unable to wait, she opened it and pulled out the contents. It was an image of a woman, her face and torso torched and unrecognizable, like she'd been attacked with an energy weapon. When Quinn looked closely, she realized the woman had *her* body, her clothing, her jawline and hair.

It was a doctored picture of Quinn.

Her heart began to pound. The lobby seemed to shift and suddenly feel smaller, like it was closing in on her.

"You alright?"

Quinn jumped at the sound of a male voice. She looked up to find Devin standing there, concern on his face. She stuffed the disturbing image back into its envelope and forced a smile.

"I'm fine. I just..." Her mind went blank and she couldn't come up with a witty lie.

"Bad news from the Federal Tax Bureau?" He smiled a little.

"Something like that."

"Tear it up and throw it away. That's what I do."

Something yanked Devin back and made him stumble. Lucifer, on his leash, trying to pull Devin toward the door. He went and picked Lucifer up. "Quit being a little shit," he said. He saw Quinn eyeing the creature and added, "You can pet him. He's a lover once he gets to know you."

Quinn petted Lucifer, his scaly skin warm and dry. But Lucifer strained against Devin's arm and squirmed like he wanted out. Devin let him down. "I think he needs to go outside. Good to see you again, Quinn." His eyes lingered on her, much like before, just a moment longer than casual.

Quinn waved. "You too."

After they left, Quinn hurried back to her place. She took a close look at the image again. Despite knowing it was doctored, it gave her the creeps. She shook her head.

A death threat? Would Noah really take things this far?

She checked the envelope for useful information: a return address, a postage scan marking. There was nothing. She slid the image back into its envelope and stowed it away.

Later that night, just as she drifted off to sleep, her phone beeped and she grabbed it. A message, from an unfamiliar number.

Did you get your picture, Quinn? I hope so. I had a swell time constructing that image. It turned out pretty good, don't you think?

Do not ever believe you'll get away with killing those men.

And with violating the code.

Then, a final one.

By the way, that picture? That's you very soon, Quinn Hartley.

Because I'm coming for you.

CHAPTER 9

QUINN STOOD AT HER WINDOW, staring out at the city lights and dark sky. She couldn't sleep. She read the message again, and then two more times.

Someone was after her. And that someone knew her full name, her phone number, and where she lived.

She stood up and began to pace.

Do not ever believe you'll get away with killing those men.

Quinn had beaten, shot, and disabled her share of enemies in her professional and personal life. But she'd only killed two: the ninjas who'd attacked her and Jones at the Lindens'. Whoever sent that message knew about that job. There were only four people there besides her and Jones that night; all four were dead.

Noah had seen her and Jones and saw their injuries, and could have put two and two together about what happened. The threat could have come from him. Or from the cops, working from Noah's intel, looking to scare her into doing something drastic so they could nab her. If so, they weren't working within the law, within the justice system Noah so passionately defended the other night.

Which left only one other option: the Black Jays themselves. They'd lost two comrades and wanted revenge.

Quinn hurried over to her computer. She would trace the call. An enemy of this sort would be too smart to call from a personal phone, but results could yield some clue that could help her. However, after running through the few tricks she had, she found nothing.

Quinn thought of Jones. If this enemy was after her, they might be after Jones. Was he receiving threats too? Unlikely. He was still paranoid about Noah coming back to haunt them, and he would have mentioned any threat right away.

Besides, she'd pulled the trigger on their enemies that night, not Jones. She'd killed the men. Based on Jones's poor condition that night, Noah was the only one who would know that.

A bad situation had just become worse. Whether the cops or the Jays, she had a new enemy after her. A formidable one.

One who could end everything for her.

Quinn packed her purple wig and her jacket into her bag and left her apartment. In the lobby, Devin strolled in with Lucifer trailing behind him. He wore a Demon's t-shirt with his slacks.

"Hey, Devin," Quinn said.

"Quinn. Hey."

When Lucifer approached, she kneeled down to greet him.

"Nice jacket," Devin said.

Quinn hesitated, then remembered which one she wore. The one with the big "El Diablo" on the back. "Thanks. It's my fave."

"It's very Downtown. Brings back memories."

Quinn looked up. "You grew up Downtown?" As soon as the words left her mouth, she knew the answer. Underneath the nice duds and the good manners was something... world-wise. Like he'd seen the things she had.

Devin nodded. "Ocotillo. Until I was fifteen."

Ocotillo. Not deep Downtown, which explained his cleaner,

tattoo-free look. Although she wondered if his upbringing contributed to his limp.

"Do you still have family down there?" she asked.

Devin hesitated. "No."

Something about his answer told her not to press. She felt his eyes on her, and she didn't know whether to feel flattered or uncomfortable. When Lucifer tried to crawl up her leg, she stopped him and he gave her a little bite. Nothing painful, but enough to make her laugh.

"No biting, you bad boy," she teased.

"Lucifer," Devin said in disapproval.

Quinn stood up. "It's okay. It was only a nibble. I know when to keep my fingers to myself." She pointed at his t-shirt. "Demons fan?"

"Diehard. The first thing I did when I got a good job was buy season tickets. Even before finding an apartment in Midtown."

"We all have our priorities."

"You ever go to games?"

She shook her head. "Not a baseball fan. No offense."

"You ever been to a live game?"

"No," she admitted.

"You might feel differently if you did..." He paused. "I was thinking about getting a coffee next door. Want to join us?"

"I'd love to, but headed out."

Devin nodded. "Maybe some other time."

Quinn waved goodbye and left.

After donning her wig and alternate jacket, Quinn headed Downtown. The air was filled with particulates and the sky looked grayish. It had been a particularly windy day and the news warned that dust levels were high. Several people she passed on the street were coughing and drinking from their water bottles. Quinn pulled out her mask. She hated wearing one, but it helped prevent dust inhalation, and offered another layer of disguise that made her feel safer.

And safety had become a huge issue, thanks to her new enemy.

She could have grabbed a taxi, but she wasn't going to waste more money on taxis when she might need it to hunt down this threat. And she avoided the train, uncomfortable with the idea of being trapped in a tube with people she couldn't escape from. As long as she walked wide when approaching any alleys, she was safest out here, on the streets in broad daylight, where she could see the enemy coming. Her hands remained in her pockets, her two friends her only solace.

When Quinn arrived at Sidewinder, Jones was already there, sitting in the corner with a root beer and an almost-empty plate of tacos. The old Jones never let himself eat out, opting to save his limited funds to support his family. Now, he could let himself have tacos, and it made Quinn happy to see.

As she approached, Jones stared for a moment, his face blank as he shoved the last bit of taco in his mouth. His eyebrows went up when he recognized her.

"I thought you wanted outta Downtown," he said, eyeing the purple wig. "Coulda fooled me."

"It did fool you, for a second there." She lowered her voice. "It's to throw off the enemy."

"That bad?"

Quinn told Jones about the image she'd received, and showed him the message. He read it, his eyes darkening.

"Fuck," he muttered.

"Yeah." She glanced around again, making sure nobody watched them.

With a sigh, he wiped his hands on his napkin and pushed his plate way. "That Linden job is gonna haunt us for the rest of our lives."

"You haven't gotten any threats, right?"

"No." He paused. "You think it's that cop you banged?"

She sighed. "Possibly. He's the only one who was there that isn't dead."

"But how's he know who pulled the trigger? Why you and not me?"

"He saw what kind of shape you were in. It makes sense to assume it was me."

He shook his head again and leaned back. "That's some crooked-ass shit, with death threats and all, which would mean he's a fucken dirty cop." She nodded at that. "But I don't know. Like you said, he let us skate that night. I'm thinkin' if he was gonna do ya, he woulda done ya by now."

"Agreed. Something about this doesn't feel like him."

"But that ain't good either, 'cause at least a cop is a devil we know. This is startin' to look like the Jays. And we don't know them guys."

"I don't know what to do, Jones."

"You trace the call?"

"Yup. Nothing."

After the server brought Quinn's drink, Jones went on. "Maybe we need to talk to the boss. Tell 'em what's goin' on."

Quinn scowled. "Are you out of your mind? They'd drop me quicker than a grenade with the pin pulled!"

"You got a better idea?"

"I do." She hesitated, knowing he wasn't going to like it. "I can call Noah, agree to be his CI. If he helps me with my problem."

Jones's eyes widened. "Are you kiddin' me? That's a fucken terrible idea—"

"He's got resources, Jones! He's got resources I don't have, and he's less risky than the Protectorate—"

"It's outta the question, Quinn. Don't even mention it again."

"What choice do I have?" she cried, feeling her frustration peak. "I—"

"There's gotta be a better way—"

"There's not. If it's the Jays, we know they have the skills to nab me. Whoever it is knows where I live, my number, my full name. God only knows what else. At least Noah works within the law. He could help me."

"At what cost? You know how cops treat their informants. Once you agree to work with 'em, they got you over a barrel forever. Yeah, they say they'll protect you and keep you outta jail, but in the end, when push comes to shove, them cops'll toss you right under the train if it means gettin' what they want. You ain't shit to them."

Quinn shook her head. "I know too much for him to try that crap on me."

"Sure about that? Girl, even if he ain't crooked, he's got a chip on his shoulder now that he knows you're the one thing he hates. You know as well as I do them jacker cops are all the same. They never stop until they get their man, until..."

"Until they win." Quinn let out a giant sigh. Jones was right. There was no way she could work with Noah. Not after everything that had happened. "I didn't work this hard to finally get to Tier One, just to get charred by the Jays. Or arrested. I'm fucking scared, Jones."

Jones paused, deep in thought. "What if you just asked for his help?"

"What? We just agreed that's a bad idea."

"No. I don't mean be his CI. Don't give him shit. I mean... just ask for his help. Be a damsel in distress."

Quinn crossed her arms, annoyed. "That's insulting. Besides, he'd never fall for that."

"The fuck he wouldn't. Not if he had feelings for you."

"Those feelings are dead. Trust me." The brunette Midtowner at his place proved that.

"I ain't buyin' it."

"Why not?"

"'Cause it's the only way to explain why he let us go."

Quinn paused at that. But then she shook her head. "Even if that were true, he's had plenty of time to change his mind. Which is why he's trying to lean on me. Plus, I may have pointed a weapon at him and threatened to ruin his career. So I don't think he's in a helping mood."

Jones crossed his muscled arms. "Then we only got one choice."

"What's that?"

"We gotta find out who's doin' this on our own."

Quinn hesitated, uncomfortable with pulling Jones into a dangerous situation. But two heads were better than one, and if the situation were reversed she would help Jones without question.

"Okay," she agreed. "But you're behind the scenes only. I don't want this rubbing off on you."

"Right now, we put it aside. We got a job to plan."

CHAPTER 10

QUINN COULDN'T BELIEVE her eyes.

It was big, blue, and filled with an obscene amount of water.

A swimming pool.

She'd heard about them, but had never seen one. And judging by Jones's raised eyebrows and stare, he hadn't either. Swimming pools were the stuff of myths and dreams, read about only in books. They played no part in Quinn's life or in the city of El Diablo... unless you lived north of 90th Street and out-earned ninety-eight percent of your fellow desert-dwellers.

"Fuck me," Jones muttered.

Quinn nodded. That about summed it up.

The pool lay quiet, turquoise with white sparkling stone, surrounded by waterfalls and lounge chairs. A solar-protected dome let light in but blocked heat and UV radiation, allowing a view of the troglodytes below who could never afford to patronize The Oasis. It was early in the morning on a Saturday, and the pool wasn't open for business yet.

Jones, dressed in overalls and a hat, began his pool-cleaning duties while Quinn snuck inside one of the changing rooms to put on her server's uniform. A few well-planned words and a wad of cash allowed them to replace the daytime server and pool maintenance worker.

It was always nerve-wracking to bribe workers, even ones the Protectorate had worked with before. You never knew who would turn you down out of fear, or decide that they didn't like you enough to take the money. But the heavily-tattooed supervisor, Benicio, took one look at Jones and nodded, pocketing the cash without argument. It was the only reason they could pull off the job at The Oasis instead of somewhere even riskier.

Quinn finished dressing and straightened her purple wig before checking herself in the mirror. As she stared at her reflection, there was something strangely comforting about her appearance, about embracing where she came from, even if only for a few hours. Besides, maybe these rich old guys would find her low-class look charming and fun.

She was betting on it, actually.

When the place opened for business, it wasn't long before the pool and lounge area were filled with people. Wives, husbands, and lots of children, all in their swimwear. The shallow end of the pool with the slide and maze was filled with younger kids screaming and splashing, the middle with older kids playing pool games, and the rest filled with adults swimming the neat lanes or lounging on the steps or under the waterfalls that now flowed.

"Excuse me, miss," came a nasal voice. Quinn turned to find a middle-school-aged girl in a one-piece suit and silky coverup. "Can I get a root beer?"

"Of course," Quinn said. Quinn turned to fetch the soda from the cooler, but didn't get far when she heard the voice again.

"Wait. Um... can I get two, actually? You can put it on the Underhill tab. It's my father's tab."

Of course it was. "So that's two root beers?"

The girl fidgeted. "Actually, my brother might want something. Joseph!" she shouted into the pool filled with kids.

"I'll get those root beers and be back," Quinn said.

Jesus, Quinn thought. The real servers better earn good tips for putting up with this kind of drudgery. After retrieving two sodas and two glasses of ice, she found herself getting thirsty. She pulled out a third bottle, opened all three, and took a big swig from one before hiding the bottle in the corner, charging all three to Mr. Underhill's tab.

Quinn returned to the table, only to find that the girl was nowhere to be found. She dropped the sodas and glasses on the table and left. She had a job to do, damn it. She made her way over to the adult end of the pool, where pale, soft-bellied men lounged in their expensive swim trunks and talked to one another or on their phones. Then she spotted him.

George Hatch. CEO of Scorpio Cooling Systems.

He was mid-fifties and fitter than most of the other men, and sat there on his lounge chair talking on a portable phone device tucked into his ear. He had a businesslike expression and spoke softly, but there was a calm confidence about him that was different than the goal-driven intensity of men like Jonathan Stilwell or Gary Linden. It was the confidence of the supremely wealthy and powerful.

It wasn't time yet. She needed to catch him between calls.

She served a few nearby adults, bringing them everything from bottled bubbly water to scotch neat, none taking any real interest in her other than to transact, which was fine by her. She needed to be forgettable, and the purple wig ironically achieved that. She was, to them, just another Downtownie.

On one errand, she passed Jones, who was heading to the water to test its temperature.

Finally, when George Hatch seemed to stop talking, indicating he was off the phone, he closed his eyes for a moment, as if centering himself.

"You look like you could use some refreshment," she said, smiling at him.

He looked up at her. "You read my mind. How about one of those veggie smoothies? With the cactus juice?"

Hatch was a healthy type. Quinn was almost impressed. "Coming right up, sir."

She returned with his beverage, then went back to the service area and took a few long pulls of her root beer. Despite the temperature-controlled environment, she was hot. She realized it was due to the humidity created by the pool.

She sent a quick message to Jones. *I'm up to bat.*

When Jones acknowledged, Quinn felt her heart speed up. It had been a while since they'd done a real job, and she'd missed it.

She headed straight for George Hatch. When she approached, he looked up.

"I'm sorry to bother you, Mr. Hatch. But I'm supposed to let you know it's time for your massage."

Hatch glanced at his watch, then gave a nod. He stood up and headed toward the massage rooms after letting his wife know. Quinn messaged Jones again.

Ball in play.

She waited, then followed him. But when she arrived, Jones and Hatch were standing in the hallway, and she could immediately tell something was wrong. Hatch looked annoyed. And Jones looked nervous.

"Is everything okay, Mr. Hatch?" she asked.

"This isn't my usual masseur. This isn't Peter." He wasn't whiny or angry. Only suspicious.

She knew why. Men of Hatch's status knew to suspect anything amiss, as they were huge targets for mind thieves. Particularly after having already encountered them.

"Jeremy is new here, sir," she said. "But I will page Benicio.

Maybe he can tell you if Peter will be available later today, if you like..."

"Good," he said with a single nod, and he turned and left.

Quinn ran off and found Benicio, telling him the situation and offering a way around it. Benicio nodded and went to find Hatch. Quinn waited, holding her breath. The two men spoke for a moment, then Hatch nodded and followed Benicio back toward the massage rooms.

Relief flooded her. It had worked. What Hatch needed wasn't Peter, it was to know he was safe. Benicio's promise to remain in the massage room had solved that problem, as Benicio had worked at The Oasis for years, long enough to earn Hatch's trust.

And so it was. Before long, Quinn got her cue. She entered the massage room and sat down on the floor next to where Hatch lay sleeping. After attaching her nodes, she looked up at Jones, who smiled wryly.

"Ready for a good ride?" he asked.

She nodded, and closed her eyes.

It felt cool but comforting. Soft, fluid... strange.

Wet.

She was in the pool, submerged up to her neck.

But it was dark. She felt the water surrounding her body, with nothing underneath her feet. Somehow she kept her head above water, her arms and legs slicing through it this way and that, treading water.

How weird it felt! She'd been submerged before while jacked in, but it had never felt like this, so real, so comforting... so womb-like.

The only light was in the distance, a golden glow, a beacon calling to her. She paddled toward it.

She kept going, slowly, wondering when she would reach the side of the pool and smack into the unforgiving concrete. But she didn't, and the pool seemed to go on and on, toward the light. She kept looking around, waiting for Hatch's defenses to kick in, for some creature to appear out of nowhere and swallow her whole. But there was nothing but water, and that glow. Then something seemed to urge her forward, like the pool contracted somehow.

It was the most relaxing initial jack-in she'd ever experienced. It seemed Hatch's outer calm reflected an inner one that he'd honed over many years. It impressed her. If only she could achieve such mental control.

When Quinn reached the light, she was bathed in gold—warm, soothing, healing gold—and she felt herself smile.

Suddenly, she was thrust through the light, and next thing she knew she was plummeting into blackness... no water, no flight device, no nothing. Down she fell, falling so fast that it stole the breath from her lungs and she couldn't scream or even breathe. Fear spread through her as she fell faster and faster, so fast she had no control over her body and was cast about by the nothingness. Panicky feelings rose, knowing that once she collided with anything—the ground, the water, anything at all—she would not survive.

A scream came out of her, silent as she thrashed about. And then Quinn remembered. This was all an illusion, carefully constructed by Hatch's mind to prevent her from accessing what she'd come for.

You're fine. You're safe. Just fall, then land.

In the pitch-black darkness, she let herself fall, mining her own memory banks for something pleasant. The taste of a diablo with real lime. Air conditioning after being out in the three-digit heat all afternoon. Her new apartment in Mayfair.

Soon, she fell no more and found her footing. There was another light; she walked toward it until she saw a door. She looked for locks or other security measures, the kind she typically had to figure out a way around, but there were none. And when she turned that door handle, it opened easily.

On the other side, she found another door. Then another. She opened doors one after the next for so long it became rote, and she knew she was stuck in a mental loop, Hatch's training chipping away at a jacker's most valuable commodity: time.

Quinn quelled any sense of panic and closed her eyes. *Focus on the task. Find your way in.*

She reached into her pocket, feeling her energy weapon. She retrieved it, then cut through the wall to bypass the endless doors, unsure if it would amount to anything other than more doors. When finished cutting, she gave the cut panel a push.

The flood came. Feelings, thoughts, memories... whizzing past her like Downtown taxis in low traffic.

Workouts. Darkness and candles and a small water bath... a homemade meditation room. Vigorous sex with a good-looking spouse. And time at the pool with the kids, showing them proper swim form and making sure they only drank one soda and no more. Odors of food and cologne and herbs.

Then, work. Meetings, lots of them. Phone calls, even more of those. All taking place while Hatch was on a treadmill or doing some sort of physical exercise.

Finally, colleagues around a conference room table: men and women in expensive suits, some familiar to Quinn. Powerful people with concerned faces, all talking mumbo jumbo.

A few images swept past, snippets of them: men in black, approaching, accosting...

One was clearer than the rest. She focused on it, something telling her it was of crucial importance, and would lead her to the answers. When a hallway appeared, she walked down it until it grew dim.

Then she stood in an apartment, old and cheaply furnished,

with a rust-colored couch that had a tear in its cushion, the white stuffing trying to escape. The place felt hot, stifling even, like it had no air conditioning. Men in blue—paramedics, maybe—carried someone on a stretcher. Quinn watched, her eyes drawn to the person, whose body was still. She saw a feminine hand, then a pale face. Too pale.

Quinn's breath left her body and pain seared through her chest, like her heart had split in half.

It was her mother's face.

"Mom," she cried, knowing her mom wouldn't respond but still repeating it again, then again. She ran toward the body but someone grabbed her from behind.

And she started to scream.

Then it was gone. All of it.

"Quinn," came a whisper.

Someone shook her. She opened her eyes, wondering why they felt wet. Jones kneeled in front of her, his blue-green eyes staring into hers with a strange mixture of concern and impatience.

"We gotta go," he said. "Right now."

CHAPTER 11

"JOB DONE. DATA COMING."

Quinn sent off the message before she and Jones hopped off the train at 28th Street, the closest stop to Sidewinder. They changed in the restroom and grabbed the gear they'd stored in a locker, and headed to the bar.

They said nothing on the way, never knowing for sure who could be nearby and listening. And silence was fine with Quinn. She was still haunted by what she'd encountered in Hatch's supposedly calm mind.

When Jones had pulled her out, Quinn, still disoriented, had jumped up, delivered the custom transitional memory of the hallway and massage room to Hatch's mind, then followed Jones out the back door. They left Hatch's slumbering body there with only moments before he would awaken to find Benicio. They'd scrambled down the stuffy, overheated stairwell and made for the train.

Finally, in a booth at Sidewinder and beverages in hand, Jones ignored his computer and their data device and looked at her.

"What happened in there?" he said.

66 / C.A. HARTMAN

Quinn closed her eyes for a moment, the imagery still vivid and disconcerting. "How did you know?"

"You started squirmin', and then cryin'. Scared the shit out of me."

"That makes two of us." Quinn pushed away the disturbing imagery. "Hatch got the platinum package for mind protection. It starts out calm and lulls you into a false sense of security, and then it drags your calm ass into free-fall and a long series of other obstacles... then to reliving the day your mother died and they rolled her out of our apartment on a gurney." She bit back the tears and took a swig of her diablo.

"Fuck."

"It was so real. It was like I was really there."

Jones stared at her. "How's that even possible?"

"I don't know. Somehow, the training stimulates the amygdala, so your most intense fear-based memories resurface."

Jones shook his head and leaned back in his chair, as if trying to wrap his mind around the idea. In all their years in the business, no mindjacker had ever reported having relived a personal memory, unless chosen intentionally to prevent drowning and getting lost in another person's mind.

"I don't get it," Jones said. "The Protectorate designed them templates that Psyche uses to develop the mind-invasion training, so they woulda told us if they'd developed something like that."

Quinn shrugged. "Psyche has probably developed new and better programs on their own since then. And what better way to stop an invader than to access their most painful memories?"

"Yolanda and the other ops managers need to know about this. They need to warn people."

"I'll let her know and post on the forum. Just... don't tell anyone the specifics, okay? Just say it was a bad memory." She shook her head. "And Hatch... I'm telling you, he's Mr. Perfect, his mind all neat and organized and filled with images of him working out and drinking turmeric shakes... and he turned out to be the most evil of all." She glanced at his computer. "Let's take a look at that data. Did we get enough?"

"I hope so. It took forever to get anything. That's why we ran outta time."

Quinn grimaced. "Sorry. I forget sometimes how hard it is for you, to sit there and wait for shit to go wrong."

"Yup. We takin' care of business while you jackers are busy playin' around in someone else's head." He winked.

Quinn snickered. Jones inserted the data chip into his portable computer and began uploading it. "Yeah, we got plenty."

While Jones began parsing the data and getting it ready to hand off to the Protectorate, Quinn took a few deep breaths and ordered herself another drink. Just when she got herself into a comfortably numb state, Jones's brows went up again.

"What do you see?" she said.

"Fucken Black Jays, that's what. Looks like Hatch mighta been tellin' the truth."

"Well, send it off. The sooner you do, the sooner we can get some answers."

"It's done." Jones closed his computer. "Not to bring up a sore subject, but we still gotta talk about how we're gonna deal with that other thing."

Her stalker. "Right. Meet tomorrow night?"

Jones nodded and stood up. "I gotta get home. You alright?"

"I will be after one more of these." Quinn pointed at her drink.

Jones hesitated. "You ain't gonna make self-medicatin' a habit, are ya?"

"No."

It was true. Quinn would never let herself follow in her father's footsteps.

Later, when she arrived at her building, Quinn half-drunkenly eyed her mailbox and decided to avoid it. She couldn't take another hit to her brain's fear centers that day. As she waited for the elevator, she felt a hand on her shoulder and spun around quickly, hands on her weapons.

It was Merritt.

"Jesus, girl," she said, suddenly sober. "You shouldn't sneak up on people like that."

"I'm sorry," Merritt said, her eyes wide. "I was just having fun!"

Quinn glanced at her watch. It was after nine. "What are you doing here so late? Shouldn't you be off by now?"

"Work never ends," Merritt said, tossing a braid over her shoulder. "How are you? Do you want to go get a drink?"

A drink was the last thing Quinn needed. "No... I can't. I had a rough day and just want to go to bed."

"Are you sure?" She looked disappointed, like she hoped Quinn would feel bad and change her mind. "Just one?"

"I can't. Sorry."

The elevator dinged and Quinn got in. She half-expected Merritt to follow her inside, but instead she just stood there, waving at Quinn until the doors shut.

When her phone rang the next morning, it took Quinn a few foggy, hungover moments to find it. Her head hurt a little.

"Hello?" she said, her voice thick and gravelly.

"Quinn," came Yolanda's businesslike voice.

"Good morning, Yolanda."

"I hear you took quite a journey with Mr. Hatch yesterday."

"That's one way to put it. And pardon me for saying this, but what the fuck? When did Psyche develop targeted amygdala attacks? And how is that even possible?"

"We are looking into that. And before you ask, no, we didn't know and then decide not to share that information with you and Jones just to make your life harder."

Quinn frowned. She knew the barb was somewhat justified after the drunken warning she'd posted on the forum last night, but it annoyed her anyway. The training sessions with Remi were bad enough, but to face that in the field, when actual lives were on the line? Quinn would do just about anything to avoid repeating an experience like that, one she had no way of preparing for. And Yolanda, in her protected little Midtown life and her cushy management job, could never understand that.

"You have no idea what it's like, Yolanda."

"I asked you if you were ready. You said you were."

Quinn gritted her teeth. "We got the data, didn't we? Do you have an update, or did you just call to torture me?"

"I have an update. But before I tell you what it is, I want you to remember something. You're a Tier One agent now, Quinn. One recommended by me. You may want to rethink how you conduct yourself on our forum. And in general."

Quinn sighed. Yolanda had a point. She'd made headway building trust with Jones, but Yolanda? Quinn didn't know if she would ever fully trust her, or the Protectorate. But trust or not, she wasn't some underdog Tier Two apprentice anymore, trying to prove herself. She was part of the elite now, and paid accordingly, and she needed to start acting like it instead of like some rebellious, tattoo-laden Downtownie with a bad attitude.

"Loud and clear," Quinn said. "Won't happen again."

"Good. We sorted through the data and found fragments of an attack by two men in black, corroborating Mr. Hatch's story and what we found in our previous pass. Which means they're targeting him. We also found an episodic memory of a meeting with other leaders in the utility business—"

"Yes! I remember seeing Carrie Anne Halstead from Saguaro Energy and that guy from El Diablo Water..."

"Hector Olmos."

"Right. They're all power players who have monopolies that have become extremely valuable since the drought. But that seems kind of suspicious. Why would they all meet?"

"Actually, they meet monthly and have for years, and this memory dates back to their last meeting."

"Do you think the Jays will target them all?"

"It's too soon to know that, but it's something we are considering."

"Anything else?"

"That's all for now. I'll contact you when the next job comes."

"Sounds good."

"And Quinn?"

"Yes?"

"Go see the therapist. That's why we retain them. I need you in top condition."

"I'll think about it."

After they hung up, Quinn sat on her bed. She had no intention of visiting the Protectorate's therapist, whom she'd learned long ago was some dorky Midtowner who couldn't relate to the tribulations of the job, much less her and her background. Besides, she didn't need a therapist; she needed for people to quit rooting around in her limbic system, drumming up bad memories.

Putting that aside, Quinn reflected on the Hatch job and realized they'd made progress. Progress was good.

Now it was time to tackle another problem.

CHAPTER 12

IT WASN'T WORKING.

Over the years, Quinn had become adept at hacking into various secure systems and getting the information she needed. But the El Diablo Police Department didn't mess around when it came to cybersecurity. She couldn't break in.

Her phone pinged.

Quinn glanced at it, only to find a breaking news headline glaring at her.

"*Two dead after another shooting in White Sands, the fourth in a year.*"

Quinn grabbed her phone and called Jones.

"Yeah," he said, sounding tired.

"Hey. You guys okay? With the shooting and all?"

A big sigh. "Yeah. But Jeffrey's hiding in our bedroom and he won't come out."

"You want to postpone? I'm having a hell of a time trying to get the information I need, so no big hurry."

"It's alright. They got the shooter in custody, and I could use an excuse to get outta here for a while. Be there in thirty."

Quinn got back to work. But by the time Jones arrived, she was no closer to breaching EDPD's systems.

Jones wore jeans and a button-down, and he sported a scarf to hide his neck tattoos. He'd grown hair on his shaven head. If it weren't for the fact that he moved like a Downtown thug, he looked just like a Midtowner. He didn't dress that way to fit in with her Midtown neighbors—he couldn't care less what they thought of him—but did so to avoid looking memorable. The last thing they needed was for people to remember his face or associate it with hers. Normally they only met Downtown, but today's task required privacy.

He looked distracted, even annoyed, as he walked in. Quinn began to wonder if he resented helping her with her stalker situation. He had enough problems of his own without adding hers to his plate. Quinn got him a root beer before he could ask.

"Nice joint," he said flatly.

He was trying to be polite, but she knew he disapproved of the entire notion of living in Midtown. Yet, she could tell by how long he looked around, how he seemed to calm a little in the nice space with a decent view, that he too could appreciate the upgrade in living situation. But it would violate his thug code to admit that to anyone, because no self-respecting thug would ever admit to wanting to leave his neighborhood, even if it was in his best interests.

Jones took a seat while Quinn toiled some more. Finally, she let out a whoop. She was in. She located what she was looking for, and copied the necessary documents to an external drive.

"That everything?" Jones said. "The report, too?"

Quinn nodded. "We need to know what Noah and the other jacker cops saw that night at the Lindens' place. They obviously didn't report everything to the news. Something about that night doesn't add up."

"Assumin' the report has everything in it..."

Quinn shrugged. "It's an internal document..."

"Cops bend the rules when they need to. Your boy is proof of that."

She gave him a look. "He's not my boy."

"Coulda fooled me," he muttered.

Annoyance began to prickle at her. "Don't start. It's not my fault that..." She didn't want to say it.

"That of all the guys in this city you coulda banged, you picked a jacker cop?" Jones said.

"I told you I didn't know he was a cop," Quinn snapped. "And why are you on my ass all of a sudden? We've pretty much ruled him out as the one sending me the threats."

"He's still showin' up here, kidnappin' you... probably waitin' for the right time to come after us and threaten our livelihoods." Jones set down his root beer with a loud crack.

Quinn stared at him. "If you don't want to be part of this, you don't have to."

"It ain't that."

"Then what the hell is wrong with you tonight?" Suddenly, it hit her. "It's the shooting, isn't it? You made it sound like no big deal, but it rattled you."

"It didn't rattle me," he growled. "Just drop it, alright?"

Quinn took a deep breath to control her temper. She wanted to press it, but something told her that beneath Jones's snarling lay a deeper worry.

"Jones," Quinn said, softening her tone. "Whatever's bothering you, you can tell me. You'll feel better if you get it off your chest. You've seen me have a total meltdown and I've seen you half dead. We should be past fronting, and there's nobody who wouldn't be a little freaked out by a rash of shootings in their own neighborhood. So spit it out."

Jones slumped in his chair. "It ain't me, alright? It's Jeffrey."

"What about Jeffrey?"

"He's... havin' issues. It ain't just the shooting, either. We got these new neighbors and they get wasted and fight a lot. It upsets him and he's been difficult as fuck lately."

"Is there something I can do to help?"

Jones fiddled with his root beer. "No. We gotta move. But Jeffrey hates change, and truth is I don't wanna deal with it. He doesn't get that change means he won't have all that shit that upsets him anymore because we'll be livin' in a nicer hood. He can't think that way..." He shook his head. "I don't know what to do. If it were up to me, we'd stay in our place. It's good enough for me."

"I know it is," Quinn said. "What about moving to Sunnyside, like we talked about before? It's safer, it's still Downtown, and they have that place—Solera, I think?—that offers education and activities for adults with mental disabilities..."

"I've tried. They ain't takin' new clients. And I don't wanna move and put us all through that if we can't get him services."

"Do they have a waiting list?"

"Dunno."

"Well, find out. You have to bug these people. And maybe you should move, and wait until they take new clients again. They have to eventually."

"Maybe. But I got the feelin' they prefer a different kinda client, if you know what I mean."

Quinn nodded. She did know. When given a choice, sometimes organizations, even those with a mission to help, preferred higher-class clientele to Downtownies. It was as if they feared those from the poorer neighborhoods would bring all their problems and poverty with them, like an airborne disease.

"It would still be good for you guys to get out of White Sands, Jones. A quieter, safer neighborhood would benefit Jeffrey. And I'm more than happy to help you look for a place, and help you with moving."

"You can't be helpin' us. You got more problems than I do and you gotta keep a low profile."

"That's what wigs are for." She grinned at her own joke, but Jones didn't smile back. "Look. I'll tell you something my dad told me after my place got burglarized, after I found out Noah was a cop and the Borelli job went to shit. He said people stay stuck in bad situations because they hate change. I didn't get it at first, because I wanted change. I wanted to make Tier One and get out of Downtown and change all kinds of things. But I was resisting change by clinging to what felt familiar, by trying to get my old partner back and not giving you a chance." She paused. "This move of yours, if it happens, is a huge change for you and your family. You'd be leaving behind what you've always known, even if it's not that great. You just have to take it one step at a time."

She waited for Jones to brush off her mini personal growth seminar, but he didn't. He just sat there, contemplating. Finally, he spoke.

"You ever get..." He shook his head. "Never mind."

"Ever get what?" When he hesitated again, she said, "Scared? Sometimes. Pissed off? On a regular basis—"

"Lonely," he interrupted, turning to her again. "You ever get lonely?"

Quinn looked down for a moment. "Every day."

Jones blinked a couple of times. "At least you fit in a hookup or two. I can't even do that, not with my situation at home."

"And look how that turned out for me," Quinn said with a wry smile. "And the ones before him..." She shrugged. "It's satisfying at the time, but afterward you wind up feeling even lonelier."

Jones grunted at that. "So that's it? A life without, until we got enough saved to survive on low-paying work? Assuming we don't die or wind up in the clink..."

Quinn nodded. She'd had the same thoughts, many times.

But she'd always pushed them aside, knowing there was no real solution to them. A lot of people in their business avoided relationships, or lied to their partners. Quinn wouldn't lie, and she knew Jones well enough to know he wouldn't either.

"At least you got options at the Protectorate, with most of the agents bein' guys and all," Jones went on. "There're only a few women, and none of them want a thug like me." He eyed her. "So why ain't you choosin' from that pool?"

She shrugged. "They aren't for me."

"Ain't no one good enough for Quinn, huh?"

"It's not that. I just... I don't feel it."

"Feel somethin' with the cop?"

Quinn's face began to heat up.

Jones raised his eyebrows. "For real? You weren't just nailin' a Midtowner for fun?"

"At first, but it took an unexpected turn."

"Jesus. That's why he's hassling you."

Quinn shook her head. "I can handle him. We've got bigger problems." She pulled up EDPD's images of the two Black Jays, bloodied and dead on the Lindens' white rug. "Do you think it's a coincidence the news only reported that two 'suspect individuals' were dead, but didn't identify who they were, mention their tattoos, or even mention the Black Jays?"

She then scrolled through the internal report until she found what she was looking for. "See, right here. It says they couldn't identify the men, that prints and DNA yielded no matches in their system or the national registry, and that the guys didn't have any IDs on them. There's a mention of the bird tattoos, but that's it. Even the cops don't know who they are or know anything about the Jays."

Jones nodded. "Which means we gotta hunt these guys down the old-fashioned way. And I know just the guy."

CHAPTER 13

Quinn stepped into her heels and straightened her shift dress. It was a nice dress, but it lacked the elegance of her red one, her former favorite, sullied by a dumpster filled with garbage and ruined forever. But her current black one served its purpose by making her look like a Midtown professional woman. Along with a long black wig and heels, those who hunted her wouldn't recognize her.

Neither did Jones, until she smiled at him.

"Ain't as nice as the red one."

"Don't remind me."

They got on the train and made their way to the outskirts of town, where concrete metropolis suddenly transformed into desert. Quinn could hardly stand to look at it. It was lush once—by desert standards, anyway—with tall green cacti, ocotillo, shrubs, and wildflowers that came alive when even a small amount of rain came. Now it was all gone, faded to crumbled tan dust and blown away by the dry desert winds.

They walked under the highway bridge and beyond concrete buildings, until they reached their destination. Quinn hadn't visited the underground in some time, and it was still little more than a giant abandoned warehouse that had seen better days.

They walked past a network of makeshift rooms and "offices" with corrugated walls and floors that were half concrete and half dirt, one after the other with no end in sight. Quinn took in the familiar menage of cannabis, coffee, and trash talk that permeated the place. The entrances to each space were often manned by surly-looking men and women in comfortable desert-colored clothing... in case they needed to make a quick escape if the cops showed.

But the cops rarely came out here anymore, unless something big was going on. If anything, many had relationships with some of the underground players in order to sweep for suspects or potential CIs. Quinn knew because she'd seen them here herself. Even in plainclothes, she could always tell. But the cops kept a low profile, as an arrest or display of power meant never getting a lick of useful information in the future.

Finally, they arrived at one particular nook, its door a column of hanging beads. On the other side of the beads stood a table loaded with multiple computers running off a giant power cell that was so poorly constructed that Quinn questioned its safety. At the table sat a skinny guy with dark hair down to his waist and a face covered in tattoos.

Jones gave him a nod. "Pablo. Long time."

The guy took one look at Quinn and scowled. "Who you bringin' here, man?"

"The girl I told you about. You said you needed to see her."

Quinn took off her sunglasses, and the guy studied her face. "I seen you here before."

Quinn nodded.

"Whatcha need?" Pablo said to Jones.

Jones held up a wad of cash, then pulled out his phone and produced an image, one Quinn had filched from the EDPD. It was the face of one of the two dead Jays, the one Jones had fought that night, the enhanced and bruise-free mock-up created by the

EDPD's facial reconstruction software. "You know this guy? Big guy—my size—knows how to fight?"

"Yeah. I know him."

"Who is he?"

Pablo hesitated. "I can't be rattin' people out, man—"

"He's dead. And he tried to kill me for no fucken good reason."

That seemed to be enough. Pablo lowered his voice. "Name's Carlson. Don't know much, but he was into somethin' big. I can always tell these things."

"What else? First name, address, who he associates with?"

Pablo shook his head. Then, after a moment: "Talked like a Midtowner. Mesquite, maybe Commons, if I were a bettin' man."

"So an ED native."

The guy nodded. "No doubt in my mind. Oh, and his old man was a big player for years, till he got rung up for murder."

Jones pulled up another enhanced image, the Jay Quinn had fought. "What about this one? Smaller guy, but fights like the devil."

Pablo examined the image for a moment, then narrowed his eyes. "Yeah. I seen him too, but only once, maybe twice." He turned to Quinn. "See, I don't forget a face. You know what I mean?"

"What do you know about him?" Jones pressed.

"Polite guy. Green. Like he ain't used to it, you know? Not a player."

"Know his name?"

Pablo shook his head. "Like I said, not a player. Came lookin' for a fryer. That's all I know."

A fryer. The Jay had bought an energy weapon. Probably the very one she'd given to Jones.

Jones handed Pablo the roll of cash. "Thanks, brother. And remember... we only here to buy some tech."

Pablo nodded.

Quinn exited through the beads with Jones right behind her, and they began zigzagging their way through the labyrinth of cubbies toward the exit. Suddenly, everything seemed to quiet and heads turned toward something she couldn't see. Quinn stopped and peered through an opening between offices to see what the problem was, praying it wasn't the cops on one of their rare raids. There were no men in uniform, though. Instead, someone even worse stood there.

Noah. In jeans, a black tee, and a Demon's hat. Even with sunglasses on, she knew without a doubt it was him.

Quinn backed away from the opening, only to crash into Jones. She stumbled and he caught her.

"What?" Jones whispered.

"Noah!"

Jones, needing to see for himself, peered through the opening. "Fuck. He's headed this way." He motioned to her to follow him, and they headed back the way they came, Quinn doing her best to keep up with Jones in her heels. When they reached Pablo's office, they scurried inside.

"Got another job for ya, buddy," Jones said to Pablo as Quinn tried to stop the beads from swaying back and forth.

Pablo, his eyes narrowed, listened as Jones gave instructions to go keep an eye on Noah and let them know when he left. Just as Pablo disappeared through the beads, he appeared again, walking backward as someone followed him inside. Noah.

Quinn, feeling like a trapped animal, grasped her weapons in her pockets, but praying hard she wouldn't need them. Asshole or not, she couldn't stand the idea of busting Noah's jaw or even hobbling him. Noah took off his sunglasses, putting them on his hat. His brown eyes went right to Quinn, a half-smile on his face.

"You can take your hands out of your pockets, Quinn," he said. "I'm here on business. Just like you." He glanced at Jones.

The two men eyed each other, recognition in their eyes. "Good to see you're still alive, man," Noah said to Jones, his tone cocky. "You looked a little grim last time we met."

Jones said nothing, and maintained his steely stare.

Noah turned to Pablo and stuck out his hand. "I don't think we've met. I'm Noah."

"Pablo," the guy mumbled. He reluctantly shook Noah's hand, probably deciding it was better to do so than risk the unknowns of offending him.

"What do you want, Sergeant Martinez?" Quinn said, tired of his games.

"Don't mind me," Noah said to Pablo. "I'm not here to cause you trouble. I just saw Quinn sneaking away and couldn't resist the opportunity to say hello."

"You mean like the time you drugged me and tied me up at your place?" Quinn said. She saw Jones bristle next to her, and she wondered at herself, at how her mouth sometimes worked faster than her mind.

Undeterred, Noah sat on the corner of Pablo's desk. "Got you to talk to me, didn't it? You know how much I enjoy our talks. And I think I recall you breaking into my place to stake it out before that, right?" He smirked. "How'd that work out for you, anyway?"

"How'd the kidnapping work out for you?" she replied.

Noah's smirk faded.

"There's always next time," he said coldly.

Quinn gritted her teeth. He was enjoying this. He liked knowing he had the upper hand, knowing they had no idea what he would do next. She wanted to lash out at him, tell him to go to hell and that she would never become his confidential informant, that she would never bow down to him or any other cop. She wanted to scream at him for everything—for hunting her down, for kidnapping her. For disappointing her. But she couldn't. She couldn't let him know how much he infuriated her because it gave him an advantage. And she didn't want Pablo knowing any more than he did, or he'd wind up ratting her out to some other guy offering up cash.

And the truth was, she had no idea what Noah was capable of. He probably wasn't the one sending her the violent threats, but he was still stalking her, and if he didn't get what he wanted he would begin to resort to desperate measures. Because underneath the confidence and that grin was a simmering intensity, one she didn't want to mess with.

"We were just leaving," Quinn finally said. She stepped forward, hoping that Noah wouldn't stand in her way.

He didn't. He stood aside as she left the cubby, Jones on her heels. As they headed toward the exit again, she heard Noah's voice behind them.

"Quinn."

She stopped and turned around, as did Jones.

"My offer still stands," he said. "I strongly urge you to consider it."

This time, there was no smile on his face.

"Well, look what we have here," Quinn said, staring at her computer while sipping her diablo at Sidewinder.

"A way to take down that cop boyfriend of yours?" Jones said flatly.

"Stop calling him that," she snapped.

"It ain't good that he showed up there, of all places. He was probably following us the whole time." He shoved his root beer away. "I don't need this. We can't have that guy showin' up at the wrong time and ruining everything—"

"Tell me something I don't know, Jones! What do you want me to say? That I'm sorry, again?"

"I ain't blamin' you, alright? I'm just sayin'... this guy's a problem. I get the feelin' this ain't just him bein' a gung-ho cop. This feels personal. Like he's still hung up on you."

Quinn shook her head. "He's not. He's got plenty of options, believe me. And he'll back off once he finds bigger prey to hunt."

"You sure about that?"

She wasn't, not entirely. "Look, like I said, I can hurt him just as much as he can hurt me, and he knows it. Just... give it time."

Jones shook his head, grabbing his root beer. "Real shame."

"What is?"

"Him bein' a lawman. 'Cause you two are perfect for each other. Both gotta make sure you come out on top."

"Can we move on, please?"

He nodded at her computer. "Whatcha find?"

Quinn, glad to finally change the subject, turned the computer to face Jones. "Our boy Carlson? The one who shot you that night? Pablo was right. He was a Midtowner. I traced addresses for him in Mesquite, back to his childhood."

Jones studied the data she'd rounded up on Elliot Carlson. "How'd you find it when the cops couldn't?"

"Because of what Pablo said about Carlson's father being in prison. I started with him and followed that trail to some Midtown General birth records. Dad's name is Jake Carlson, resident of Chihuahua Prison for the last seven years." She pulled up Jake's mug shots and showed them to Jones.

"They look alike... but how do you know it's him? There's lots of Carlsons..."

"Sure, but how many have fathers in prison and a Midtown accent? Plus, why would the Black Jays risk coming after me when I'm no more of a threat than you or anyone else? Yes, they could be targeting us one at a time, trying to defeat their enemy, but the threats I've gotten feel personal. Like they're coming from someone angry about losing his only son. In his messages, he used

"I" instead of "we" and made it clear he wanted revenge for the men *I* killed. Who's more motivated than a parent? And who's more suspicious than a felon with a murder sheet?"

"This is all real useful, Quinn... but we got one little problem."

"What's that?"

"He's in prison. He can call you and send you shit, but he can't do nothin' else. And any phone they got in prison could be traced unless he's in deep with one of them underground guys. And you said them packages didn't even have postage. That don't sound like it's comin' from Chihuahua."

Quinn smiled. "It's not. Jake Carlson got out on parole two months ago." Jones raised his eyebrows. "He's our guy. And... I know where he lives."

CHAPTER 14

WHEN THE WIND kicked up another gust, dust and debris blew against Quinn's sunglasses and hat, and she pulled on her mask to avoid breathing in too much dust.

A dry thunderstorm. Quinn could barely recall the days when a thunderstorm actually produced precipitation. Sometimes it was just a sprinkle, other times a flash flood, but now it was nothing but particulates and electricity in the air.

But that was good for her. Again, the weather allowed Quinn to cover herself without looking like she was trying to hide from the growing number of dangerous men after her.

Quinn finally arrived at Hole, descending into the dark, cool cave as electronic music greeted her. She looked around at the tattoos and bright hair, and smiled. It felt strangely good to return to her old haunt.

Daria saw her and waved. She wore a bright pink tank with her knee-length cargoes, and she looked... happier. She stood up when Quinn approached.

"Hey, girl," she said.

"Hey, Dar."

They hugged, and Quinn held onto her for a few moments, hardly believing this was her childhood friend and former tech partner. She'd been so upset by Daria turning her back on her and their livelihood, and had hoped to win her back, but with time she'd come to see that Daria was never cut out for the business.

They sat down at the table, and before long Soo came over and grinned at Quinn. "Hey, girl! Haven't seen you in a while! Too good for us now?" She winked.

Quinn laughed. "I'm still around, but I'm working north now."

Soo made a point of clearing her throat as she looked at Daria. "By north, she means Midtown, right?"

Daria laughed. "Two diablos. The good ones. Quinn's buying."

"Ooh!" Soo said, her eyes wide. "I'll be right back."

"So how are you?" Quinn said. "How's nursing school?"

Daria beamed. "I love it. It's hard, though. You know I hate getting up early, and my chemistry class..." She made a face. "But I already get to work at this clinic for a few hours every week, and some of the kids have special needs, and they're so fun to work with!"

Quinn nodded, reminded of Jeffrey.

"How are you? How's the mind-fucking business?" Daria arched one eyebrow.

Quinn hesitated at her tone. "Since when do you call it that?"

"Since I've been doing legit work that actually helps people, rather than pretending it does."

Ah. So Daria was in that sort of mood today. Before she could respond, Soo brought their drinks and set them down, winking again before she left.

"It's... it's fine," Quinn said.

"No one's tried to kill you lately?" Daria joked.

Quinn forced a smile, not wanting to let on just how close Daria had come to the truth. "No, but give it a few days..."

"How's your dad? Did he mention we ran into each other?"

"He did. And, he's fine. He's sober."

"For Joe Hartley, that's outstanding news."

Quinn smiled. "That's the truth."

"He still dealing?"

"Yeah. But I'm trying not to be judgmental. Especially considering the reality of my life."

Daria snorted. "Well, look who's gotten off her high horse."

Suddenly, anger rolled through Quinn. "What the hell is your problem, Dar? I was looking forward to seeing you, but you're all over my ass the minute I sit down."

"I'm just messing with you!"

"Well, don't."

Daria's smirk faded. Quinn realized the gulf created by Daria's leaving their business not only still existed, but had possibly widened when Quinn moved away.

"Sorry," Daria said. "I guess I'm a little mad that you moved to Midtown, and thought I'd throw you a little Downtown-style razzing, just to keep you honest..."

Quinn's anger dwindled. "You know me. I'm always honest. And even though I moved, I'm still me."

"Have you met any nice people up there?"

"Not really," Quinn admitted. "Well, the building maintenance worker. And this one guy... Devin. He's been pretty nice. Plus, he has a pet iguana." She sipped her drink. "He's really cute."

"The iguana or the guy?"

Quinn giggled. "The iguana. His name is Lucifer." Daria cracked up at that. "Although the guy isn't bad either..."

"It didn't work out with the Midtown guy?"

"No." Quinn never told Daria the truth about what happened with Noah. She'd always trusted Daria completely, but things were different now. "I'm abstaining from now on. Too complicated."

"Maybe I should too. I mean, is finding a goodhearted thug too much to ask for?"

"They exist, but you have to search hard."

"Exactly. And without you around to scare away the assholes, it's even harder."

Quinn laughed. They were back on track.

"Sorry if I was weird before," Daria said. "I had a dark moment. To make it up to you, I'll buy the drinks."

"No," Quinn said, shaking her head. "I've got it. But I do want to run something by you."

"What is it?"

"You mentioned working with kids who have special needs. I have a friend whose brother is developmentally delayed. He wants to move, and he's thinking about Sunnyside because there's a clinic there for people like his brother. I can't remember the name..."

"The Solera Clinic?"

"Yes! That's the place. But they told him they aren't taking any new clients and I think he and his mom are struggling to take care of him."

"How old is he?"

"Not sure. In his twenties..."

"So he's an adult. That's good. Solera doesn't take kids. One of the nurses at my clinic works there part time. Do you want me to look into it for you? Maybe find out when they can take someone new?"

"That would be great, Dar. These are such nice people—Downtownies—and they could really use the help."

"So who is this guy?" Daria gave a cheeky grin.

"Just a friend."

How could she explain? Daria knew how the Protectorate

worked and had sworn to keep its secrets, but Quinn didn't know if Daria had ever crossed paths with Jones and didn't want to reveal his identity without his permission. Just asking for help on his behalf was risky enough.

"I'll talk to Nurse Haley about Solera," Daria said. "Let me see what I can find out."

As Quinn left, she checked her phone and had a missed call from her dad. But when she tried to call him back, service was down. It didn't matter. She was headed that way.

The winds finally died down just as the sun disappeared. Quinn kept her head scarf and sunglasses on, determined to remain as incognito as possible.

As she walked in the fading light, she occasionally patted her pockets to ensure her weapons were inside. She missed the days when her main concern was Downtown thugs with their probing eyes and brash comments. Now, she didn't know who would be around the corner.

Finally, she arrived at her father's building in Westgate and entered the code he'd given her for the building. She headed downstairs to the lower level and knocked on the door. When there was no answer, she knocked again, louder this time. Still no answer.

Finally, she banged on the door with her fist. A neighbor's door opened then, and a scrawny man with leathery skin gave her an annoyed look.

"He ain't there, so you can quit bangin' on the door."

Quinn sighed in annoyance. "Do you know when he's coming back?"

"Nope. But if you need somethin', maybe I can help ya..." He looked at her expectantly, a look she understood immediately.

Great. Apparently, this was the drug dealer's floor. Easy in and out for customers.

"I don't need anything," Quinn snapped. "I'm his daughter."

The man looked surprised for a moment, then shrugged and went back inside.

Quinn checked her phone. Service was back up, and sure enough there was a message. Her dad had to "go to work" for a while. He would catch up with her soon. Quinn shook her head and left. Before she was even a block away, her phone rang, and Quinn hoped it was her dad. But it was Jones.

"Hey," she said.

"You at home?" Jones sounded rushed, like he needed something.

"No. What's going on?"

"I gotta bead on Carlson."

Quinn stopped walking. "How?"

"By trackin' his phone."

"Where is he?"

"Some bar in Coyote. He just got here."

A tingle ran through Quinn. Then she made a face. "I'm all the way in Westgate. With no equipment."

"Just get here as soon as you can. This is our chance."

CHAPTER 15

QUINN ADJUSTED her wig as the taxi headed Downtown. The purple wig would do this time, along with her torn-up gray cargoes and jacket filled with the equipment she would need.

But it was the neck tats—fake—that would help her most tonight.

She needed to fit in Downtown, but more importantly she needed to not look like herself. Jake Carlson couldn't recognize her, at least not until it was too late, or the jig was up.

When the taxi stopped, Quinn handed over some cash and headed to the alleyway that Jones had communicated to her. She took a deep breath and entered the dark alley, every instinct in her resisting doing so. Heat emanated from the asphalt and concrete buildings, and the alley stank of urine.

She clutched her weapons until her knuckles ached, and her pace slowed to a crawl without her even realizing it. When she heard a noise and saw a hulking figure in the shadows, her heart began to pound.

It was Jones. Quinn let out her breath, not realizing she'd been holding it.

"You alright?"

She nodded. "Alleys aren't my favorite. Especially in Coyote."

"Shit. Right. Figured it was safest here..." He was right about that. People generally didn't wander in alleyways in that infamous neighborhood.

"Did you find a back way in?"

"Yep," Jones said. "All you gotta do is wait for him to go take a piss, send me the signal, and we got him."

"Do I look alright? I'm screwed if he recognizes me."

Jones glanced at her again and nodded. "Yeah. You look like a proper Coyote girl. All you need is a cig."

Quinn smiled, patting her pocket. "Got 'em."

"Good girl."

Quinn stuck the earpiece deep in her ear, so Jones could hear everything that was going on. Just as she turned to leave, Jones grabbed her arm.

"Be careful. Don't be a fucken hero. If anything looks wrong, get out and run north. I'll be right behind you."

She nodded, hesitating. "Thanks. For doing this. I know it's a lot to ask, especially when this isn't your problem. If I can make it up to you in some way—"

"Hey, you're my meal ticket. I can't have you dyin' on me."

Quinn wondered at that. Jones was making a joke, but she couldn't deny that there was truth to what he said. Losing her meant probably getting partnered with a Tier Two for a while, and the low pay that came with it.

She left the alley and headed around the block to the entrance of Canine. It was a small establishment in an old stucco building with chipped tan paint and no windows. It had a beat-up, faux-wood door with a mural of a wild dog with red eyes snarling at whoever entered, its canine teeth dripping with saliva. She took a deep breath and opened the door.

Inside, it was barely cool enough to be tolerable. The place was long and narrow, the bar along one side and tables along the other. Music chugged in the background, overwhelmed by loud voices. The seats were filled with people with facial tats and rows of empty glasses in front of them, the air clouded with smoke of all kinds.

Several people turned to stare at her, whether to ogle a new piece of female meat or because they recognized that despite her cultivated Coyote appearance she wasn't a regular. She donned her Downtown scowl and headed toward the bar. She suppressed the urge to cough at all the smoke.

It didn't take long to spot him. Jake Carlson sat at one of the tables with another guy, his face lined and his hair grayed, but his frame solid and hardened, like he could easily hurt someone. Suddenly, he stood up from his seat and headed back, disappearing around the corner. He was already headed to the restroom. Quinn froze for a moment. This was her chance.

But it was too soon. She couldn't just stroll into a place where nobody knew her and immediately head to the bathroom. It would look suspicious to anyone who watched. Which meant she would have to wait until nature called again, assuming it did before he left for the night. She forced herself to look away and found a seat at the bar.

There, a shaven-headed, tatted-up-to-his-neck bartender raised his chin at her.

"Twenty," she said flatly.

That was how you ordered in Coyote. By ounces, not size. They had several cheap tequila options and some sodas, but beer was the only real option for that night.

When Carlson returned to his seat, she watched him in the reflection of the mirror behind the bar. He was big, bigger than Jones. He wore monochrome prison tats and a noticeable scar that started at his hairline and traveled through his eyebrow, down his cheek, and all the way to his jaw. He didn't look like a

Midtowner. But he hadn't been one in years, not since before his prison days. Nor did he have the ninja-like look of a Black Jay. Then again, he wasn't a Jay. He was seeking revenge for one.

Three minutes hadn't passed before the guy sitting next to her turned and gave her the up-and-down. It was the Downtown way.

"How you doin', girl?"

Quinn ignored her initial defensive reaction. "Alright," she said. She raised her glass, a definitive sign that the overture wasn't unwelcome. He did the same and they drank.

They chatted a little, Quinn doing her best to stay in character, suddenly glad to befriend a thug. He made her look more legit when she was up to no good, and helped her pass the time before Carlson's bladder called to him again.

Eventually, it did, and Quinn excused herself.

"Game time," she muttered.

"On it," came Jones's voice in her ear.

Quinn headed to the back of the bar, where the din of smoke and noise mellowed, as did the light. Her heart began to pound like crazy, and dread nipped at her, making her hesitate. What was wrong with her? This was what she did best, and she'd done it countless times.

But this was different. She didn't have the backing of the Protectorate. And Carlson wasn't a target she was being paid to jack; he was the father of the Jay she'd fried that terrible night at Linden's place, the one who'd shot Jones and tried to shoot her. And someone who wanted her dead.

They would only have one chance at this. The moment she entered that restroom, there was no going back. They would corner Jake Carlson, they would jack him and get the evidence they needed on the Jays, then wipe any memories he had regarding her. It wasn't a perfect solution. But it was the best they had.

She rounded the corner toward the men's restroom, numerous possibilities running through her mind. Would there be other men inside? Would there be urinals to make things hard, or stalls to make things easy? Would Jake recognize her once he got a better look at her? Whatever the case, they would adapt. That's what they did.

She stopped at the men's room door and took a deep breath, glancing behind her to make sure no one followed.

Game time.

Quinn reached for the door. But just as she did, it opened forcefully, banging into her and shoving her backward until she crashed into the wall. Someone was coming out. Just as her mind quickly formed an excuse for her presence there—silly her, she was wasted and got the restrooms mixed up—a hulk of a man grabbed her.

"Goddamned jacker whore," came the gravelly voice before a fist crashed into her face. She went flying back and slammed against a stack of empty boxes. Just as she went for her weapon, Carlson fled toward the back door... and right into Jones.

She managed to recover herself and reached for her injector, ready to stick Carlson and drag him back into the restroom. But before she knew it, Carlson had somehow gotten past Jones and disappeared out the back, the metal door slamming into its doorstop with a bang.

Jones sprinted after him and Quinn followed. They could do this in the alleyway if they had to, assuming no one from the bar heard the scuffle and followed them outside. They wouldn't need much time; someone like Jake wouldn't be trained to prevent mind invasion. But once she got outside, she stopped in her tracks.

Jones stood there, a scowl on his face as he panted. He was alone. She looked in both directions... but Jake Carlson was gone.

Quinn cursed under her breath, the desire to run and hunt

Carlson down intense. But she didn't. He could have gone in either direction, and he could easily lose them in Coyote's circuitous alleys. Plus, chasing him exposed them both in a situation where neither could afford to attract attention. If Carlson waited around some corner with a weapon, or friends, the situation could turn ugly.

She turned to Jones, who was more silent than usual as he stuffed his energy weapon back into his pocket. He had the same scowl on his face, but Quinn quickly realized it wasn't quite a scowl. It was a grimace. When she looked down at his shirt, she saw why.

Blood. Lots of it.

CHAPTER 16

QUINN SAT WAITING at the Coyote med clinic. She squirmed in her seat, then got up to pace the lobby. She sat down again when people began looking at her funny.

Flashbacks of Daria's head injury returned, followed by those of a half-dead Jones getting rolled away on a gurney at Midtown General. It was a swirl of bad memories, accompanied by the bad feelings that came with them, all bombarding her like she'd invaded a target's mind. But this time they were her own thoughts, and she couldn't escape them. Because once again, Quinn sat and waited while her partner faced serious injury. And this time it felt worse because the injuries weren't due to the job. They were due to her.

It all happened so fast. One moment she faced that men's room door, and the next she stood in that putrid alley watching Jones's t-shirt turn bright red.

"You! Purple hair!" came the shout.

Quinn jumped. A doctor with glasses and bedraggled hair stood waiting, looking tired and impatient. When she approached him, the doctor didn't say anything, only turned and walked down the hallway, motioning for her to follow.

"Is Jones okay?" Quinn said when she caught up to him.

"He'll be fine," he muttered. He turned the corner and pointed to a room, then continued down the hallway.

Quinn hesitated and looked inside the room. There was Jones, resting on the bed, shirt off and pads on his wound. She hurried over to him.

"You okay?"

He waved a hand at her. "I'm fine. They did a quick surgery to fix the damage."

Quinn sighed, shaking her head, knowing it could've been much worse. "You shouldn't have to go through this. This is my fault—"

"Girl, you know how many times I been stabbed?" He lowered his voice. "That fucker saw us comin' and did what he had to do. I shoulda known better. Shoulda been prepared for that. Workin' these rich bastards for the Protectorate has made me soft."

She sat down, relieved he wasn't angry. "If that's true, how did he know?"

"Dunno. Probably recognized you. You looked Coyote to me, but them people know an outsider when they see one. Or he could be trackin' your phone. I'll look at it later."

She grabbed his hand. "I got this. I'll pay for it."

Jones gave a laugh. "You don't gotta pay. We got the decent insurance now, remember?"

Quinn stared at Jones. He was right. This would cost them little to nothing, far less than what Daria's head injury cost her and what Jones's surgery cost the Protectorate. She'd grown up living in fear of a medical situation ruining her financially, and she'd forgotten she wasn't in that situation anymore. "I'll cover whatever insurance doesn't."

Before Jones could respond, the doctor returned. "We need

to take one last look. If you check out fine, you can go, stabby." He looked at Quinn. "Purple hair, time for you to get out."

Quinn stood up and turned to Jones. "I'll wait until you're done."

"No. Go home. You can't be here."

As much as she hated it, Jones was right. Carlson or any of his associates would know about the injury and could come looking for them. She needed to get out of Coyote as soon as possible.

Quinn stared out the window of the taxi as it drove north. She'd had to wait for a ride, since taxis almost never roamed through Coyote. Nobody in Coyote could afford one. And Coyote types rarely had the need for transportation because they rarely left their neighborhood. Their motto was *Live in Coyote, Die in Coyote*.

Quinn watched in silence as the taxi passed by one of the Protectorate safe houses. Part of her wanted to tell them the truth, but she couldn't. Not until she'd solved the problem and had something to offer them. Them finding out any time before that meant she became a liability to them and they would cut her loose.

Tonight, she and Jones had screwed up. Jake Carlson had escaped their clutches, and without much effort on his part. He'd outsmarted them both and got away without a scratch. Jones was right; Carlson had seen them coming.

Even worse, they no longer had the element of surprise in their favor. Now, he knew she was on to him, and that she had the means—and the cojones—to pursue him. In the future, he would take measures to ensure she got nowhere near him.

Quinn gritted her teeth. Setbacks were part of life, and part of her work. But she hated them anyway. Especially when they threatened her livelihood.

When the taxi passed 30th Street and the landscape began to change, she started to feel better. Midtown, friendly or not, had fewer dark corners for someone like Carlson to hide in. Men like him stood out like a rose garden in the desert when they came to Midtown, with those tattoos and that huge facial scar.

No, if Carlson came after her, he wouldn't do it in Midtown. He'd proven that by only leaving her mail and sending her messages, never showing his face despite knowing where she lived. Then she had another thought. Bungled or not, tonight had one positive point: despite Carlson knowing she was coming after him, they were now on equal footing. She could find him, just like he'd found her. A smart man would realize he'd lost the advantage and back off. Only time would tell if Carlson was smart.

When the taxi stopped, Quinn paid cash for the fare, mentally tallying up how much she'd spent on taxis that day. Normally she would have cursed wasting so much money on a failed errand. Now, she wondered if that money wasn't well-spent after all. Carlson now knew who he was dealing with. They'd been unprepared this time, but that would never happen again.

She got out of the taxi wearing her Midtown best—a sundress and light jacket, her neck tats scrubbed away and the rest of her Coyote attire stuffed into a bag. As the taxi drove away, Quinn began walking the three blocks to her building.

Suddenly, someone grabbed her from behind. A hand covered her mouth and beefy, strong arms wrapped around her and pulled her off her feet. She knew immediately who it was.

Carlson.

She thrashed about, her screams muffled by his hand. As he dragged her into a narrow passageway between buildings, Quinn prepared her best self-defense quickly. If alone, Carlson couldn't kill her while also restraining her and covering her mouth, and she had a narrow window to turn this around.

She bit down on his finger as hard as she could. Teeth plunged through skin and sank into muscle until her jaw ached and she tasted the acrid flavor of blood on her tongue. He grunted loudly and cursed, then his fist slammed into her face.

A burning pain exploded in Quinn's nose, and then she saw nothing but darkness and fury. She kicked back her foot and landed on something hard—maybe a shin or a kneecap—and Carlson's grip loosened enough so she could get free.

In a moment, Quinn had her brass knuckles in hand. Without enough room in the narrow space to get a full hook, Quinn took the uppercut to his jaw, or what she hoped was his jaw, since it was too dark to see much. The crack that resulted told her all she needed to know. She pulled out her weapon, ready to deploy it, knowing it was the only thing that would ward off the steady stream of deadly force that Carlson would level at her. But instead of retaliating, he stumbled back, just enough so that the streetlight illuminated his face. And that's when she saw it.

Darker skin tone. No facial scar. Her attacker wasn't Carlson.

When he saw her weapon, he dropped something and ran off. Quinn stood there for a moment, not knowing what the hell just happened. When she looked down, her bag lay there, her purple wig and a few other things scattered about.

A mugger. He'd targeted her, tried to steal her bag, and found himself battling a former Downtownie with a few tricks up her sleeve instead of a defenseless Midtowner.

Shaking, Quinn gathered her things and left the narrow passageway, adrenaline racing through her as her eyes darted back and forth. The street was empty. She hurried to her building, and when she was almost there, she heard her name.

She jumped, looking up to find Devin and Lucifer, out for

their late evening walk. When Devin saw her face, his expression shifted to surprise.

"What happened to you?"

As if on cue, pain throbbed in her nose. She put her hand up to her face and felt warm blood. Devin picked up Lucifer and came closer, taking a good look.

"I... I got mugged," she finally said.

"Jesus," he said, looking her over and noticing her bag. "What did he take?"

"Nothing. We scuffled and then he ran off. I don't know if he heard someone coming, or what..."

She wanted to tell Devin the truth. That she did as much damage to him as he did to her, if not more. But she couldn't. She couldn't let on that she could fight well enough to scare off a man twice her size. Not in Midtown, where people—even former Downtownie Devin—would find that suspicious.

"Do you want me to call the cops?"

"No," she said a little too quickly. "I... I'm fine. It was dark and I didn't get a good look at him anyway. It's a waste of their time."

"Then let's take you inside and get you cleaned up."

As Devin watched her, Quinn wanted to argue, but didn't. Jones's words about loneliness returned, and the prospect of Devin helping her sounded pretty good after the day she'd had.

Devin led her inside. "Let me drop off Lucifer and I'll come over."

She told him her apartment number and headed home. Back at her place, Quinn examined herself. The bleeding had stopped and her nose wasn't broken. It just hurt.

When the doorbell rang, she froze. She realized she couldn't let Devin in her apartment. Her things were everywhere as she'd scrambled to prepare for going after Carlson, and there were many suspects wigs, outfits, and technical gadgets that would make Devin suspicious.

Never get dimed. Never let people even wonder about you. You have to seem like everybody else.

That mantra had been burned into them during training, and ever since. It was a sobering reminder, one she needed right now. She'd botched a job by underestimating an ex-con looking to kill her. Then she'd lowered her guard and gotten attacked by a random mugger. And she'd been moments from letting Devin see too much of her personal life. Jones said he'd gone soft... apparently, so had she.

She opened the door and stepped out into the hallway, closing it behind her. "Hey, Devin. Look... I appreciate the offer for help. But I'm tired, and the wound isn't anything a little ice and a drink won't fix." She smiled.

Devin hesitated, his expression changing. Like it wasn't the answer he wanted to hear.

But he only nodded. "I understand."

"Hey you two!" came a feminine voice.

Quinn turned to find Merritt at the end of the hallway, waving eagerly with a grin on her face.

"Hey Merritt." Quinn gave a brief wave, but an uncomfortable feeling settled in at Merritt's sudden appearance, right when Devin stood at her door. When Merritt disappeared into the stairwell, Devin pulled out a slim leather wallet from his pocket and took out a card. "This is my number. Call me if the pain gets worse, or if you feel nauseated or dizzy or anything out of the ordinary. Understand?"

She nodded, taking the card. "I will. Thank you."

Quinn slipped back inside and closed the door. She grabbed a bottle of tequila and the fixings for a diablo. Before she could make the drink, she heard a knock again. She smiled and peered through the peephole.

It was Devin again.

"What are you doing tomorrow?" he said when she cracked open the door.

"Avoiding all alleys?"

He smiled a little. "Feel like going to a Demons game?"

CHAPTER 17

QUINN AND DEVIN stood in line with a crowd of people clad in black-and-silver baseball jerseys and hats. She looked around at couples of all ages, fathers with their sons, groups of men... and started to wonder what she'd been missing for twenty-eight years.

She could never afford to attend a baseball game growing up. The games got prohibitively expensive after the drought came, once Demon Stadium got bought out by private investors and rebuilt to protect spectators from the deadly heat. As such, she'd never developed much of an interest in the game. It probably didn't help that her dad had spent more time watching the games on TV with a bottle in his hand than paying attention to her.

Devin presented his phone to the ticket checkers, who scanned them both in. Next, they stood in line for security scans: an electronic scan followed by a pat-down that she suspected was for alcohol more than anything dangerous. The stadium owners also owned a large liquor company and wanted to ensure spectators bought only from them.

Once they entered the once-forbidden stadium, Quinn couldn't help but stare. It was huge, for one thing. And nice, with comfy seats and plenty of food and drink options. Best of all, it was air-conditioned. She felt Devin's eyes on her.

"You've never been here before," he said.

"First time."

"Welcome to El Diablo's favorite pastime."

She smiled. "Thank you for inviting me. I could use the distraction."

His expression darkened. She knew why—she'd developed some bruising, thanks to her alley encounter and Carlson's punch. Hearing a woman talk about an attack was one thing, but seeing the evidence was another. He put his hand on her back to steer her toward a vendor selling Demons clothing.

"Let's get you a hat. Everyone's looking at me funny, like I'm the one who punished you for being a bad girl."

Quinn chuckled. Yet, despite being used to coarse male humor, the joke seemed a little off. She couldn't help but think Noah would never say something like that. Then again, Devin was different, and part of her liked that about him.

Soon, Quinn wore a baseball cap like everyone else, and she was grateful for the partial camouflage. Especially since she had no idea if her enemies were there that night. It was paranoid, sure, but Quinn learned that maybe a little paranoia was justified.

They found their seats and the game began. Quinn was rusty on the rules, but Devin gave her a quick rundown and it all came back pretty quickly. After an inning or two, Quinn found herself enjoying the game—the easy pace, the crack of the bat hitting the ball, the crowd cheering when a Demon got a base hit or caught a foul ball. She understood now: it was a dome-shaped, air-conditioned escape from the realities of life in El Diablo.

There were times when she felt Devin's eyes on her. Like he was trying to decide if he liked her, or whether she liked him. He'd grown on her, but there was a distance there, like he didn't get close to people easily. She could relate to that. He didn't have the effect on her that Noah had. Then again, that hadn't turned out so well.

"You alright?" he asked.

"Yeah. Why?"

"That was a pretty big sigh."

"I'm fine."

Soon, Quinn decided she was thirsty.

"I'm going to grab a drink. Want anything?"

Devin shook his head. Quinn headed up the stairs, keeping her eyes out for anyone staring too long or any sudden movements from the crowd. It was a difficult task with a crowd this large, which was why she chose to go during the inning, where she would encounter fewer people.

She went to the restroom first. On her way out, she halted when she saw someone unexpected. There, leaning against the wall, was Noah.

Quinn's heart began to pound, her hand immediately heading toward her groin, where her energy weapon lay hidden in its holster. Another brilliant thing about the illegal weapon: it was impervious to routine security scanners.

"I'd keep that thing hidden," Noah said. "I could get you four years easy just for bringing it to a game."

"What do you want?" she growled at him.

"You know what I want."

"I already told you I'm not interested in being your fucking snitch."

"I didn't ask whether you were interested." He took a step closer to her. She knew that move, the "I'm bigger than you and want to see if you'll back down" move, classic among Downtownie men.

She had few options. She could back away and create the space she needed, but that showed weakness. She could stay put and let him closer to her, risking that he'd pull a sudden move, rendering her unconscious and in his clutches again, with the expectation that he wouldn't make the mistake he did last time.

She did neither. Instead, she did the craziest thing possible.

She stepped closer to him. So close that she could feel Noah's body heat, smell the faint odor of his natural musk, the one she'd enjoyed many times, back when everything was different. Her eyes were locked with his, and she didn't look away for one moment or even blink.

It had the effect she'd hoped for. Noah froze, his eyes locked with hers and his breathing a little too still. She leaned close to him and spoke, putting her hand softly on his arm.

"I know how much you love to win. And I've always admired that about you." She smiled. "But you know me, and you know I will never let you control me. And something tells me that, deep down, you don't really want to."

Noah grabbed her so suddenly and with such ferocity that she let out a gasp. His dark eyes glimmered in anger, and when she tried to pull away, he held on.

"Let me go," she hissed.

Suddenly, she was free. Someone had shoved Noah away. It was Devin, his jaw set as he stared Noah down. Noah stared back, blinking in surprise for a moment before he quickly recovered.

"Back off," Noah growled. "This is police business."

Devin looked Noah up and down. "Then where's your badge?"

Quinn intervened. "It's okay, Devin. Noah and I were only catching up, and he was just leaving. Right?" She eyed Noah.

Noah pulled out a badge and flashed it at Devin. "Miss Hartley and I have business to discuss, so walk away." When Devin didn't comply, Noah took a step toward Devin, attempting the same move he'd tried on her.

Devin didn't budge. Instead, he held up his phone. "Well,

Officer Asshole, I've got a pretty good video of you assaulting her. I'm sure my friends in the media would love to get their hands on it."

"Blackmailing an officer isn't going to help your case," Noah said.

Devin only stared, and the coldness of that stare gave her chills. For a moment, she forgot he walked with a limp and wondered if he would attack Noah. But he didn't. Instead, he grabbed Quinn's hand, nudging her toward him and away from Noah. "Go fuck yourself."

Quinn followed as Devin led her away. Her heart was still pounding. She glanced back, afraid Noah would come after them and create a scene. But he didn't. He just stood there, glowering at them, and she knew she hadn't seen the last of him.

Back in their seats, drinks in hand, Devin said, "You in trouble with the cops?"

"No. Just that particular one."

"Were you two involved?"

Quinn hesitated. "Yes. Before." She didn't want to admit that, but Devin had proven he could stand up to Noah's intimidation, and now she had a witness in case Noah's tactics grew worse.

"If he's violent or abusive, you need to—"

"He's not. We just... had a misunderstanding."

She wondered at her choice of words. Thus far, Noah had stalked her, drugged and abducted her, grabbed her. But maybe tonight was a good thing. If Devin really did have friends in the media, his threat might ensure Noah left her alone.

She hoped so. As much as Noah was pissing her off, she didn't want to turn on him like that. She'd never turned on Wyatt, despite the many questionable things he'd done, despite the fact a little jail time might have corrected Wyatt's ways or even saved his life. It wasn't the Downtown way.

She only hoped Noah wouldn't force her hand.

. . .

Later that day, Quinn sat in her comfy chair, sipping a diablo. After the game, Devin had walked her to her door and asked to come inside her place. She declined. He tried to hide his disappointment, but she could see it.

Part of her wanted to let him in. Devin had been nothing but helpful—helping her after the mugging, taking her to a game, intervening with Noah. But there was a wall there, one she couldn't get past. And she knew why. Her profession—and her life—had turned her into someone unable to get close to anyone. The cost of doing so was too great. She'd lost her mother, lost Wyatt, and the closest she'd come to anything promising since had devolved into a power struggle between two determined people on opposites sides of the law. Again, she thought of Jones's confession about feeling lonely. It was something she'd long learned to accept, but at that moment it seemed harder than ever.

Her phone rang. Quinn glanced at it, praying it wasn't someone looking to torment her again. She sighed with relief when she saw it was Jones.

"Hey," she said. "What's up?"

"We got another chance at Carlson."

"When?"

"Right now."

CHAPTER 18

"GAME TIME," Quinn muttered to Jones, who stood next to her in the alley filled with broken glass.

Quinn peered into her viewing device, the one that allowed her to see around the corner. Even though the daylight was fading, she spotted Jake Carlson turn onto 20th Street. He was headed their way, and would pass by their alley in less than a minute, en route to a visit with his parole officer.

Jones had tracked Carlson's phone calls and managed to intercept part of one where he and his parole officer planned their meeting. It was a rare opportunity to catch him alone, rather than in a bar filled with witnesses. They had little choice but to do an old-school snatch-and-jack right there in the alley, with Jones keeping watch.

Another thirty seconds and Jones would strike, sticking Carlson with the sedative and pulling him into the alley in one quick swoop.

"Half a block," she said.

Jones rustled around behind her before he drew closer to the alley entrance, waiting.

Then, she saw it. The one thing she didn't want to see.

Noah.

He wasn't far behind Carlson, walking down the street in a Demons hat and sunglasses, like he was on a mission.

"God damn it," she said through her teeth.

"What's wrong?"

"Noah."

"Seriously?" Jones hissed.

She let out a breath and pushed Jones away. "Get out of here." When Jones hesitated, she whisper-yelled, "Go! You can't risk it! I'll deal with him."

"Don't do anything stupid."

Jones turned and ran deeper into the alley until he disappeared. Quinn backed away from the street and hid behind a dumpster. She hunched down and extended her device. A moment later, Jake Carlson skulked on by, his hands balled into fists, as if waiting for someone to jump him. Quinn stuffed her equipment into her pockets, grabbed her weapon, and headed to the establishment next door. Where there were witnesses.

Once inside, she realized it was a sex shop. She headed to the corner, where she was surrounded by a display of giant dildos. When Noah appeared, as expected, he joined her and glanced around.

"So this is your thing, huh?"

"What the fuck do you want?" she growled.

"Why so angry? Did I foil your chance to grab Jake Carlson?" She must've shown some surprise, because he smiled, showing just a hint of those dimples. "Mr. Carlson called us to report a suspected mindjacking attempt at a little joint in Coyote. The description of his attackers sounded very familiar. Plus, I figured only you would be crazy enough to go after an ex-con in a place even I would hesitate to go in."

"You have no real evidence it was me, and you know it."

"I have two witnesses who described your face and build, one of whom said you carried brass knuckles. Seems that's your signature. I saw the damage you did to those men at Linden's place, and it was obvious a pair of knucks broke the jaw on one of them. Not to mention a short but distinguished list of knuck-induced busted jaws and broken noses, all taking place Downtown by women whose descriptions all sound very similar..."

He had her there. But again, the evidence was circumstantial at best.

"I'm sick of this shit, Noah. You need to quit stalking me, or else you'll force me to resort to desperate measures."

"Oh yeah? Like what?" He crossed his arms and waited.

"Try me and find out."

"I'm not going to stop until you give me what I want. Because like you said, I really, really like to win." His eyes shot daggers at her. "The real question is, if I were to cuff and search you right now, what would I find? Would I find a mind reader and nodes? Data storage devices? Other paraphernalia that would implicate you?"

Dread fell over her.

Noah went on. "That's all I need to bust you, Quinn. I don't need any of the other circumstantial evidence I have on you— which is growing by the day—although it wouldn't hurt my case one bit. And before you say it, any dirt you have on me is more than cancelled out by what I've got on you now."

Fear coursed through Quinn, and then turned to anger. "You are such a fucking hypocrite! You're no better than I am and you know it. The only reason you're leaning on me isn't because of some bullshit need for justice, it's because you want to hurt me."

"Why would I want to do that?"

"Because I hurt you. You liked me, and I hurt you. I'm the one goddamned thing you hate because of what happened to your father, and you keep hoping that messing with me will make it all go away. But it won't. You can't scapegoat me for someone else's crime."

Noah's eyes flared with anger. "Don't try that shit on me, Quinn. I invented that." He stepped closer to her. "And don't ever bring up my father."

When a customer approached, she took one look at Quinn and Noah and backed away.

"Why not?" she hissed. "What happened to your father is terrible, Noah, but if you had any damned clue about the people you hunt, you'd know that no mindjacker would ever do that to someone. That was a mind thief—"

"So you've said—"

"No." She pointed at him. "Listen to me. Mind thieves are dangerous and not like us—"

"Who's us?"

Quinn stopped herself. She had to be careful. "What *I* do... there's a code. You haven't been able to nail people like me because we're good at what we do, and we don't hurt people! And my targets... they're guilty one hundred percent of the time."

"So there's honor among mind thieves, huh?" he scoffed. "It's still wrong, rooting around in someone's fucking head like that. And if you don't know that—"

"Oh, to hell with your pious crap, Noah. You've stalked me! You drugged and abducted me and you've threatened me—"

"I'm allowed to do all of that!" he hissed back. "In case you've forgotten, I'm a cop and mindjacking is felony!"

"Really? You're allowed to drug a female suspect, take her home, and tie her to your bed?"

Noah hesitated. "I had to. I knew it was the only way you would listen to me, the only way to get through that stubborn head of yours."

"Listen to what?"

He let out a breath. "I wanted to give you a way out, okay? Because if you keep this shit up you're going to wind up in prison, or worse."

Quinn blinked at Noah's honesty. "Look, Noah. I cared about you—"

Noah shook his head. "I don't want to hear it—"

"It's the truth. I cared about you. A lot."

He rolled his eyes. "Right. That's why you hid the truth from me, about what you do. Knowing I would hate it."

"I didn't—"

"You did," he said coldly. "You didn't look surprised to see me that night in that Uptown alley. See, that's when I figured it all out. That's when I realized that during the entire Linden job I was chasing you. You knew before I did." He stared at her. "So how long? How long did you know I was a cop?"

Before Quinn could answer, he went on. "Never mind. I don't fucking care because you're evil, Quinn. All your kind are—"

"If I'm so evil, why let me go that night?" Quinn pressed, knowing she pushed her luck about as far as it would go.

"Because I was an idiot." He pulled out his handcuffs. "Turn around."

Shit. Nothing she said had helped at all. There was no way she was getting out of this without resorting to extreme methods... methods that turned her stomach to consider. When Noah came toward her, she held out her hand to stop him.

"They're Black Jays," she blurted out.

Noah stopped. "What?"

"The dead men in black at Linden's... they're called Black Jays. They're an organized group of mind thieves. That's why they wear those blackbird tattoos. They're the ones you want, not me."

"How do you know this?"

"I know a lot of things." Noah gave her a look. "I can't tell you that. But I can tell you Jake Carlson is the father of Elliot Carlson, the larger of the two men in black who died that night. The one with the busted jaw."

"How'd you find that out?"

"Through a friend."

"Your partner? The tatted-up one?"

She sighed. "Look. That's a lot more information than you and your fellow officers could come up with, even with all your training and resources. This is a huge lead, Noah. Follow it up."

"You know the other stiff's name?"

"No. But he was a newbie among players, and my source said there's not much on him."

"And you're trying to nail Carlson so you can jack him and get information on your enemy."

"Not exactly."

"Then what exactly?"

She couldn't tell him. He would assume she was manipulating him, telling him about Carlson coming after her so he would feel sorry for her, and right now that kind of thing would only backfire. Plus, the last thing she needed was to confess to murder, with an illegal weapon no less. Noah suspected she killed those men, but he had no proof.

"You have to give me more than that if you want to stay out of prison," he warned.

Quinn raised her chin. "Let's get something straight, Officer Martinez. I gave you that information to prevent things from getting ugly, and to make up for... the past. Maybe I should have given it to you sooner. But under no circumstances will I be your CI, or let you put me under your thumb. We're done here, and you're going to let me walk away."

He chuckled, shaking his head. "You have some nerve on you, woman. I don't even know if I can believe a word you say."

"Follow up on what I just told you. You'll see it's true, and it will open up a whole new avenue for you to pursue. The kind of avenue that could lead to something huge." Noah still didn't look fully convinced. "Even if I'm lying, you've made it clear you can find me and make my life difficult. You can keep on torturing me and trying to catch me in the act—which you'll never do—or you can take the gift I just gave you, see it through, and who knows... maybe there'll be more in the future."

"Why Carlson? He doesn't have the bird tattoo."

"Don't worry about him. That's my problem to deal with."

"Is he after you for killing his son?"

"I'm done answering questions." She forced her way past Noah, but he grabbed her arm. This time he didn't look angry or controlling. He looked concerned.

"That's it, isn't it?"

Quinn yanked her arm away.

Noah stepped closer to her, his eyes darkening. "Who's the guy?"

"What guy?"

"The one at the game earlier."

She rolled her eyes. "I didn't ask you about the woman you brought back to your place, did I?"

"I don't like him."

Of course he didn't, not after Devin had stood up to him while showing no sign of intimidation. No cop liked that. But Noah would never admit it, and the last thing Quinn wanted to do was say anything to damage the fragile peace treaty between them.

"He's not part of my world," she said.

"I have a bad feeling about him."

"Based on what?"

"Based on years of being a cop."

"Devin isn't someone to worry about. Worry about the names

I gave you. Worry about the Black Jays. Because if things go the way I think they're going to, those guys will be a huge problem for everybody. Including people like us."

With that, Quinn left the sex shop, turned the corner, and ran.

CHAPTER 19

IT WAS PITCH DARK. Dark in Quinn's place and dark outside. A power outage.

Quinn was no stranger to power failures. They happened on a regular basis in Downtown during summertime, when too many people were trying to cool hot apartments and businesses, and Downtown's power grid lacked the ability to handle the load.

Phone service was down too. Third time in two weeks.

But at that moment, she was glad for the darkness and quiet. It had been a difficult day. Running into Noah at the baseball game, then again Downtown as he ruined what may have been their only chance to nab the man who'd been threatening her life, was bad enough. But it got worse when she came home to yet another threat in her mailbox.

This one had an image so violent that it turned Quinn's stomach. She almost tore it up just to destroy its existence in the world, but instead stuffed it back into its envelope and stacked it with the others. She might need that information if forced to solicit Noah's help. It would also come in handy for detectives if she wound up dead, and the stench of her rotting corpse wafted out into the hall for someone—probably nosy Merritt—to find.

There was another note, too.

Tired of failure yet, Quinn? I almost have you.

Somehow, he knew. Quinn shook her head at the irony. By thwarting their takedown of Jake Carlson, Noah had prevented her from obtaining useful information she could have fed him. And it was only a matter of time before he would want more.

If only she could tell him the truth. Why she did what she did. How the Protectorate worked underground to ensure some kind of justice.

Quinn sat in her chair and sipped on her diablo, stripped down to undies and a tank top in her hot apartment, her battery-powered fan blowing in fresh air from her open window. It reminded her of her old apartment, where the fan whirred day and night, bringing in more hot air but also air that was fresh instead of recycled. She found the whirring and the warm air strangely comforting.

As she stared out at the night, she noticed something. Dots in the sky, sparkling like little diamonds. Stars!

She went to the window to get a better look. Between El Diablo's dust and the city's light pollution, stars just weren't a part of her viewing life anymore, despite spending an inordinate amount of time outside at night. She loved stargazing as a kid, and growing up, she and Daria would sit and stare at the sky for hours. Quinn would search for familiar stars and constellations, but Daria never cared about that. Instead, she would see animal shapes and make up a story about each one. Sometimes, Quinn's mom would come outside and stargaze with them. She was the one who taught Quinn the constellations and planet names. How she knew such information, Quinn never knew. At that age, she took it for granted. She took everything for granted, including having a mom... until she was gone.

Quinn's mind returned to Noah. She felt torn between

resenting his anger and threats, and understanding them, and she finally let herself admit the truth.

She missed him. She missed the feel of his body against hers, the way he understood things... understood her. But it didn't matter. That, like everything in her personal life, had gone to shit. All she had was her job, and if she didn't get control over this Carlson situation soon, that too would be threatened.

Nothing had gone like she thought it would. She thought she'd be safer in Midtown, that her life would get better. But she'd only exchanged one set of worries for another, one set of annoyances for another, one set of dangers for another.

She heard a beep. Her phone. They had service again. When she checked it, she had a message from an unknown caller.

Home alone in the dark, Quinn?

Fury flooded her. Carlson again. She hit reply and typed out "Go fuck yourself." But before she hit send, she hesitated. She erased the message and blocked the caller, knowing he would just find another phone.

Her sense of peace destroyed, Quinn shoved her chair up against her door, and got into bed with her energy weapon next to her. That night, she dreamt of being attacked in a dark place by a man with a giant scar on his face.

When her phone beeped the next morning, Quinn felt a pit in her stomach. It was him again, new phone already in hand, ready to scare her. But it wasn't Carlson. It was Daria:

You awake yet?

Quinn called Daria, wanting to hear a normal voice.

"Hey, girl," Daria said, sounding chipper.

"Hey."

A pause. "You alright?"

"Fine. Just... waking up."

"So, I have some news on Solera."

"Solera?"

"The clinic. For your friend with the disabled brother?"

Quinn sat up in bed. "What did you find out?"

"Apparently there is a waiting list, but they also give preference to locals. They don't advertise that, obviously. My guess is they probably brush off people from the bad neighborhoods because they assume they can't afford to pay."

Quinn sighed, rolling her eyes.

"Stupid, I know. But I'm told it helps when you can pay a few months in advance, and they prefer clients who've been assessed by a medical professional. To ensure it's a good fit."

"What does that involve?"

"A nurse or doctor does an interview and some tests with— what's his name?"

"Jeffrey."

"It costs money, but—"

"Can you do the assessment?"

"Me? I never thought about that. I've learned a few things through my internship, though..."

"Find out. I'm happy to pay you..."

"I can't take money during my internship, Quinn. It's unethical."

"Okay... well, can you get credit for it or something?"

"Let me find out."

"Dar, he's the sweetest guy. And his brother and mom are the nicest, most hardworking people you've ever met. Dad died years ago and they've been struggling to survive ever since. Jeffrey's struggling because of noisy neighbors who fight all the time, plus all the shootings in White Sands—"

"They live in White Sands?" she cried.

"Yeah—"

"How can they afford Solera?"

Quinn hesitated. "I... they're moving because they've had a change in circumstances. You can ask them yourself when you come meet them." She held her breath.

"Let me see what I can do."

Quinn heard a beep. Another call. Her stomach curdled, but it was only Yolanda. "I've got a call, Dar. Talk soon?"

"Sounds good."

Quinn switched over to Yolanda. "Good morning, Yolanda."

"You ready for another job?"

"You bet."

After Quinn finished up with Yolanda, she got cleaned up and saw that she had a message from Daria. She listened to it, then called Jones.

"You better not be callin' me from jail," Jones said.

"Nope. Not yet, anyway."

"What the hell happened last night? You like to dance with the devil, girl."

"I don't like it. It's just what I have to do these days."

"How'd you get out of that one? Or do I wanna know?"

"If you're suggesting I fucked my way out of trouble, fuck you."

"Hey, I ain't judgin', if you're safe at home."

"Depends on your definition of safe. I got another threat from Carlson, taunting me for failing to nab him. And another doctored imagine, this one so awful—" She stopped, choked up.

"We gonna get this motherfucker one way or the other," he said.

Quinn nodded. She hated involving him, but she had little choice.

"You there?" he said.

"Yes."

"Just hang on. This guy's dangerous, but he ain't that smart 'cause he's still using the same phone and I'm still trackin' it."

"This, from the guy whose messages I can't trace."

"Yeah, seems weird to me too, but it is what it is."

She sighed.

"We'll get him. You can stay here if you don't feel safe—"

She couldn't do that. "I'll be fine here."

Jones paused. "So whadya have to do to get the cop off your ass?"

"I gave him information." When she got nothing but silence, she added, "I had to. He was going to arrest me."

"What information?"

"That the dead guys were Jays. Told him Carlson's name, too." She heard a sigh. "He knew we were after Carlson, that I had equipment on me. It was the only way. Once he pulls at that thread, he'll be off hunting and leave us alone."

"Until he wants more."

"Don't worry about him."

"I don't trust him."

"I didn't call to argue about Noah. I have good news."

"I'll take some of that."

She told Jones about Daria and Solera. Jones was silent for several moments.

"Really?" he finally said.

"Yeah. She just left me a message, too. They told her she can do the assessment as part of her training. It will take an hour or two, including breaks in case Jeffrey gets tired."

"When?"

"Tomorrow at ten. I'll come too and introduce you."

"Who'd you tell her I was?"

"A friend. But I should mention that she's my former partner.

She left because she wasn't cut out for the job. So she might recognize you or make assumptions."

"She ain't ratted you out?"

"She would never. Besides, you know the oath we sign doesn't end when we leave the job."

"Alright. See you tomorrow."

When Jones opened the door to his place, he glanced at Quinn briefly before his eyes went to Daria. He stared for a moment. Like he recognized her.

"Hey Jones," Quinn said, trying to sound like a normal friend and not a close one. "This is Daria, my oldest friend."

"Hey," he said, holding out his hand. "Good to meet you."

Daria shook his hand. "Good to meet you, too." She smiled, but showed no look of recognition. When still with the Protectorate, Daria never went to meetups or other events for techs, where they talked shop without jackers around. It was entirely possible they'd never met.

"Come on in."

They walked inside the small but neat apartment, the temperature comfortable but not cool. Christa approached them and Quinn made more introductions.

"Nice to meet you, Daria," Christa said. "We really appreciate you coming. We've wanted to enroll Jeffrey at Solera for a while, and now that we can finally afford the place—"

"Hi Quinn!" came Jeffrey's adult but still childlike voice as he appeared next to Christa. He held out his hand like Christa and Jones had taught him.

Quinn put her hand in his and held on for a moment. "Hi, Jeffrey! It's good to see you!"

Jeffrey glanced at Daria and froze for a moment. He stared at her, his blue eyes studying her like he wasn't sure whether to be afraid or fascinated.

"Jeffrey," Quinn said, "this is my friend, Daria."

"Daria came over just to see you," Christa told him in an encouraging tone.

Quinn waited for Jeffrey to turn away in shyness, or even retreat to the far end of the worn couch. She'd warned Daria that was a likely scenario, but Daria said she had ways to handle that.

But he didn't withdraw. Instead, he said, "Daria." Then, "You're pretty."

Daria's smile widened. "Well, thank you, Jeffrey!"

Christa's eyes lit up while Jones watched Daria and Jeffrey, fascinated. Quinn couldn't believe it herself.

"I have some questions for you, Jeffrey," Daria said. "And some games. Would you like to sit down with me and play?"

Jeffrey hurried over to the table and sat. Soon, Christa got beverages for them while Jones led Quinn into the bedroom to talk, closing the door behind them.

"I don't think she recognizes you," Quinn said quietly.

"Huh. 'Cause I remember seein' her before, during training."

"That was a long time ago. You remember that far back?"

"I remember her." He glanced toward the door. "What's her story? She single?"

Quinn raised her eyebrows. "Seriously?"

He scowled. "Comin' from someone who nailed a cop."

"I'm not lecturing. I just... you don't even know her."

"Gotta start somewhere. Did you see how Jeffrey took to her? He's a good judge of character, better than anyone I know."

"I'll try not to take it personally that it took me weeks to get that kind of greeting from him."

"It ain't personal. He knows you're part of what takes me away from him and puts me in danger. He's intuitive that way. So, Daria. She single or not?"

Quinn sighed. "She is. But she left the organization for a reason. It's hurt our friendship, and she's still prickly about it all. If she learns what you do right away, it'll scare her away."

Jones sighed. "I hear ya."

Quinn smiled. "Did you just admit I'm right? Because it sure sounded like you're telling me I'm right."

"Don't start."

Quinn laughed, and she swore she saw a tiny smile on Jones's face.

"You talk to Yolanda?" Jones said. "We gotta job or what?"

"She called earlier. It's on."

"Who's the target?"

"The CEO of Saguaro Energy."

CHAPTER 20

QUINN WIPED the sweat from her forehead, already overheated. They'd had a heatwave that day, where the temperature soared to 120 after everyone had gotten used to it being under a hundred. The tall buildings of El Diablo, even the nice shiny ones Uptown, radiated heat like an oven.

It didn't help that she was dressed in full-length pants, a jacket, and a wig. She'd worn similar in hotter temperatures many times, but her body wasn't used to it after months of good weather. She glanced over at Jones, his face glistening and red. His hand sweated in hers as they walked, and when Jones finally pulled his hand away, she felt relief.

Fortunately, they would find respite indoors soon.

Once they reached 109th Street, they headed west into a part of town Quinn had never visited. It was so posh that the alleys were paved in pale brick instead of heat-absorbing black asphalt, lofty cacti with built-in drip systems lined the sidewalks, and tall gates kept the public away from gorgeous buildings with sandstone facades, huge windows, and giant succulent gardens.

Finally, they turned north again before reaching their destination. Quinn glanced around before she grabbed Jones's hand and pulled him into the alley and giggled, making it look to any potential onlooker like they were up to something naughty. That, the handholding, the uncomfortable clothing... it was all part of the act. It was what they needed to do to avoid attracting the wrong kind of attention, but tonight it felt exhausting.

Deeper into the quiet alley they went, and Quinn marveled at how strange it smelled. How clean. No stench from garbage or some rotting bodily fluid. She even felt safe—unheard of for her—like there was no threat that lay deeper in the darkness.

This was Uptown. Any threats here didn't lurk in alleyways or bars... they sat in bedrooms and boardrooms, offering a whole different sort of peril, the kind that impacted everybody rather than one vulnerable victim. The kind that nobody recognized until it was too late.

Carrie Anne Halstead, CEO of Saguaro Energy, was one of those perils. A third generation Uptowner from a family of business school magnates, Halstead was part of the one percent who controlled the other ninety-nine once the drought came and everything got worse. Yet, confirming Quinn's prediction after the George Hatch job, Halstead was another Black Jay target. They'd already come sniffing around, hoping to steal information and God only knew what else—wipe her memories, influence her decisions—and she too was scared.

It was official. The Jays had targeted the CEO of a cooling systems monopoly and were now sniffing out Halstead, CEO of an energy monopoly. Not only power players, but the most powerful in the city, controlling the resources everybody needed to survive. Quinn couldn't help but wonder if the Jays were activists of some sort, looking to challenge the inequities of their city. Could the black-clad men be nothing more than rebels looking to scare these CEOs into breaking up their monopolies? The justice of it intrigued her.

But then reality hit her. These same "activists" had tried to kill her and almost killed Jones, had murdered Borelli and the

Lindens. Nobody capable of that kind of mayhem could be trusted, even if their beliefs leaned in the same direction hers did. It was more likely they were just greedy ninja shitheads looking to steal the power of the one-percenters and make it their own. And who better to aim for than those who controlled the most crucial resources for survival in their city?

They arrived at the alley entrance to Halstead's martial arts studio. The hidden entrance allowed for privacy, so members could come and go quietly. Quinn didn't have to jack Halstead to know why she trained, that she benefitted from the discipline while also honing the skills needed to protect herself from mind thieves. And being a woman meant she had to train twice as hard.

Recon on Ms. Carrie Anne had made it clear she visited the studio every Monday and Thursday, staying for hours at a time. Quinn recalled her "training" sessions with Wyatt—she was exhausted after an hour, ninety minutes tops—but Halstead trained for longer despite being twenty years older. Quinn couldn't help but admire that too.

No one else seemed to come or go from the studio during those hours, which made sense, as Halstead could afford private lessons from a top-notch instructor.

After Jones breached the studio's security system, they went quietly inside, an excuse at the ready in case anyone unexpected saw them. But the place was quiet. And gorgeous.

This was no ordinary studio or dojo. It was a spa, with natural wood floors, floor-to-ceiling mirrors, sleek furniture, and warm lighting. A sign told them what was on what floor: the swimming pool, the steam rooms, the massage tables, the various classrooms. The dojos Quinn had seen in the past were little more than hot, stuffy concrete rooms in basements with mirrors in various sizes pasted together on the walls.

Quinn glanced at the time. It was 10:00, at least thirty minutes before Halstead would emerge, with or without her instructor. She and Jones had agreed if they couldn't get Halstead alone, they would jack both. It never hurt to have extra data, even though her instructor probably wouldn't provide much that was useful.

As they approached the ground floor training room, a light was on and Quinn heard a grunt. A feminine grunt, the kind that came from exertion. Then another, and again. As they drew closer, Quinn hesitated. Something didn't sound right about the grunts. They didn't sound like training. They sounded like something else.

She turned to Jones, whose eyebrows were raised.

"What the..." Jones mouthed.

Quinn shrugged.

The two of them stood just outside the studio door, the sounds getting more and more intense. Quinn could barely look at Jones, but she knew one thing. If there was ever a time to go in and surprise these two, it was right now, when they were most vulnerable.

Quinn unzipped a jacket pocket and pulled out an injector. She pointed toward the door. Jones reached into his pocket and nodded. The door was locked; Jones quickly decoded it and in they went.

Halstead and an extremely fit man were tangled in carnal bliss up against the mirror, both so engrossed that they didn't see the door open. Quinn felt almost guilty interrupting them at such a key moment.

Quinn hurried over as quietly as she could. When she was only a foot away, Halstead's eyes opened and spotted Quinn. She froze, and Quinn injected the male while Jones aimed for Halstead. A couple of moments later, both went limp.

Quinn caught Halstead's pale form before she tumbled to the wooden floor, and Jones did the same for the instructor. They laid them down on the floor, next to one another. When Quinn finally got a look at the man's face, it wasn't familiar. It wasn't her husband's face.

She rolled her eyes. These power players... they were all the same.

"Who is that?" Jones mouthed, pointing at the man, seeing what she saw.

Quinn shrugged but said nothing. They needed to remain silent to prevent leaving any mental traces in the minds of their targets. She glanced at their naked, sweaty bodies, the instructor's erection still at full mast. Quinn found a couple of yoga mats and covered them.

Quinn sat down and leaned against the mirror, and hooked her nodes to the base of her skull. Jones kneeled down next to her and waited for her nod.

It was hot, even stifling. It smelled of lavender, so much so that Quinn held her breath and her eyes watered.

Her mother loved lavender. Lavender dish soap, hand soap, bath oils. And she'd forgotten that until right now. It made her smile, and it was as if her mother were right there with her, with her own smile and kind words. It was like everything was right in the world again.

Then she remembered being lulled into relaxation in George Hatch's mind. That the positive, calming moments were temporary. This time, they wouldn't catch her by surprise.

It was steamy and she could barely see her hand in front of her face. The heat and humidity suddenly engulfed her, making her feel claustrophobic, like she was trapped in a muggy box where she could see nothing and hear nothing. But that passed quickly, and soon she spotted light in the distance, through the fog, beckoning to her.

She walked toward it.

Just as she drew close to the golden light, so close she could almost touch it, she plunged into darkness. Hard, fast, endless. This time, it took her less time to right herself. When the falling ended, she broke her way through to the good stuff, and braved the flood of thoughts and feelings that assailed her.

Meetings. Selecting which tailored suit to wear that day. Kissing her husband. Stress, power, greed, happiness... and peace, when at the studio. And lots of amorous feelings and images, Halstead and her lover trading fluids six ways to Sunday in that studio, one giant orgiastic mish-mash of images, so many that Quinn wondered if the woman could fight at all or if she'd spent all her training time fucking herself into a frenzy.

Lucky her, Quinn thought drily.

Then, two men in the shadows. Fit and wearing all black. Watching Halstead. The Jays, hoping to make their move but not able to yet. And another flash, brief and slightly blurred... but familiar. The conference room meeting with the El Diablo power players, including Hatch and Hector Olmos of El Diablo Water. Their monthly meeting, Halstead's version of the one in Hatch's mind.

Then the image grew more crisp, focusing in on Olmos, who stood up and walked toward a door. He opened it and she followed him through.

On the other side, Quinn stood in an institutional-looking room: white walls, clean floor, strange chemical smell. A strong— almost overwhelming—feeling of dread came over her, like she was waiting for her own death. Rows of drawers lined the wall as far as the eye could see. Someone in a white coat opened one of the drawers, then looked right at Quinn, a strange look on his face. Like he expected something from her.

Quinn took a step toward the drawer, unable to see inside. She didn't want to look. Something told her it wasn't the kind of thing she wanted to see. But she stepped forward anyway, as if compelled.

Another step. And another.

Closer.

Until she was there. She looked inside.

A body covered in a white sheet. The person in the white coat peeled back the sheet, and when Quinn saw who it was, she gasped.

Wyatt.

Eyes closed. Grayish pale. Lifeless.

A flood of emotions bowled Quinn over, and she crumpled to the cold, hard floor where she buried her face in her hands. Despair overtook her, took the breath from her lungs. He was gone. Forever. It was all gone and nothing good ever came of anything.

Then it all disappeared. She sat there, staring. Blinking. Her eyes moist with tears. A face stared at her.

Jones.

He watched her, eyes studying her, brow creased. She looked around the room. The dojo. The Halstead job. Halstead and her instructor out cold and covered in yoga mats. She'd drowned and Jones had pulled her out. Again.

"Don't make me talk about it," she whispered.

Jones shook his head. "Ain't no time. We gotta get moving."

"My tranny's no good."

"I can shoot some footage of the hallway and the training room," he whispered. "That's as good as we gonna get."

"Do it."

As Jones created footage for the new transitional memory, Quinn jacked the instructor, pulled some data, then uploaded the tranny to both after wiping their brief memories of Quinn and Jones.

As Quinn finished up, she focused on the tasks at hand,

trying to ignore her shaking hands and the terrible hangover of sadness that haunted her. The memory of identifying Wyatt at the morgue was real, but it was one she'd forgotten, blocked by her mind in its attempt to protect her from another crushing loss.

Finally, they put the yoga mats away and left the two lovers next to one another. Quinn turned Halstead to face her instructor and slung her arm over him. Then they left.

On a train headed south, Jones finally spoke. "Wanna talk about it?"

"No."

"She had the platinum training like Hatch did?"

Quinn nodded.

As the train quietly cruised through the underground tunnel, Quinn pushed the horrible memory away and focused instead on the niggling thought that kept running through her mind: how similar the Halstead jacking was to Hatch's. It made sense; the two targets were part of the same club, high-powered people with high-powered mind invasion protection. Yet, something about the two jobs nagged at Quinn, and she couldn't quite put her finger on it.

She shook that off, too. After reliving that horrible memory, everything would seem off.

Instead, she chastised herself for her failure, for getting caught up in what was nothing more than some programmer's way of protecting his or her clients. One way or another, she needed to get a handle on it.

Otherwise, someday it could cost her her life.

CHAPTER 21

QUINN STRODE down Sonora Avenue in the dark, ignoring the sweat building up on her as the heatwave marched on.

"You almost here?" came Jones's voice in her ear.

"A few more blocks."

"Any sign of loverboy?"

"No."

And there better not be. Quinn had already decided if Noah showed up and tried to sabotage her again, she would resort to harsher measures. She would drug him, tie him up... whatever it took. Better to face an enraged Noah than lose what was probably their last chance to nab Jake Carlson.

And nab him she would. No matter what it took. She was sick of it all—the messages, the doctored images, the bad dreams. And looking over her shoulder night and day, not knowing if or when he would strike.

Quinn had believed that nothing much could really scare her anymore. That with her wits and weapons, she could handle anything that came her way. She'd broken into the private spaces of some of the most powerful people in El Diablo, pounded men far bigger than her, fought through the chaos of someone else's mind without them ever knowing. She'd faced loss, abandonment, poverty, loneliness, even the possibility of death. But none of it scared her more than knowing she could die a senseless death at the hands of some stranger looking to do unspeakable things to her.

The only thing that kept Quinn sane these last several weeks was having discovered the identity of her tormentor. She'd made mistakes, but she always knew she had the means to cut this malignant growth from her life, no matter what it took. And she was going to do it tonight.

Jones would help her. Again. Quinn shook her head as she walked, still not feeling right about his involvement. Why would he do this for her? Why risk himself, especially after what happened at Canine? But she let him help. She did so because this was one thing she couldn't do alone. Besides, it would be over soon.

Finally, she spotted Jones a block away, his meaty build and aggressive, don't-fuck-with-me stride making clear it was him despite plain clothing, dark hair, and sunglasses.

They joined up and headed east, toward their destination. When they reached a tall stucco building with dark windows, Jones quickly bypassed the security console. They entered the hot stairwell and made their way up the stairs, climbing them at a rapid pace until sweat poured from her. When they reached Carlson's apartment on the third floor, Jones picked the door lock.

Quinn drew her weapon and went to open the door, but Jones held her back. She gave him a questioning look, and he quietly opened the door and headed in. She grabbed him, shaking her head. Jones scowled and gave her a warning look. He'd never done that—not to her, anyway—so she backed off and let him go, hoping she wouldn't regret that choice.

They tiptoed inside the studio apartment, weapons drawn. The place was spare, with only a couch folded out into an unmade bed, a TV, and a coffee table lined with empty liquor bottles, several takeout burrito containers, and an ashtray over-flowing with cigarette butts. It was hot and stuffy, and smelled of dirty socks and cigarette smoke.

Quinn shook her head. This was the guy who'd stalked and tormented her? Someone too lazy to throw out his garbage or fold up his bed?

The bed was empty, which left only one place to look.

Come out of that bathroom, Jake. Come out so I can stick you with this needle. And then you're mine.

That was the plan. Find him, jack him, wipe any memories related to Quinn and Jones. Clean and simple. But somehow it didn't feel simple. It felt personal, and far more stressful than any job she'd done.

But it was quiet. Dead quiet. Either Carlson was as still as a frightened mouse, or he wasn't there. Jones approached the bath-room, peeking into what he could see through the partly ajar door. He quickly shoved the door, hoping to hit Carlson if he were hidden behind it. But it only hit the doorstop. Jones took another last look around, knowing as well as she did there was nowhere else to hide.

"He ain't here. We gotta wait it out."

"Didn't you track him here?" Quinn whispered.

Jones looked around, then found it. A phone, peeking out from underneath Carlson's pillow.

Frustration overcame her, and all she wanted to do was punch something. Instead, she began to pace, her mind flooded with too many thoughts.

"It's alright," Jones said. "We knew this could happen."

"It's three in the fucking morning! His phone is here! Why isn't he, sleeping off whatever the fuck he drank at Canine tonight?"

"Keep your voice down," Jones said through his teeth. "He's

gotta come home eventually. You're agitated tonight and that ain't good. If you wanna get this done, you gotta calm down."

Quinn sighed. Jones was right. She *was* agitated, and she knew why.

"I can't take this anymore, Jones. I can't live like this. It's only a matter of time before the coyote finally catches the rabbit off guard and sinks his teeth in."

"You ain't no rabbit, girl."

Quinn sat down on the floor and leaned against the wall. Jones sank down next to her.

"We got this," he said. "We'll wait until he comes home."

"What if he saw us come in?"

"Then we'll get him some other way. He won't be huntin' you anymore 'cause we'll be huntin' him, and he'll know it. Besides, he's an ex-con, and ex-cons are trackable."

Quinn nodded. She hated it, hated having to prolong what she'd felt sure was a forgone conclusion tonight. But she knew better. There were no forgone conclusions, not in her world.

They sat in silence, waiting. An hour passed, Quinn fidgeting and growing more restless by the second. She did her best to fight it, to remember the discipline she had when she was working.

It's no different. It's just another job. We'll nail him eventually.

Then, close to five, they heard footsteps. Big, heavy ones, getting louder and louder. Then the footsteps stopped.

Jones stood slowly, as did Quinn, each reaching for the necessary tool. When the door unlocked and then opened, a large figure emerged. Jones reached over and stuck the injector right into Carlson's shoulder before he had a chance to react.

And down he went.

Quinn kneeled on the dirty tile floor while Jones stood aside, keeping watch as he stifled a yawn. Jake Carlson lay flat on his own bed, slumbering away in cargo shorts and tee, a pair of nodes attached to the base of his skull.

She stared at the scarred face, the thick hands that had taken lives, the prison tats. How easy it would be to end him right now, to ensure he never bothered her again, or anyone else. But she couldn't do that. Even if she felt okay about it, which was questionable, she couldn't take the chance that Noah or someone else was watching. She could claim he'd threatened her and produce all the evidence, but nobody would care. But if she and Jones did their job right, Quinn would cease to exist in Carlson's memory.

After the data was downloaded and stowed away, she finally started to see the light at the end of the dark hallway. But she wasn't there yet. She still had one crucial task.

She pulled up the images of her and Jones to help her mind reader locate the matches, then targeted the hippocampus with a date range that extended back to the showdown at Gary Linden's home. She then realized she should go back further, just in case Carlson or the Jays had done recon on her before that night. It was a long span of time, with countless memories to search. She leaned against the bed and rested. This would take a while.

She could just wipe them all, take the easy way out like a mind thief would, but she refused to do that. She wouldn't do to Carlson what someone had done to Noah's father. Carlson had been wrong about her; she did have a code.

To her surprise, the search took only a few minutes. When she studied the results, it had produced only five matches, all recent. There should have been far more.

She looked up to find Jones's tired face giving her a questioning look. Quinn shook her head. She was tired too, and fatigue caused mistakes. She re-entered her parameters, double-checking the dates, and reran the search.

And got the same result.

"What's the matter?" Jones whispered.

Quinn motioned for him to join her in the bathroom. They couldn't chance leaving any traces for Carlson's mind to pick up on.

"It doesn't make sense," she said.

"What doesn't?"

"It only produced five matches."

Jones made a face. "You do it right?"

"I ran it twice. Same result."

He shrugged. "Not every memory gets stored. Them five must be the good ones."

She began looking through the memory fragments, each a different size, ranging from brief to extensive. The larger one was from that night at Canine, near the men's room. The smaller fragments had the same time signature as the large one. There was nothing from the night at Linden's place, or thereafter, until Canine.

"Did they block his memories somehow?" Jones asked, looking at her in disbelief.

Quinn scowled. "One way to find out. Give me five minutes, no more."

They left the bathroom and sat down near Carlson's bed. Quinn put on her nodes, and within moments she was in the disarray of Jake Carlson's mind. There were random images of Canine, conversational fragments, snippets of attractive women in revealing clothing, the odor of alcohol and smoke, meetings with other rough-looking men. The mindjacking equivalent of a stroll through Downtown on a Saturday, and nothing more.

She waited, knowing the good stuff took time. It eventually came—men in prison uniforms with monochrome tattoos, brief fragments of Midtown back when there was still a tree or two, images of a teenage boy. Elliot Carlson, Jake's son.

His memories of Quinn weren't blocked by some fancy technology. Which meant that unless they were buried in the mass of data they'd downloaded, it was becoming less and less likely he was the one who'd been stalking her.

After Jones pulled her out, Quinn wiped any memories of her, Jones, and the injection. Then they gathered their belongings and snuck out the back door of Carlson's building before going their separate ways.

When Quinn got home, it was light out. She peeled off her jacket and stowed away her equipment, her mind blank and her emotions run dry. She sat down on her bed, too tired to think but too disturbed to sleep.

Then her phone beeped. Maybe Jones, making sure she got home okay. But it wasn't, and deep down she knew it wouldn't be.

Out looking for me again, Quinn? You're wasting your time. By the time you find me, by the time you can do anything about me... it will be too late.

It couldn't be Carlson. He wouldn't wake up for several more hours.

Carlson wasn't her stalker. And she had no idea who was.

CHAPTER 22

"It ain't him."

Jones was sitting at Quinn's kitchen table, hunched over his computer, parsing the data they'd pulled from Jake Carlson.

Quinn stood by her window, staring out at the sky, its blue marred by dust on that windy day. She nodded. She'd known Carlson wasn't her stalker the moment she'd gotten that message, if not before. But they'd mined the data anyway, hoping for some nugget she'd missed. There wasn't one.

"Try to find some data on the Black Jays," she said. "Maybe this wasn't a complete loss. I'll go get us something to eat."

By the time Quinn returned and they ate, Jones hadn't found anything. Finally, he shook his head and cursed.

"Fucker didn't even know his son was a Jay. The memories of his kid are old, from before he did time."

"So they weren't even close. But... he saw me coming, Jones. Saw us coming. He even called me a jacker whore!"

"Them prison guys are paranoid about gettin' jacked. They hear all sorts of stories from other guys inside. Most of 'em are lies, but some have been jacked by mind thieves lookin' for cheap information or a way to blackmail." He shrugged. "Even after they get out, most of 'em are still up to no good, so they learn to be on the lookout for any sign of a jacker."

Frustration building in her, Quinn kicked her boot, sending it across her floor. "How the hell did I get this wrong? Am I losing it?"

"Nah. The guy had the rap sheet and the motive... and the timing was right. Had me fooled."

There was a knock at Quinn's door. She stared at the door in surprise, her blood turning cold.

Calm down. The stalker isn't going to show up here in broad daylight and knock on the damned door.

She tiptoed over and peered through the peephole. It was Devin. She opened the door just a crack.

"Hey," he said. "I just wanted to stop by and see if you wanted to get dinner later... maybe take Lucifer out for a late-night gander?" He smiled a little.

"I'd love to, but something came up at work and it's going to take a while to fix it."

Devin hesitated, glancing past her, as if trying to get a glimpse inside. He knew something was up, and it showed on his face.

"Is everything okay?" he finally asked.

"Yeah. It's just work." At least it wasn't a lie.

Devin nodded. "Give me a call tonight if you want."

"I will, Devin. Thank you for checking on me." She smiled, then closed the door.

Jones sat there looking at her, one eyebrow raised. "Gentleman suitor?"

"That sounds strange, coming from a thug." Jones chuckled. "He's a neighbor. He's been nice to me and he has the cutest pet iguana. He even took me to my first Demons game."

"He a cop?"

"No, he's not a cop. I checked."

"I like him already."

Quinn grabbed a bottle of chilled water from the fridge and refilled their glasses.

"He knows you were lyin'. About bein' busy with work."

"It wasn't a lie," she said, annoyed.

Jones's phone rang. He checked it and stood up. "Hey buddy." His tone changed completely, and she knew it was Jeffrey calling. "I'm with my friend. I'll be home—" Pause. "No. Everything's fine, I promise. There's no need to get upset." Pause. "Alright, alright. I'll be home soon, okay? Be good for Mom." Jones hung up and closed his eyes for a moment.

Guilt tore through Quinn. Jones was missing out on time with his family because of her bullshit. "Look. You did all you could, Jones. I'll deal with this on my own from now on. It's too dangerous for you and it's taking too much time away from your family."

"You can't take on this stalker alone."

"Thanks for the vote of confidence."

"It ain't about confidence! This guy's fucken dangerous, and he's skilled as shit if *we* can't even find him."

"This isn't your fault or your problem. It's a waste of your time—"

"Stop sayin' that," he growled at her.

"Why? Why not say it? I can't take the pressure of having you involved anymore."

"Pressure? I've been workin' my ass off for you, riskin' myself, and it's a fucken annoyance to you?" He shook his head. "Fuck this." He snapped his computer shut and began packing.

"Why are you being an asshole?" she cried. "I'm trying to look out for you."

"No, you ain't. You just want to do everything your way, like usual. It's like you don't even know what partnership is."

Quinn took a deep breath and kept herself from blowing up

at him. "I know exactly what partnership is. This may come as a shock to you, but if something happened to you because of me, because of my situation, I couldn't live with myself or face your family."

Jones set down his bag. "This is what I'm talkin' about. Yeah, you pulled the trigger on them guys, but we both did 'em in. I'm as responsible for them dyin' as you are. You say you couldn't live with yourself if somethin' happened to me, but you don't get that I couldn't live with myself if you handled this alone and somethin' happened to you."

Quinn went silent at that. Jones made a good point, and she was touched by his loyalty. But she still struggled with it. The illegal weapon she'd used that night had saved their lives, but she'd chosen to kill the two men when she could have hobbled them. Her tormentor knew it, and that's why she was in this mess. Her choices had landed them here, not Jones's. Besides, responsible or not, she had no one depending on her like Jones did. But... even she knew this was no time to argue.

"I'm sorry," she said. "I never thought of it like that. If you want to help me solve this, okay. Just... be careful, okay?"

"I'm always careful."

"I know."

Jones sat back down, and Quinn followed. "Listen," he said. "We played in the bush league. Now we gotta play in the bigs. This guy's probably a Black Jay, and we gotta think different if we're gonna nail him."

Quinn nodded. "I was thinking the same thing. It's the only explanation." She stared at her water glass, swirling it round and round.

"Hey," he said. She looked up at him. "It's him or us... and it ain't gonna be us."

Quinn hesitated, a chill running through her at how much Jones sounded like Wyatt at that moment. She nodded.

"I gotta favor, though," he added, smiling a little. "Consider it payment for my services."

"What's that?"

"Get me a date with Daria."

Quinn rolled her eyes. "Seriously?"

"Yup."

"Jones, you have to understand. Daria... she's smart, she's trustworthy, but she's unpredictable, and her moods shift as often as El Diablo's winds."

"How's that different from any woman?"

Quinn smacked him on the arm.

Jones snickered. "Come on. Unpredictable is my life. You've met Jeffrey, right? Besides, if it turns into something, no need to explain what I do or lie about it."

"Assuming she's okay with it... which is a big *if*."

"I'll take my chances."

Jones was right. For all Daria's moodiness, she would be a welcome break from the challenges of Jeffrey. And Quinn couldn't imagine a better man for Daria.

"Fine. I'll do what I can, but no guarantees. I think I know where to begin."

"Where's that?"

"She'll eventually report back on Solera. When she does, I'll schedule a meeting for you guys, and I won't come."

He frowned. "That ain't a date."

"Trust me, Jones. I know her better than anyone. You don't want to rush this."

"Alright."

After Jones left, Quinn found the card with Devin's number on it and called him.

"Hey, Quinn," he answered.

Quinn hesitated, not expecting that. "How'd you know it was me?"

He paused. "You have a Downtown prefix. I don't get a lot of calls from that prefix. And you said you'd call."

She chuckled. "Good point."

"Did you get your work problem solved?"

"For now."

"Feel like getting some fresh air? I was just about to take Lucifer out for a walk."

"I'd love to."

Down in the lobby, Devin and Lucifer were already there when Quinn arrived. Lucifer lunged toward her, so Devin let go of the leash and Lucifer scuttled over. When she bent down to meet him, he ran up her leg and then her arm, his weight heavier than she expected and his feet half-tickling, half-scratching her bare skin. Quinn cried out in surprise, laughing.

"Lucifer," Devin said sternly as he came over to relieve Quinn of her new reptilian friend. But when Devin reached out to take him, Lucifer bit his hand. Devin scowled.

"Oh my God, he's so cute!" a female voice called out.

Quinn turned to find Merritt heading their way, her tool belt askew and her eyes lit up like a child's. She reached a hand out for Lucifer.

"Careful," Devin warned, but it was too late. Merritt was already petting Lucifer, keeping her hand far from his mouth. "Ladies' man," Devin muttered.

Quinn laughed and Merritt giggled too, cooing at Lucifer like he was a newborn baby. "Can I hold him, Devin?" she said, looking at Devin with pleading eyes.

He looked like he wanted to say no. "Just be careful. He's not a puppy."

Merritt took Lucifer from Quinn, looking as happy as could

be as she played with the iguana. Moments later, Devin reached for him.

"He needs to go outside." He took Lucifer and turned to Quinn. "You ready?"

Quinn nodded, taken aback by Devin's chilly treatment of Merritt. She waved at Merritt before following Devin outside. They headed south, their pace slower than Quinn was used to due to Devin's limp. He glanced in the lobby window, as if looking for Merritt.

"Does it bother you when people touch Lucifer without asking?" she asked, taking a guess.

"As long as they don't get upset when he chews a finger off, not really."

"You seemed annoyed before," Quinn said.

Devin was silent for a moment. "I don't like her."

"Merritt? Why not?"

"There's something about her that seems off. Like she isn't who she seems."

"Because she's a Downtownie?" Quinn said, feeling a smidgeon of defensiveness.

"You're a Downtownie and I like you."

"Then what?" Quinn too had noticed something off about Merritt, but assumed it was her own paranoia, a result of her lifestyle.

"She's too friendly." When Lucifer began straining to get out of Devin's arms, Devin finally let him down to walk on his own. "Like she's a little too interested in people. And she shows up at the most convenient times, like she knows who's coming and going, and when, and then acts like it's coincidence."

Quinn had noticed that too. "Maybe she's just... friendly. She probably does it with everyone."

"She doesn't. Only some people, including me."

"Maybe she likes you."

"I doubt it. In my experience, people like her aren't what they seem. They're usually up to something. Something dangerous."

Quinn stared. "How do you know this?"

"I just do," he replied, not looking at her. "I could be wrong, but I would be careful around her. And be careful what you say."

Quinn did a mental tabulation of all her interactions with Merritt. Her being there when Noah came looking for Quinn, appearing when Quinn happened to be in the lobby even late at night, and twice now when Quinn was talking with Devin. And at least twice Merritt had been present when Quinn had gotten her hate mail.

Devin went on. "How many times has she been in the lobby when you came home or were leaving for something other than work? She's not the building's only maintenance worker, but somehow she's always around. She even asked me about you once, like she was trying to get information about you."

Quinn frowned. "Huh."

"She even asked about your work, since it's clear you aren't a nine-to-fiver."

A chill ran through Quinn. "What did you say?"

"I said not everybody works in an office. She thinks you're an undergrounder."

Quinn would have laughed at that if she wasn't so creeped out. "I agree, it's strange. But she doesn't strike me as dangerous."

"No, she doesn't. But that makes it even more powerful, especially for a woman. Young, friendly, working a menial job... perfect way to do recon or other clandestine work. No one would suspect her."

"And I thought I was paranoid," she joked, trying to hide her concern.

He turned to her, eyes boring into hers. "What do you have to be paranoid about?"

Quinn backpedaled. "I... all Downtownies are paranoid. It's bred into us. Plus, I got mugged recently..."

"Something tells me there's more to it than that."

She wanted to tell Devin. She wanted someone besides Jones to know she was being tormented by an angry stalker. It never hurt to have someone else looking out for her. But she couldn't. To tell him that would give away that *she* was the one doing clandestine work.

"I saw you out really late a few nights ago," he said. Quinn stopped walking and Devin stopped too. "I wasn't watching you, Quinn. I keep weird hours and so does Lucifer, and I went downstairs and happened to see you just leaving—"

"Speaking of right place at the right time," she countered, crossing her arms.

"It was one time, unlike Merritt. I was about to call out to you, but you were in a hurry and you looked... upset. It's not my business. I'm not exactly a nine-to-fiver either. All I'm saying is if you ever need anything—*anything*—you call me, okay?"

Quinn's annoyance began to fade. "Good to know. Thank you. For that, and everything." She felt scratching on her leg and looked down to find Lucifer trying to climb up her leg. She bent down to pick him up. As she petted him, trying to process all that Devin had said, her phone rang.

She pulled it from her pocket to see who it was. Yolanda. Yolanda never called this late.

"I need to take this," she said, handing Lucifer back. "Thanks for the walk."

They said their goodbyes and Quinn headed back to her building before taking the call.

"Yolanda. What's up?"

"Go to the West Side safe house, right away. Call Jones and tell him to do the same."

Quinn halted. "What's going on?"

"You'll be briefed at the safe house."

"Am I fired?"

Yolanda hesitated. "No. We've lost an agent.

CHAPTER 23

QUINN CHOSE a stool to sit on, since the couches and chairs had been taken by other agents. Jones stood behind her, leaning against the wall. Everyone murmured amongst themselves, speculating on what had happened.

Quinn did a quick count, but many of the Tier Ones weren't in attendance, making it impossible for her to guess who they'd lost. There were also a few techs there, sitting near their partners. Behind a closed door, she could hear Yolanda and someone else talking. She looked back at Jones with a questioning look. He shrugged.

Finally, the door opened and everyone went silent. Yolanda emerged, followed by Marshall Talbert, a long-time ops manager with cropped gray hair and vigilant eyes.

Marshall spoke first. "We've lost John Romero."

There was a collective silence, and Quinn closed her eyes for a moment. John Romero had been the first agent Quinn trained with during her mind invasion practice runs. He'd given her good tips on how to deal with the onslaught of a target's thoughts, and had taught her to drum up pleasant thoughts or memories when things got too tense. He was a good man and a good agent, and now he was gone.

"What happened?" said Perry, a jacker with a chiseled face and a cocky way about him.

"Murdered," Marshall said. "By the Jays."

Quinn's entire body tensed, and a gasp traveled through the group.

Marshall went on. "He was following a trail. A warm one. A group of men accosted him and Bodie, and took John. Bodie followed protocol and called it in. We tracked John, but they anticipated us and left the scene just before we arrived. By that time, they'd done too much damage and we couldn't save him."

"How do we know it was the Jays?" said Javier, another agent with dark, chin-length hair.

"Bodie said they were dressed in black and were skilled fighters. John didn't have a chance. And when we jacked in..." Marshall hesitated, a wrinkle between his brows. "They'd taken data."

"How much?" Quinn said.

"Everything from the last two weeks. Thanks to great blocking, they didn't have time to get more."

More silence in the room as everyone weighed the pros and cons of that.

"Where's Bodie?" Javier asked.

"In treatment."

And would be for some time, Quinn thought.

Yolanda spoke. "This is terrible news. John Romero was an outstanding agent and this is a great loss to the Protectorate. His burial will be handled, and his girlfriend will receive a stipend."

A stipend. That was all immediate families or partners got if an agent or tech perished.

"So if they have his data and memories," Perry said, "that means the Jays know about us."

"Sharp as always, Perry," Marshall said. "That's why you're all here."

"You're the only agents who were involved in this particular aspect of the hunt for the Black Jays over the past few weeks, which means you're all compromised," Yolanda said. "It's possible they already knew your identities, but we're keeping you here until we can regroup and come up with a strategy to deal with them."

"We're stuck here?" Javier said. "For how long?"

"We don't know. As long as a week."

He groaned, and several others shook their heads.

"No whining," Marshall said. "It's for your own safety. You're no good to us if you're dead. And Romero's death did yield two pieces of important info. First, Bodie swears one of the Jays who attacked them was a woman. We've assumed an all-male crew based on spec ops data, but Bodie said he heard a woman's voice and saw a strand of long red hair. Red hair isn't common in these parts, so we got a lead."

Quinn furrowed her brow. Red hair.

Merritt. Merritt had long red hair.

"What else?" Javier said.

"The Jays left something at the scene." Marshall lifted his hand, and between his thumb and index finger was a small black figurine.

Quinn's stomach lurched. She knew that figurine, even from ten feet away. She could almost feel Jones's eyes boring into the back of her.

"It's a black jaybird," Marshall said. "Could have some special meaning, a token they leave to send a message. But it's the first we've seen it, so it could indicate a splinter group, a group within the group. Maybe one targeting the Protectorate."

Quinn's mind reeled. The figurine. Just like the one left in her old Downtown apartment, by whoever was stalking her. Could it be? Did her tormentor kill Romero and leave that figurine Marshall held up to them today?

"There was a note as well," Yolanda added. "It said, 'There will be more.'"

Another collective silence, and Quinn could tell that even the most experienced jackers, the Perrys and the Javiers, had gotten their cockiness doused with fear.

Marshall spoke again. "Do not go outside. Stay away from the windows. And power down your phones until I say otherwise. If you need to contact loved ones, we will provide you with phones. Keep the conversations short."

"We'll keep you informed," Yolanda said, and the two of them left.

Quinn paced, too restless to sit or to watch the baseball game in the living room with the others. Jones sat in a chair at the conference table, his legs spread wide as he stared ahead, an earpiece in his ear.

"I know, buddy," he said in a soothing voice, or what was soothing for Jones, anyway. "It shouldn't be long." Pause. "I don't know. Work got real busy again." Pause. "Mom's got your back, buddy." Longer pause. "I know you don't. I promise I'll make it up to you when I get back. We'll go get ice cream." A tiny smile appeared as he waited in silence again, as if the promise of ice cream finally worked to assuage Jeffrey.

When he got off the phone, he set it down on the table and let out a giant sigh.

Quinn sat down next to him. "He must be worried."

Jones nodded. "If I could give him an exact day, he'd probably be alright. It's the not knowing that makes him nuts." He smiled a little. "He asked about Daria again."

Quinn laughed. "The Jones brothers have a crush on Daria."

"That little fucker's got me beat, too. He's got more charm than I'll ever have."

"Well, he is very cute." Then Quinn had an idea. "Hey, why don't you have Dar check in on Jeffrey while you're out? Maybe she can vouch for you and say that you're okay."

His eyes got a flicker of hope. "Think she'd do that?"

"I do. Just say you got caught up with work and won't be back for a few days."

"You mind askin' her? I don't feel right about it."

Quinn gave Jones a shove. "I'm not asking her! You're the one who likes her."

"I ain't askin' her for a favor. It ain't right. Especially since she already doin' for us."

"Oh, come on. Drop the tough guy act for one minute. She's a compassionate person. Plus, doing a favor for you will make her see you differently, in a good way." Jones shook his head. "You want her or not? You have to trust me on this."

She snatched the phone off the table and shoved it into his hand.

Jones rolled his eyes. "What's her number?"

Quinn smiled and told him.

He dialed. "Get outta here. I don't need you breathin' down my neck."

Quinn did as ordered and went into the kitchen.

As Jones talked on the phone, Quinn peeked into the freezer, pleasantly surprised to find a box of ice cream sandwiches. She grabbed one and began to pace some more. She wanted to puzzle through this Black Jay figurine tormentor stuff—the connection between her case and Romero's, how her stalker knew she'd pulled the trigger and not Jones. None of it made sense. But it looked more and more like her tormentor was a Jay.

Noah suddenly sprang to mind.

She stopped in her tracks, wondering where that sudden thought had come from. Then she realized it was her ice cream sandwich, which was chocolate chip. Noah's favorite. He'd told her once that was what he'd always bought from Leon the ice cream man back in his Downtownie youth. That, and Noah had called while she was on her way to the safe house two days ago. She'd let the call go to voicemail, but she never got a chance to listen to the message before Marshall ordered them to power down their phones.

What would Noah think if he knew the truth about her tormentor? That it wasn't Jake Carlson, but possibly an enemy far more dangerous than any of them had imagined? She wondered if she should tell Noah about Romero. To keep him happy, but also to possibly enlist him to help nail an elusive, dangerous enemy.

She shook her head. Her of all people, entertaining such thoughts. She'd already violated an ironclad Protectorate rule by getting dimed by a jacker cop, telling herself it didn't count if he wasn't arresting her. But sharing Protectorate secrets with him? That was a much bigger violation, one the Protectorate would need to "deal with."

Yet, at the same time, if Noah proved himself useful with the information she already gave him... he could be a powerful asset for her. For *them*.

It was risky, on several levels. She and Noah were natural adversaries, after all. Yet, what was the one thing that could unite two adversaries? A common enemy. An enemy that threatened them both, where both benefitted from that enemy's defeat.

But there was nothing she could do right now. She was locked away with no way of contacting Noah, not without putting herself and her people at risk.

Just as Jones set the phone down, one of the others came in to use it. But when he went to dial, he made a face. "What's wrong with this thing?"

"Service is down again," Jones told him.

"Again? Fuck." He marched out.

She turned to Jones. "Did you ask her?"

He nodded.

"And?"

"Said she'd do it."

While Jones and the others watched baseball, Quinn spent the next few hours thinking through everything—the Jays, her tormentor, Noah, Merritt.

Merritt. Red-haired Merritt. Devin's observations about her had gone from thought-provoking to downright disturbing.

But as the night dragged on, Quinn grew restless again. She didn't want to be stuck in that safe house any more than the rest of them. Her only solace was the brief respite she got from watching her back every moment of every day, waiting for her tormentor to strike.

But that respite was only temporary. Every moment she remained in that safe house, her enemy drew closer.

CHAPTER 24

QUINN TOOK another swig of her water as she continued reading. She realized she'd read the same paragraph three times now and finally tossed the e-reader aside.

She peered at her colleagues. They sat here and there, looking fidgety and glum as they pretended to enjoy another Demons game on TV. Their gazes shifted eagerly toward the door any time the wind rattled it.

Jones was off talking to Jeffrey again, and a few of the others would glance at him from time to time and then look at one another, as if disapproving. To them, whoever Jones spoke to every day was an attachment and therefore a weakness that, to them, made him somehow less of a pro. They had no idea Jones's "attachments" made him better than any of them. Better than her.

When Jones got off the phone, Quinn took it and called Daria.

"Hey girl," Daria said.

"Hey Dar. What are you up to these days?"

A pause. "You sound bored. What's the matter?"

Quinn chuckled a little. "Nothing. I'm just between jobs."

"Did you get in trouble again?"

"No more than usual. What's new?"

"I talked to Hammond earlier, if that's what you're wondering. Jeffrey is doing fine and seemed real happy that I visited. But I could tell he misses his brother."

Quinn raised her eyebrows. Daria called Jones by his first name. She grinned.

"Why the silence?" Daria asked.

Quinn rolled her eyes. Did the girl miss anything? "To be honest, I forgot that was Jones's name. He was pretty adamant about me not calling him that, from the start."

"I asked for his first name once I realized Jones was Jeffrey's last name. I don't like calling people by their last names."

"How very obliging of him to do that for you."

"Are you trying to play matchmaker, Quinn?"

"Of course not. But even if I were, would that be so bad? He's an amazing guy. Don't let the thuggish appearance fool you."

"Appearances don't fool me. Unlike you, I don't fall for troublemakers."

Quinn rolled her eyes, but didn't argue. Mostly because Daria was right.

"I do admit he's cute," Daria said.

Quinn sat up a little straighter. "How cute? Like baby iguana cute? Or like you want to see him naked cute?"

"What is it with you and iguanas?"

"I like iguanas. And you didn't answer my question."

"It doesn't matter. You know how I feel about your business."

Quinn was silent for a moment. "What do you mean?"

Daria scoffed. "Don't play games with me. He's with the organization."

Quinn sighed. "How'd you know?"

"How? I've known you since we were kids, Quinn! I knew he couldn't be some new friend because, well, you don't have friends. You have work. And he's work. My replacement, I assume. I'm surprised you chose someone so thuggy, though..."

In what rainy, water-clad universe did she believe she could fool Daria? Jesus, she really had lost touch with reality. "He wasn't my first choice, believe me. But he's amazing. I don't know what I would do without him."

"I appreciate the effort, Quinn. But I've got enough going on right now without adding him to the list."

Quinn nodded and left it at that. Stubborn or no, the seed was planted. If Daria didn't like Jones, she would have made it clear. Now it was just a matter of time.

After she hung up, Quinn went back to reading.

"Can we watch something besides baseball, for the love of the devil?" Javier cried.

"Like what?" Perry argued.

Others chimed in and yet another argument broke out. The fourth within a few hours. Quinn looked at Jones, who just rolled his eyes.

"Too many wild animals cooped up for too long," Quinn said.

"Fucken crybabies," he muttered.

But when the door opened and Marshall appeared with Yolanda, the squabbling ceased and all eyes focused on them.

"Gather 'round," Marshall said.

The agents and techs assembled, and Javier shut off the game and yelled for his tech, who hurried out of the restroom, still zipping his fly.

"I have news," Marshall said. "Spec ops set a trap for the Jays, and we nabbed one." A few triumphant cheers from the group. "Two of our best jacked him and pulled everything we could get. The data didn't have all we'd hoped for—these Jays have top-notch blocking—but we got enough." He looked around at all of them. "You're all cleared to return to work."

More cheers and slapping of hands.

"What about the Jay?" Perry asked. "What did we do with him?"

"What we do with anyone who crosses us. We threw him to the wolves."

"Which wolves?" Perry said. "There're a lot of wolves out there."

"The cops," Quinn offered.

Marshall glanced at Quinn for a moment, then nodded. The others looked surprised at that, and for good reason. The Protectorate never worked with the police, had always considered the EDPD an adversary, if not an enemy. Even if the Protectorate kept their role anonymous, which of course they would, handing over a perp to the police still had risks, not to mention gave the police more information about their business.

But the move made sense. Especially to Quinn, who'd already begun working with the police in her own way, even if it wasn't her first choice. The Protectorate knew the EDPD would investigate and could be an ally in their cause, even if they didn't know it. And now that Noah had the information Quinn had given him, he could take that busted Jay and exploit him for all he was worth. That is, if Noah was as smart as he let on.

"What are the fucking cops going to do with him?" Javier asked. "They don't know anything about the Jays."

Marshall frowned. "They do now." When Perry went to argue, Marshall held up his hand. "That's all you need to know."

"So we're safe to get back to hunting these guys?" Javier said.

"We are. You aren't. All of you will be reassigned to other projects, and other agents will take your place."

Frowns and chuffs around the room. Even Quinn let out a sigh.

"Let me guess," Quinn said. "You found data confirming our involvement in the operation."

Marshall gave a nod. "You're all compromised. Until we solve this Black Jay problem, you will steer clear of any project involving them."

"But that leaves us with all the dumbass jobs," Perry griped.

Yolanda finally spoke, her steely gaze aimed at Perry. "Until we discovered the Black Jays only months ago, you seemed more than happy to take those 'dumbass jobs,' Perry. It may surprise you to know that our mission as an organization isn't to keep you entertained. And if you don't want the assignments, I'm sure we can find some eager Tier Twos to take them..."

Perry scowled. "No, I'll take 'em."

Quinn suppressed a smile, happy to see Perry get dinged a little. He was typical of many Tier One agents—from Midtown, privileged, doing the job for thrills. And Quinn was also glad that, for once, Yolanda was giving the smackdown to someone besides her.

"Your new assignments will come tomorrow," Marshall said. He waved them off. "Go home and wait for our call. And watch yourselves."

Everyone began gathering their things. Quinn did the same, feeling her own disappointment at being removed from the Black Jay op. It was the kind of op they all yearned for, and it came with good pay and status. But there was nothing they could do. At least she could get out of this place and get back to doing what she did best. Not to mention they'd finally—*finally*—made headway in what had seemed an insurmountable challenge.

Just as Quinn went to say goodbye to Jones, Yolanda approached them. "You two, please follow me."

Quinn glanced at Jones, whose brows knitted together. That couldn't be good. Had spec ops found evidence of their moonlighting on the Carlson case? Or worse, Quinn's "meetings" with

Noah? Her heart pounded as they followed Yolanda into one of the other rooms. Yolanda closed the door.

"We have combed through every inch of the data we extracted from this Jay," she told them. "Somehow, you two did not appear in any of it."

"How is that possible?" Quinn asked.

"Your recent assignments were special, and different from the others. You've focused on the power players rather than on jobs designed to lure the Jays. As such, you've managed to remain under the radar. Which means you both can continue on this operation until further notice."

Quinn smiled in surprise, glancing at Jones again, who nodded.

"However," Yolanda added, "the danger factor has increased. You will both need to be even more cautious. We will arm you with weapons, also until further notice."

Quinn nodded, somewhat surprised but never letting on that she and Jones had already armed themselves with weapons that outstripped whatever the Protectorate would issue them. She felt a wisp of doubt, and began to wonder if she should tell Yolanda the truth. About her stalker. About Merritt. Maybe even about Noah. Was it the right thing to do?

But something stopped her.

She said goodbye to Jones and hopped into a taxi. When she turned on her phone, she had several messages from Noah. They all said the same thing: it was time to meet. She cursed, deleting them all. Maybe it was time for a new phone number.

As she watched the city go by, she pondered Yolanda's decision to arm them. It was about damned time. If Quinn hadn't violated the Protectorate's strict rule about weapons, she and Jones would be dead and their ashes mingling with the desert dust by now. Sure, the Protectorate hadn't known about the Black

Jays yet, but that was the point. Weapons were insurance against the unknown, at least in their world.

And the truth was, as much as the Protectorate had done for her, and Jones, their lives were as disposable as John Romero's. If the worst happened, the Protectorate would feel bad, offer up stipends to their beneficiaries, and find someone to replace them the next day. For that reason, Quinn decided to tell Yolanda nothing.

She'd taken care of herself all her life, had learned how to survive by doing as Wyatt taught her and trusting nobody unless absolutely necessary. She didn't trust the Protectorate with that information, and for good reason.

Quinn hopped out of the taxi and into the warm air of Midtown, glad to finally be outside again and far away from that safe house.

She walked the few blocks toward her building, her shaded eyes scanning everything around her. From now on, she would be on full alert, ready for any mugger, Black Jay, redheaded secret agent, or any other enemy who dared try to rob her of her freedom and life.

Quinn sighed. She missed the days when her biggest enemies were Downtown thugs and cops. How simple things were then.

She turned the corner to her block. When she saw a suspect-looking plain car nearby, she eyed it just in case. Sure enough, a familiar-looking figure sat inside it.

Noah.

CHAPTER 25

NOAH STEPPED out of the car, looking both angry and sexy in his slacks, white t-shirt, and mirrored shades. Too hot to be a cop, too confident not to be.

She shook her head at him. "Not here."

"You gave me no choice," Noah said, his jaw set.

Quinn glanced around, and then crossed the street and headed around the corner. She entered an electronics store, then found her way into a listening booth and turned on some electronic music. Noah followed her in, taking off his sunglasses and hooking them onto his t-shirt.

"Do not show up at my building again," she said, pointing at him. "Or you will get *nothing* from me."

"Don't threaten me," he shot back. "I can still bust you any fucking time I want."

She gave a bitter laugh. "Okay. Sure. How about this? You threaten me, and then I'll threaten you, and we can keep up this stupid little game and have yet another one of our standoffs."

"You can stand down anytime," he said.

"Never happen."

His dark eyes bore into her. "You haven't returned my calls."

"I had good reason, Noah—"

168 / C.A. HARTMAN

He laughed. "What's that? Jacking emergency?"

"Kind of, yeah."

His expression grew serious. "Anything to do with that asshole someone dumped at headquarters? With the blackbird tattoo?"

Quinn crossed her arms. "What have you done with the information I already fed you? Find anything? Or have you spent the last several days waiting for me to come home?"

"Oh, so it's me giving you information now?" He shook his head, like he couldn't believe her gall.

"You want the choice cuts of meat, you have to prove you can cook, *sergeant*."

He eyed her for a moment, a strange look crossing his face—almost like concern—but then it passed. "I know Carlson's not your guy, despite the motive and timing."

She arched an eyebrow. Maybe Noah did have the goods after all.

"But there is a guy," he went on. "And you have no idea who it is."

A chill ran through Quinn. "How do you know that?"

"A suspicion. Until now."

Shit. Quinn shook her head. Her tormentor had such a hold on her that she'd fallen for the oldest trick in the book. Or maybe Noah really was that good. "Forget about that—"

"Tell me everything you know," he said, stepping closer to her. "I can help."

She sighed in exasperation as the next song came on. "Which do you want more, Noah? Details on something you can't do a damned thing about, or the kind of juicy information you've been waiting for?"

Noah paused, watching her. "What do you have?"

Quinn glanced out the window of the sound booth, making sure nobody watched them. "The special delivery at your headquarters, with the tattoo... he was part of a crew who killed someone I know. Stole a lot from him, and I don't mean his wallet."

"A memory wipe."

"Like I said before, these guys are dangerous. They're the ones you want. You've followed up on what I gave you already, right?"

"I have. We've got stuff in motion." He paused. "You know these people? The ones who brought us this little gift?"

"Does it matter?"

"Ah, so you're not just a rogue agent. You've got people. Which we've suspected for a long time. My question is, why work with us now, after this long?" Then his eyes lit up. "These Black Jays have you turning in circles, don't they? You need us."

"Let's not get carried away. Follow that lead and see where it takes you. That's all I have—"

"Why were you out of commission for so long?" he pressed. "To hide out after the murder of one of your guys? The package isn't talking, by the way..."

"All I know is you need to quit following me and pursue that lead. He was seen with a woman with long red hair. Which means you need to take a closer look at the maintenance worker in my building. You talked to her before, when you were looking for me."

Noah cocked his head. "Merritt?" Then, "Ah. The red hair."

"Just check her out, okay?"

She turned to leave, but Noah stopped her. "I'm not done yet—"

He was close enough that she could feel his warmth, smell his clean smell. She backed away. "We can't be seen together, Noah. It's bad for me... and it's bad for you too."

He narrowed his eyes. "How is it bad for me? I'm a cop, doing my job."

Quinn bit her lip. There was no way she could tell Noah that being seen with him meant risking her job, possibly more. But more than that, she couldn't tell him she feared for him, that being seen with her could put him at risk. Why she cared, she didn't know. He didn't care about her, other than the information she could feed him. And he'd made it clear he was as clever and tough as jacker cops were rumored to be. Yet, if Merritt was a problem and her overly friendly behavior just an act, she knew Noah was connected to Quinn, and hurting Noah could be another way the Jays could mess with her. She would do anything to avoid that.

"What are you not telling me?" Noah said, picking up on her hesitation.

"You have everything you need to know for now."

"Maybe I should check out that asshole you were at the game with while I'm at it."

Quinn groaned. "Come on. These guys we're after... they're super fit and as skilled as ninjas. Devin's got a significant limp, and I've been alone with him on several occasions and he's never laid a finger on me."

Noah contemplated that, the look in his eye one she didn't understand. When she tried to leave again, he blocked the door.

"Let me go!" she snapped.

"How long did you know I was a cop?"

"What?" Quinn asked, confused.

"How long did you know, back when we were dating?"

Quinn grew angry. "Oh, now you want to know! Because last time we broached that topic, you wouldn't listen and then told me I was evil!"

"How long?" he demanded.

"I saw you from inside the dumpster," she said quietly. "The one behind Voila, the one you banged on."

Surprise filled his eyes. Recognition. But then Noah's jaw tightened. "If you knew, why not just end it?"

"I did!"

"No. You called me back about brunch the next day. Talked to me about work. Said you weren't feeling well because of your period. Like you were playing a game. You didn't end it until after all that. Why?"

Fuck. The guy missed nothing.

"Give me a fucking answer," he growled.

"Because once I found out what you do, I assumed you'd been using me the whole time. To get information about... my kind. I thought I could play along, but realized I couldn't do it." She looked down, embarrassment washing over her at how stupid that sounded now.

Noah stared at her. "You thought that?"

"Until I saw you in the alley behind the Lindens', yes."

"You don't trust anyone, do you?"

"No."

Noah shook his head. "That's pathetic."

"I know," she said, still unable to look him in the eye.

She nudged him aside and opened the door. This time, he didn't stop her.

Back at her building, Quinn took the elevator up to her floor, her eyes scanning constantly for Merritt. There was no sign of her. When she entered her security code and opened the door, she found an eight-by-ten envelope on the floor. Her stomach churned.

Another set of doctored photos, even more violent and obscene than the previous ones. The temptation to call Noah gnawed at her. Maybe he could run the pictures or envelope for prints, or through some other forensic analyses.

No. For one thing, it would do no good. Nobody at this level would be stupid enough to leave prints or forensic data like a rookie. And why would Noah want to help her, now that he knew the truth? That she thought so little of him—and herself—that she'd assumed he faked his regard for her? No. This was her problem, and she would deal with it on her own.

She cursed, stuffing the pics back into their package and putting them away with all the others. It was the first time the images hadn't arrived in her mailbox. Her tormenter had grown bored of that game and taken it to the next level by delivering them right to her door, sliding them underneath so nobody but her saw them. Which meant he—she?—had access to the building.

It was a message. Her enemy was inching closer.

She ran through the possibilities. Gaining access to her build-ing... not easy, but possible with the right skill set. Possible for the Jays. Fortunately, getting into her actual apartment would prove almost impossible without her knowing, thanks to a few modifi-cations.

Quinn considered Devin, for no other reason than Noah's suspicions. He had access to the building, obviously. But he wasn't Jay material, at least not physically, and now more than ever she believed Noah's negativity toward Devin was probably personal in nature. And by now, Devin had seen plenty of oppor-tunity to harm her.

The strongest evidence pointed toward the Jays. The threats mentioned revenge for her killing two of theirs, and their stealth methods suggested better than average skill. Not to mention the blackbird figurine she'd found in her old apartment, just like the one found on John Romero. Yet, spec ops data had shown repeat-edly that the Jays worked in pairs or small groups, never alone. And their dealings with them so far showed they didn't play games or make threats, they simply tiptoed in, jacked you, and killed you.

No, this felt like some dark agent, working alone. Someone who took pleasure in psychological torture and fear tactics, who enjoyed the power of it all. Someone who didn't seek data, but instead wanted to make her suffer until she did something desperate. Someone who could put on a good show if necessary, like a serial killer putting on the charm, appearing even harmless, while luring another victim to her death.

Maybe someone like Merritt.

What once had seemed ludicrous now seemed compelling. Merritt had full access to the building, a disarming way... and long red hair.

When her phone beeped, Quinn immediately knew who it was.

Get my package, Quinn? Hope you liked the images. That will be you, sweetheart. Very soon.

Now, Quinn could almost hear Merritt's sing-song voice behind the words.

Then she did something crazy. She replied.

I look forward to seeing you. Again.

Let her tormentor think she knew. Two could play at this game.

And Quinn knew just where to begin.

CHAPTER 26

WHEN QUINN's phone woke her the next morning, she grabbed it, ready to see if her tormentor decided to take things to the next level. But it was Yolanda.

"Good morning," she said.

"Quinn. I've got an assignment for you."

"Hit me."

"Hector Olmos."

"The CEO of El Diablo Water? That Hector Olmos?"

"The very one."

"Let me guess. He sought us out because the Black Jays attempted a jacking."

"Yes and no. We spoke with Carrie Anne Halstead, who mentioned that Olmos had an encounter with the Jays, but that nothing happened. However, Olmos is unwilling to contact us, for fear of angering them."

"Don't you find it a little suspicious that these very capable mind thieves keep missing opportunities with these power players?"

"We considered that. But the 'power players' have busy lives and families, and they're trained to watch their backs constantly, so they're difficult to isolate. Your success was helped by an inside man at The Oasis, and having caught Miss Halstead with her pants down, so to speak. More importantly, the Jays didn't attempt to attack Mr. Olmos. Instead, they left him a token."

"The figurine."

"Yes."

"Hmm. Same drill, then? Sneak up on Olmos, face my worst memories, and find nothing helpful about the Jays?" Quinn knew Yolanda wouldn't appreciate her sarcasm. But she couldn't help herself. This would be a difficult and risky job, more so than the others because Olmos didn't patronize pool clubs or martial arts dojos, and spent most of his time with his colleagues or family.

"I'll give the job to Javier, then."

"No, we'll take the job. I just... it seems unnecessarily risky for no real gain."

"It may appear that way, but we found certain patterns in the data from your other two targets. A third, assuming it's consistent, gives us confidence to do what we have planned next."

"What's that?" Quinn asked, intrigued.

"Finish this job and you'll find out."

Quinn sighed. "What did you tell Halstead you would do?"

"We said we would investigate."

Quinn nodded, but said nothing. Something nagged at her, something she couldn't put her finger on.

"Quinn?"

"I'm here. It's just... something about this feels off."

"How so?"

"All these power players being targeted at once, but none fully jacked or harmed. And the figurine... they left it after killing Romero, but left it for Olmos without going after him? And why didn't the others get figurines?"

"It's too soon to know the significance of the figurine. And, as I mentioned, isolating people like Olmos is difficult. It is also possible the Jays seek merely to frighten these leaders, then wait for them to do something desperate."

Just like her tormentor was doing to her.

Yet, while Quinn wasn't an easy target, she was often alone and more accessible than the CEOs. Again, Quinn wanted to mention the figurine she'd received, to tell Yolanda the truth. But doing so was risky and would encourage more questions, questions she didn't want to answer. And with the limited information they were working with, her confession wouldn't yield anything useful anyway.

"Whatever the case, Jones and I will take care of it."

"Glad to hear it."

After Yolanda hung up, Quinn paced her apartment. Maybe Yolanda was right. Maybe the Jays had planned it this way all along, had decided to switch methods. If so, it made them an even more formidable enemy.

But more importantly, Olmos receiving a figurine intrigued Quinn. Something told her mindjacking him would produce something worthwhile. Including information that could lead to her tormentor.

That, by itself, was worth the risk.

Quinn stomped on the gas, grinning as she took the corner just fast enough to slide a little, but not so fast that she lost control.

"God damn, girl," Jones said over the whine of the engine. "You tryin' to get us killed?"

Quinn laughed. "Just having a little fun. I haven't ridden in a dune buggy since I was a teenager and my old boyfriend stole one for the night."

"That's great. But I'd like to make sure my mom and brother have an income comin' in, so slow it down, will ya? We don't need to be drawin' attention to ourselves."

Quinn sighed and eased off the accelerator. She could see his point. Sort of. Although they were out in the open desert, where few dared to tread. And safety? Hell, that wasn't an issue. She knew how to drive a dune buggy, and even if the occasional rollover took place, the buggy was equipped to handle it and keep them safe. Wyatt wouldn't have told her to slow down. He'd have pushed her to go faster. Then again, Wyatt was dead.

It was a beautiful night. The late-night hour and leaving the concrete jungle of El Diablo had cooled the air to something downright pleasant. Out here, there was nothing to store heat and radiate it back to them, other than the sandy desert floor. The stars were out too, with no light pollution to obscure them.

But this was no joyride. This was work. They were heading to the desert escape of one Hector Olmos and his family. Like many of the highest-level power players in El Diablo, Olmos had a place outside the city, where only the wealthiest could afford to drill deep enough to reach water and afford the generated power to keep the air conditioning and other luxuries running.

Quinn had never been inside, or even near, one of these places. They were scattered in the hills outside town, buried in the landscape and far enough from one another to feel like a real escape. The closest she'd ever come to seeing one was when she and Daria invaded the home of one rogue military man, the one whose energy weapon Quinn had secretly stolen. And his place had been nothing but a small, modest home, now little more than a skeleton of dried wood and concrete that lost its battle with the unforgiving desert.

"I see it," Jones said.

Quinn slowed down and looked ahead. There, in the distance, were lights. Soft lights, almost like little candles, lining the drive up to Olmos's weekend home. There wasn't much to see, as the home was mostly submerged into the earth, allowing for maximum privacy and escape from the elements. However,

178 / C.A. HARTMAN

even from a distance, Quinn could spot the landscaping. Plants, trees, lighting. All requiring power, and water.

"What's up with the landscaping?" Jones said drily. "Good ole water CEO, settin' an example."

Quinn chuckled. "Exactly."

She killed the lights. They would pull off into a spot behind a hill they'd marked on their topo map, and travel the rest of the way on foot. No need to alert the Olmos clan, or anyone else, that they were coming.

As she and Jones began checking their belongings one last time, Quinn's phone beeped. She shook her head and ignored it. It was probably her stalker, hoping to continue their fucked-up little game. Quinn didn't have time for that now.

But when another louder beep came, followed by several more, she froze. So did Jones. They knew that signal. She looked at Jones and he looked at her, and she picked up her phone and called Yolanda.

"Quinn," came Yolanda's voice.

"What's wrong?"

"Where are you?"

"Near Olmos's weekend place. What's going on?" There was no response. "Yolanda?"

"... abort..."

"What? You're breaking up."

"... abort the..."

"You want us to abort?" Jones's eyes widened as he watched her. Then the line cut out. They were too far out, where coverage was spotty at best. Her phone beeped as a message came through: *Abort. To headquarters, immediately. Only you. Confirm.*

"What is it?" Jones asked.

"We have to abort. And I have to report to headquarters."

"You? Or both of us?"

"Me."

"What the hell?"

Quinn shook her head. This had never happened before.

She confirmed the message and they returned to the outskirts of the city and dropped the dune buggy off. Jones asked Quinn to let him know what happened as they parted ways, and Quinn took a taxi to headquarters.

Quinn tried to think about what had gone wrong. What would warrant aborting such an important mission at the last minute, after all that planning? It could be a host of things, most of which revolved around protecting their safety or that of the Protectorate. But if that were the case, why couldn't Jones come too?

When she reached headquarters, she entered the code and stepped inside, the cool AC offering relief from the city heat. She marched down the stairs and into the underground tunnels, going through a series of checkpoints to ensure she had the necessary credentials. When she arrived at Yolanda's office, she expected to see Yolanda sitting there in one of her pretty printed dresses, her fancy handbag next to her and her hair perfect. Instead, three male agents—all spec ops—stood there, weapons in their hands. Yolanda stood nearby.

"What the hell is going on?" Quinn asked.

Yolanda stepped forward. "We have evidence that you've been collaborating with the El Diablo Police Department." She pulled up an image.

Quinn felt a pit in her stomach. The image was of her and Noah, inside the soundproof booth at the electronics shop.

"It's not what it looks like," Quinn said.

"No?" Yolanda nodded at one of the ops guys, who pressed a remote.

A video projected onto the wall. Her and Noah, the camera capturing her face. And her lips.

"So you believe our lip readers are lying or incompetent?" Yolanda went on.

Quinn stood there in silence, her heart pounding and sweat forming in her armpits. Then she said the three most useless words ever. "I can explain."

When Yolanda pointed at Quinn's pockets, the ops guys approached her.

"Hands up," one of them ordered.

Quinn put her hands up, and they began going through her pockets, pulling out all her equipment. When they were finished, Yolanda turned to her.

"Quinn Hartley, you're no longer a member of the Protectorate."

CHAPTER 27

QUINN SAT in her nice apartment, sweating in the afternoon heat that blew in from her window. She'd turned off the air conditioning. She couldn't afford it now that she had no job.

How had it come to this? She'd gone from favored Tier One to outcast in a matter of a moment.

They'd canned her and confiscated her equipment. When she pointed out that she'd paid for that equipment, Yolanda merely said in her usual flat tone that Quinn would be reimbursed.

Quinn could have said more. But what was the point? She'd collaborated with a jacker cop, and spec ops found out. They'd followed her, just like they'd followed her that time when Daria had assisted her remotely on a couple of jobs instead of joining her in the field. Despite Quinn being the Protectorate's special pet and getting the premium jobs, they still didn't trust her and went looking for a reason not to.

She'd broken two steadfast rules: never let the police know what you do, and never collaborate or share information with them. Even more, they knew from that conversation that she and Noah had been more than collaborators. That didn't help her case.

Quinn set down her diablo, already a little loopy from the high-quality tequila she would no longer be able to afford. She stood and began to pace.

There was a solution. There had to be.

But there wasn't. Not for this. Even if Yolanda listened to her explanation and could see her perspective, there was still no way around the fact that she'd lied about important things, had gotten herself dimed by a jacker cop who, at least from their perspective, could turn on her anytime he wanted. Justified or not in her choices, she was now a liability the Protectorate couldn't afford.

Now, it was a matter of what the Protectorate would do with her. Relieving her from duty wasn't enough. The documents she signed, the tenets she agreed to... they weren't enough to ensure she wouldn't become a threat to the organization. They would have to take stronger measures, measures that would be named later.

In the meantime, Quinn agreed to wear a tracking device, to let them monitor her movements.

She paced back and forth like a restless animal in a cage. She was out. Out of the only job she'd ever cared about. Out of income. Out of a future. And soon, out of a place to live. Of course, all that assumed Merritt wouldn't sneak in and gut her in her sleep.

She wiped the sweat from her brow. As harsh as all that was, it didn't mask another problem, one that still haunted her. There was something about the power player jobs that nagged at her, like a thirst she couldn't quite quench. Like she was missing some key piece of the puzzle, a piece she may have found if she'd done the Olmos job. And the more she paced, the more the idea took hold in her mind like an iguana's feet clung to a rock.

She thought about Lucifer and wondered how the quirky little beast was doing. How Devin was doing. She'd been so busy that she hadn't had a chance to call or return the message he'd left.

She picked up her phone and messaged him: *Hey Devin. Things have been a little nuts. I'll call you soon. Give Lucifer a kiss.*

A few minutes later, there was a knock on her door. It was Devin, with Lucifer in his arms.

"Or you can kiss him yourself," he said drily, smiling a little.

Quinn grinned and stepped into the hallway, closing the door behind her. Lucifer looked at her curiously, so she took him from Devin, his scratchy feet abrading her arms and tickling her a little.

"How's my boy?" she cooed, petting him. She looked at Devin. "How are you? Sorry I've been busy."

He shrugged. "No problem. I've been busy myself." He paused. "You mind if I come in? My bum leg is hurting today."

Shame washed over Quinn as she realized how weird she'd been about not letting people into her place. Besides, everything she owned that would make him suspicious was either stowed away or in the Protectorate's hands.

When the elevator dinged, Quinn glanced over, and her stomach turned upside down when the doors opened. Merritt emerged, her expression serious, even menacing in a way Quinn had never seen before. Then, when Merritt saw them, her face instantly transformed. Big smile, wide eyes. She hurried over, her tool belt clunking on her hips.

"Hey Quinn! Hey Devin! How are you?" Before Quinn or Devin could answer, she'd already turned her attention to Lucifer. "Oh, my goodness! My favorite little guy!" She glanced at Devin. "Hope you don't mind all my gushing... I just love this little guy!"

As Merritt petted Lucifer and stuck her hand out for him to bite or not bite, Quinn glanced at Devin. His eyes seemed to darken as he stood there, watching Merritt with slightly pent-up anger, like he wanted to tell her to leave but didn't want to be rude.

Then Quinn had an idea.

"You want to hold him?" Quinn asked. Without bothering to get Devin's permission, she handed off Lucifer to Merritt, whose eyes lit up even more.

As Merritt played with the creature and cooed affectionate little words that seemed more contrived by the moment, Quinn took the opportunity to observe her. Long red hair. Fit body, trim and firm, with ropy muscles in her arms. Quinn's eyes moved to Merritt's wrists, searching for a telltale tattoo that, if found, would prompt a question about its significance.

Her right wrist was bare, but she wore a leather cuff on the left. Big enough to cover the giveaway marking. Another idea came to her.

"I love that leather cuff, Merritt! Where did you get it?"

Merritt glanced at her. "From a secondhand store here in Midtown. I think it was really expensive, but I got a great deal on it."

"It looks expensive. Would you mind if I tried it on? I've always wanted to see how a cuff would look on me..."

There it was. The test. Which would win out: Merritt's innocence and eagerness to please, or her guilt and desire to hide the truth?

Merritt hesitated, her smile fading. "I... I'd rather not. The clasp is getting ready to break, and I can't afford to fix it right now."

A lie. Quinn had owned a similar cuff once, and the clasps were bomb-proof. And Merritt's expression made it clear she was lying.

Quinn nodded, eyeing her. "I understand."

There was silence for several moments, and Quinn felt a

tingle run through her. She watched Merritt, whose eyes flashed with anger for just a mere moment before she looked away and focused on Lucifer.

Gotcha, you lying bitch.

Devin finally stepped in and grabbed his iguana. "I think Lucifer's had enough attention today."

"I need to get going anyway," Quinn added. "I just remembered I have something I need to take care of." She glanced at Devin, who did not look happy. "Rain check?"

He barely had a chance to nod before she turned to Merritt and smiled. "Good to see you, Merritt."

"You too," Merritt said, discomfort now clearly showing on her face.

Back inside her apartment, Quinn took a deep breath and began to pace again.

The redheaded demon had made it clear she was everywhere, lurking around the corner and ready to surprise Quinn... and there was nothing Quinn could do about it. But with Quinn's message and now her leather cuff test, Merritt could make no mistake about Quinn's intentions.

Quinn considered telling Devin, sharing her suspicions and getting him on her side. But that would raise a whole slew of questions from Devin. Like who Merritt really was. Who she worked for. Why she'd be after Quinn.

No, Quinn was on her own. As usual.

She continued pacing, fear competing with anger at her increasingly desperate situation. Only a crazy person would stick around in the face of all this, instead of packing up her shit and leaving. But maybe crazy was what she needed. Instead of trying to do this the right way, the smart way... maybe she needed to do something different.

Something crazy.

And then, like a thunderclap on a hot day, it came to her.

An hour later, when she was finished with her preparations, she rolled up one pant leg and looked down at the tracking device on her ankle. Then she grabbed her energy weapon and began to slowly disintegrate the metal along one side, careful to avoid damaging the chip or herself. When finished, she pried the thing off and placed it in a cabinet.

She took one last look around, and left.

CHAPTER 28

QUINN STOOD on the crowded train, in the far corner where she could see everyone and everything. She wore one of her classic Downtown getups—cargos and a jacket—along with a new wig to cover her blonde hair, shocking pink this time. She hated the hair tickling her face and arms, but she had little choice. She wore prosthetics to make her hips and breasts much rounder, hoping they would prevent any cop, tormentor, or Protectorate spec ops from recognizing her. She also wore another important item: a backpack, filled with the things she would need that night.

When she got off the train in Westgate and the familiar sweat-cannabis aroma hit her, she felt almost nostalgic. But she knew that feeling resulted only from her desperate state, and maybe the desperate actions she was about to take.

Once she arrived on the outskirts of town, she headed into the underground and weaved her way through the labyrinth of makeshift offices. Soon, she found a familiar nook with a door of hanging beads, and shook the beads to announce herself before poking her head through them.

Pablo made a face. "What the fuck? Get out."

She came inside anyway. "It's me, Pablo. Jones's friend."

He eyed her for a moment before his eyes finally showed a

sign of recognition. Then he smirked, his eyes traveling down her body and back up again. "Bring me something special?"

"Cash. If you have what I need."

His eyes narrowed. "What's a pretty girl like you need?"

"So glad you asked."

Soon, Quinn was examining a black-market mind reader and nodes that seemed to be in good working order.

"How much?" she asked him.

When he told her, she gave him a hard look. "My previous guy gets them for half that."

In reality, her previous guy was a Protectorate-approved dealer. She knew the markup for buying through someone like Pablo would be significant, but that didn't mean she wasn't going to try.

"Then your previous guy's hooked into the source. I ain't. You go peripheral like this, you pay more. And you get secrecy with me, 'cause you're a friend of Jones."

Quinn handed over the cash. "If this equipment doesn't work perfectly for my client, we'll come looking for you."

"I expect nothin' less, girl."

She left and headed to her next stop, about a mile down the way. It was a former airplane hangar, hot with giant fans blowing, and filled with dune buggies. A woman with salt-and-pepper hair and arm tattoos eyed her.

"Back again?" she said.

"I need another buggy."

"How long you want it this time?"

Quinn had paid for twenty-four hours last time she rented a dune buggy, the night she and Jones headed out to the desert. One never knew how long a job would take, or what could go wrong. Bringing it back after only an hour didn't warrant a refund, either.

"Twenty-four hours," Quinn said, handing over the cash.

She was out half her savings now. The woman pointed to a buggy on the far side of the hangar, saying it was sized better for a "lady."

"I'll park it outside and come back for it later," Quinn said. "I have to take care of something first."

Quinn hurried down the street. There was only so much time before the Protectorate realized her tracking device hadn't registered any motion. They knew her well enough to know she couldn't stay in her apartment long. She needed to do what needed doing before they began looking for her.

When she got to her dad's place, he was sitting in his chair with a bottle of Snakebite soda, watching highlights from the playoffs. He was drinking the good soda she'd been bringing him, and for some reason that made her happy.

"To what do I owe the honor?" he said flatly, glancing over at her. When he saw her appearance, his eyebrows came together. "What the hell's goin' on?"

Quinn took off her pack and handed it to him. It contained everything that mattered—her computer, the note from Noah, the ruined butterfly art, the black jay figurine, all the envelopes her stalker had sent her, storage devices, money.

"Keep this safe," she said. "Hide it, and don't let anyone know it's here."

He gave her a dubious look, only glancing at the pack.

"I'm serious, Dad."

"I can see that."

She shoved the pack onto his lap. "You got any paper?"

Her dad just stared at her, then the pack, then motioned with his head toward the counter, where a small pad of paper sat. She grabbed a piece, ignoring the one with his grocery list, and wrote down a series of numbers. She unzipped the pack and stuffed the paper inside before closing it up again.

"That's everything you need, just in case," she said. "If I wind up in the clink, the information in this bag will become useful. If anyone comes looking for you because of me, don't tell them *anything*. There's enough money in here to hire someone to help if necessary, and there's more hidden in my apartment. I wrote down where's it's hidden and the code to get in, plus the security codes to my building and apartment. You got it?"

He stood up, holding the pack. "What the fuck is going on? You into something bad?"

"Yes. And tonight's my only chance to fix it."

He shook his head. "I'll help you hide, but I don't want this shit." He held out the backpack to her. "I ain't gonna stand around and wait for you to get yourself killed."

"It's the only way, Dad. You still have your gun?"

"Of course. But—"

"I'm sorry, Dad. I love you, okay?"

Quinn turned and left.

When Quinn returned to the hangar, it was almost nine. The shop was closed and her buggy waited outside.

She still had time.

She drove cautiously. She couldn't afford mistakes... not tonight.

Her phone rang. Jones again.

By now, he would know she'd been canned. They would have told him right away, to make it clear what he could and could not tell her. And he probably knew she was up to no good, doing the thing she shouldn't do... and alone. But there was nothing he could do about it now. He would be furious at her refusal to accept his help, but too bad. She wasn't going to take him down with her.

Because what she was about to do was crazy. Totally lizard-shit crazy. And she knew it.

But what choice did she have? She'd lost the only job that ever mattered to her. She'd lost the income that came with it. The Protectorate would find some way to punish her for her collaboration. She had some psychopath after her. She had no future. So why should she sit back and let her life go to shit like some broke-ass Downtownie, or worse, let her tormentor kill her?

Nope. She needed answers. And she would get them tonight or die trying.

Die with your boots on.

It wasn't long before Quinn was back in the open desert again, breathing in the fresh air. After driving a while, she spotted the hills... and then she saw them. The lights leading up to his house.

Hector Olmos's house.

CHAPTER 29

QUINN SLOWED DOWN, not wanting the buggy's quiet electric hum to reach Olmos's home. She hadn't turned on the lights this time to avoid looking like a beacon. Besides, she didn't need headlights. Outside the city, the starlight and the glow of the crescent moon gave her all the illumination she needed. Soon, she pulled behind one of the neighboring hills.

She checked her equipment one last time before heading toward the Olmos family's desert home on foot. The silence out there was unnerving. Other than her soft footsteps, she heard only the occasional sound of the breeze shuffling the dry soil. She kept looking around, then behind her, feeling far more hyper-aware of her surroundings in the abandoned desert than she did Downtown, despite the fact that there was nothing and no one out here. There hadn't been in a long time.

Her excessive awareness came from being alone. Mind-jackers weren't supposed to work alone. Ever. The few times she had, she'd had Daria in her ear. But now she was off her turf, doing something crazy, and without Jones.

He would have helped her, no question. That was why she ignored his calls. Because she'd learned long ago that it was foolish to rely on others. They died. They got murdered. They let you down. She didn't depend on anyone now, and no one depended on her.

There were times when she'd wondered if it could be different. For a moment there, she'd dared to hope it would be different with Noah. But that too was foolish. He'd cared about her more than she'd given him credit for, but that was no longer true. And by now, Jones had a reputation so solid that he'd find a new Tier One to partner with.

So tonight she was free of all attachments. Nothing and no one to worry about but herself. It was better that way.

Yet, as she walked in the warm desert air, such thoughts didn't rejuvenate her. They made her feel empty. She pushed them away.

As she drew close to Olmos's partly submerged home, she encountered a wall that surrounded the entire property. She sized it up, then took a running start and scaled it until her head peeked over the top.

Yup, just as she thought. Surveillance.

Quinn pulled herself over the wall and landed squarely on the other side. It was late, but if someone saw her, let them see her. She'd prepared to sedate the entire family and anyone else she encountered anyway; it didn't matter if she did so here or inside.

But nobody came. Which meant no one saw her coming, or they did and would wait for her inside.

She disabled the security system, and it took her twice the time it would've taken Jones. Inside, the air conditioning hit her first, cooling her light sheen of sweat. It was dark, other than a soft light source that seemed to move and sparkle ahead, offering enough illumination to see leather furniture, imported tile, and, in the center of it all, a glass-enclosed courtyard with moonlight shining into it.

Then something hit her. Something odd, but familiar. A

smell, one she couldn't put her finger on. Not animal, not plant, but natural. Her mind suddenly flashed back to the George Hatch job, where the money elite lounged by the pool. She smelled water.

Sure enough, inside that courtyard was a pool.

Quinn halted, staring, momentarily forgetting what she was there to do. The pool was dark, not bluish like the other one, its liquid surface shimmering in the moonlight and scattering tiny light reflections around as the breeze nudged its surface.

All that water. Literally tons of it, out here in the middle of nowhere, replenished often in order to keep up with the rapid rate of evaporation in their hot, arid world. Lots of water for the CEO of water.

Quinn marveled at the cost of such a luxury, which would be astronomical. The infrastructure, the water, transporting or somehow accessing the water, the upkeep.

She was pulled from her reverie by distant footsteps. Heavy, male. She quickly hid behind a chair, her temperature rising as a new batch of sweat poured from her wigged head and padded body. A door opened to the right of the courtyard, and bright light flooded into the room. She pulled out her injector, ready to strike. Whoever it was, he was likely armed and coming for her.

She waited, listening for the footsteps growing closer. But they didn't. Instead, she heard the sound of a refrigerator door opening. She pulled out her viewer and inched it out from behind the chair, adjusting until she had an image. It was Olmos himself, silhouetted against the fridge light, peering inside before retrieving several frosted bottles of water and wine.

Quinn recognized his hair—dark, thick, curly, and streaked with gray. But what surprised her was how trim and fit he looked under his slacks and t-shirt. Lean and muscled, like he worked out every day. She'd researched images of Olmos and noted his youthful appearance, but chalked that up to old images, cosmetic enhancement, or to the images only showing him from the shoulders up.

This was her chance. Sneak up on him, stick him, then sedate the family, buying her plenty of time to jack him the right way and make sure she got what she needed.

When he faced the fridge again, Quinn silently headed to the partition that separated the kitchen from the living room, topped with a counter and lined with barstools. She crouched behind it, preparing to jump him when he left the kitchen.

The fridge shut. More sounds, like he'd loaded his beverages onto a tray. She clutched the injector and got ready to spring. She inched forward, until she heard a voice. A male voice, coming from the open door Olmos had emerged from.

Olmos had a wife and three daughters. There shouldn't be any other men.

Quinn stayed hidden behind the partition and watched him head toward that door. She needed to strike before he headed through it, but her feet would not move. Olmos disappeared and closed the door behind him, leaving her in silent darkness.

She'd lost her chance. She'd hesitated and lost her chance.

But something wasn't right.

After her eyes readjusted to the darkness, she began searching the main floor of the house, including the bedrooms. She peered into one of them, a girl's bedroom with a picture of a pop star hanging over her bed. The bed was made. Quinn checked the other rooms, including the master bedroom. All empty.

What the hell?

Then she heard it. Voices. Laughter. Men, and possibly a woman. All beneath her in the subterranean part of the house. Were his wife and children down there? Were they having a party, or watching a movie? No. Those were adult voices.

Quinn knew what would happen if she went down there.

She would see them, they would see her, and all hell would break loose. Instead, she needed a way to get them under her control. And there was only one way to do that.

But first, she needed to get Olmos away from the others.

She tiptoed to the door, carefully turning the knob to open it. Voices, clearer now. At least three other men and a woman. From what little she heard, they weren't having a party. They were talking business.

She took a deep breath. "Dad?" she called downstairs, making her voice high. When it didn't carry, she said it again, a little louder. "*Dad?*"

The voices quieted. She heard something about "your daughter."

She backed away from the door. And within a moment, there were footsteps coming up the stairs. Olmos appeared.

"Alexis?" he said.

Quinn stepped toward him and injected him. The injection worked quickly, and he was out before he could get a good look at Quinn. He began to crumple, and Quinn scrambled to catch him before he tumbled to the floor, but it was too little, too late. His falling mass proved too much for her and they both collapsed to the wood floor with a loud thud.

Knowing she had only moments before the others came to investigate, she shoved Olmos away and scrambled to her feet, pulling her secret weapon from the back of her cargoes. She released the trigger on the gas bomb and tossed it downstairs, then shut the door. She grabbed the nearby dining table and shoved it toward the door to brace it as rapid footsteps clambered up the stairs. Doorknob jiggling, followed by pounding on the door.

"Hector!"

The pounding got more forceful, and Quinn jumped as an

explosion of weapons blew through the door, a gaping hole appearing where the doorknob was. She pressed that table up against the door as hard as she could, muscles straining, sweat pouring from her forehead and stinging her eyes, hunching down to avoid stray fire. Then there was a big push against her, so hard she stumbled backward, but she shoved the table forward again to thwart whoever tried to escape.

Another pushback, harder this time, knocking her onto her butt. She pulled out her energy weapon, ready to stop the stranger any way she could. She aimed... and then she heard it.

Thud. Then another. The assailants had succumbed to her gas bomb and gone down.

She stayed where she was, catching her breath, waiting for the rest of them to go down. Finally, she opened the door and let the gas dissipate. When enough time passed, she headed down. A man lay slumped on the stairs, out cold, and another just below him. She stepped over them and continued down until she reached the basement.

Three more people—two slumped in their chairs and a third in the closet, feet sticking out. All unconscious. The place smelled of acrid smoke and she coughed. She took out her handkerchief and held it over her mouth and nose, just in case. Wine and water sat on the table in silver buckets, ice-filled crystal glasses everywhere.

Quinn took a closer look at their faces. She saw blonde hair and a familiar face. When Quinn realized who it was, she blinked a couple of times. Carrie Anne Halstead. From the martial arts dojo.

She recognized some of the other faces as well, including George Hatch... and, in the closet, the mayor of El Diablo. These were the people who controlled El Diablo's energy, water, and cooling, who controlled El Diablo itself. Quinn glanced at her watch. Was it time for their monthly meeting? No. That took place during the week at the mayor's office, not late at night in Olmos's basement.

And that's when she saw it. The screen filled with names. Familiar names, including hers and Jones's. Hers had been crossed out, next to which was Perry's name. A chill ran through her.

Quinn began looking around again. She eyed Hatch's gorgeous, expensive watch, gracing the arm that lay on the table. She went over and picked up his arm, studying the watch before tugging it to peer underneath the platinum band.

Nothing. No tattoo.

She checked the others. No tattoos on their wrists, or anywhere that she could see. Then she remembered the men on the stairs. She checked them, not recognizing their faces but immediately noticing their well-developed and lean muscles. When she examined their wrists, both contained the familiar blackbird insignia.

Quinn stepped over them again, emerging from the basement to find Hector Olmos still slumped on the hardwood floor. On a lark, she grabbed his wrist, which was watch-free on that evening.

And there it was. The avian mark, black with red eyes... and swollen. Like the tattoo was brand new.

She stood there, her mind swirling, until it all began to coalesce.

El Diablo's power players were in bed with the Black Jays.

The Jays weren't using their powers to try and take down the establishment. The Jays *were* the establishment. And they were targeting the Protectorate.

She couldn't mindjack Olmos now. It was too risky. She needed to get her evidence and get out before they woke up and everything got ugly. She stepped over the mayor in the closet, peering into the large space. When she saw what was inside, her eyes grew wide.

Firearms. Energy weapons. Other weapons. Lots of them.

This was their hideout, their safe house. Or one of them.

She began rooting through their pockets, looking for phones, wallets, anything useful. She took photos of everything she could think of, then found Halstead's purse, stuffed what she could inside it, and threw it over her shoulder. Then she took another look in the weapons closet, her eyes landing on an Udi 99, a fully automatic firearm that folded down small enough to hide. She collapsed it down, found its holster, and strapped it under her shirt.

She barreled back up the stairs, stepping over the two Jays, then Olmos.

Just as she went to leave, she saw movement from the corner of her eye, out the window.

Camouflage pants and boots hurrying past. Then another set.

Someone had tripped an alarm. They were coming for her.

CHAPTER 30

QUINN FROZE, quickly trying to assess her options. Another set of boots appeared outside, possibly a third man.

She'd planned for this. For encountering multiple enemies. That's why she'd brought the gas bomb. But now it was spent. She only had her usual defenses, against multiple enemies with a potential arsenal of weaponry. But escape meant facing them in the open desert, where she had no buildings to hide behind, no back alley to escape through, no taxi to commandeer.

The city, with all its treachery, suddenly seemed so safe.

She wanted to slip through the door and make a run for it. But those men, whoever they were, would be waiting for her.

So she would wait for them.

Quinn snuck through the dark house, past the shimmering pool and into the control room. She peered at the displays, giving her a view of the property surrounding the house and beyond. One man was staked out at the wall, another passed by a camera, then another appeared at the front door. Three of them, then.

She returned to the kitchen area, hiding just behind the partition, and waited for him to break down the door. But nothing happened. So she waited.

One minute, then two.

Then two more.

Dread sunk into the pit of her stomach. The longer they waited, the more likely they were setting a trap.

A chime rang out, startling Quinn. Then again.

Quinn followed the sound; it came from Olmos. She found his phone and, after hesitating for a moment, decided to answer.

"Hello?" she whispered. It wasn't hard to sound desperate.

Silence. But someone was there. Waiting for her.

"Hello?" she repeated, still whispering. "Are you guys out there? This is Carrie Anne." Still nothing. "We're in here, trapped. Hector is down, so are the others, and it's just me and George. Someone gas bombed us. There are two of them, upstairs."

"You know their location?" came the male voice.

"I hear footsteps, right above me, above the supply closet. Should I go up there?"

Onscreen, Quinn saw one of them, muscled and tattooed, gesture toward another to the south side of the house. "Negative. Stay in the safe room until we come for you." He hung up.

Quinn went and hid behind the edge of the couch, keeping one eye on the front door. Not long after, the front door clicked and cracked open, and a man with night vision lenses peeked inside, weapon drawn. Quinn pulled back behind the couch so he wouldn't spot her.

She waited, heart pounding in her ears as light footsteps silently prowled across the wood floor, growing closer.

One step. Then another.

Quinn held still, her leg beginning to cramp and the hard floor hurting her knee. She remained crouched, weighing her options, knowing she didn't have many.

The silent steps drew closer, Quinn sweating despite the comfy temperature, and she readied herself. When a leg in camo pants appeared, she stabbed the injector into his calf. He whipped around, spotting her, then dropped with a thud.

She crouched down again, listening for weapons fire, for movement, for any sign of backup muscle. When she detected none, she ventured to pop her head over the couch. It was clear. She scurried to the door and waited. She could wait here, until the other two came to investigate, and she could pick them off one by one.

But that wouldn't work. They would know not to come that way after the first guy didn't respond to their hails. And time was ticking on her sleeping Jays downstairs, who would wake up soon enough. She needed to get out, before she turned two enemies into eight.

She glanced at her watch, estimating how much time she had. Another fifteen minutes, at best. Better make it five to be on the safe side.

Five minutes felt like an hour. Waiting, wondering, knowing she was surrounded.

But after those minutes passed, no one else had entered. Finally, crouched low, she headed to the control room again and found the location of the two guards. One waited by the front door, the other covered the south side of the house. She had only one choice.

She headed to one of the bedrooms on the east side of the house. Quinn took her energy weapon and sliced through the thick, UV-blocking glass, just enough to weaken the pane. Then she grabbed a chair from the desk and heaved it at the glass, enough to make a loud clatter.

She dropped the chair and ran into the control room. Sure enough, the guy guarding the front door headed to the east side of the house. With Halstead's handbag of goods slung across her chest, Quinn escaped out the front door and bolted for the wall.

Just as she began to scale it, she heard a man call out.

Someone saw her. She scrambled up the wall, her padding hampering her agility and the rough stone scraping against her clothing. Just as she reached the top and was about to flip to the other side, the pain hit her and she heard a sizzling sound.

They'd shot her in the leg with an energy weapon.

Somehow, she got over the wall, gracelessly plummeting down the other side and dropping to the ground with a thud. She gasped for breath, the wind knocked out of her, momentarily forgetting the searing pain in her leg.

What if I can't walk? What if they crippled me?

Then crawl, damn it!

She spotted the bag nearby, its contents partly scattered on the desert floor. She crawled over, stuffing it all back inside and tossing the strap over her head as she hauled herself to her feet. She grunted as the pain spread through her leg, readying herself to run off into the darkness like a wounded jackrabbit. But something clobbered her from behind, hard enough to send her straight to the ground again. Someone had attacked her.

One of the guards.

CHAPTER 31

QUINN ATE DUST, a puff of it shooting into her mouth and eyes as she felt the dense weight of a man on her.

She wasted no time recalling what Wyatt had taught her, and she prepared to fight. With all her force, she jabbed her elbow into the guard, hoping the shot landed somewhere useful. There was a grunt and a brief delay as she rolled over and away, buying her time to reach for her weapon. Before she could get it, however, he went for his and Quinn's eyed widened, knowing she had only a moment before she met her demise.

She drew back her leg and kicked him as hard as she could, exhaling with the effort, surprising even herself at how hard it hit, knocking his weapon from his hand. Unable to reach her energy weapon, she wasted no time getting her brass knuckles on. She considered going for the cojones, until she remembered the Jay she'd fought at the Linden home, who'd worn protection. Instead, she landed the punch in his face, forcing him back down to the ground again.

The punch wasn't enough, though, and he came for her and bear hugged her, strong arms trapping her. She thrashed about, sweat mixing with dust and saliva as she tasted gritty mud, and threw her head back until it collided with his face, a hard crack and his grunt telling her she'd lucked out. She reached behind her and began scratching at his face, searching for purchase until she found it, her fingers digging into something soft, then digging some more until he cried out in pain.

She pulled away, hoping she could break loose from his grip. When she did, she pulled out her weapon, bumbling and nearly dropping it as he lunged at her. Never looking at his face, not wanting to see the damage she'd done, she pulled the trigger and aimed it at his legs. Down he went, a flurry of dust rising as he hit the ground. Quinn took off running.

She ran west, her tunnel vision seeing only the path ahead. She finally turned to look behind her. She spotted another guard scaling the fence. She ran harder, headed for the hills.

Sweat poured from her, her gait and pace hindered by her fake hips and boobs, the latter misshapen and maladjusted like some twisted child's doll. She wheezed and her throat burned as she inhaled more dust, sweat coating every inch of her. She tripped over a rock, causing her to stumble and almost fall. Her leg throbbed, and it felt like the wound was spreading, tearing open further as she ran.

Then a crack sounded in the night air. A rifle. A round whizzed past her, way too close. The guard had chosen a traditional firearm rather than an energy weapon. Which meant she had a good lead on him. But she was also an easy target out here with nothing to hide behind.

Quinn began darting back and forth in a random zigzag pattern, making herself a more challenging target for the gunman. Another tip from Wyatt.

Forty more yards. Then shelter.

Another round whizzed past her as she zigged right, ducking down as far as she could, sucking in air as fast as her lungs could process it. Then something hit her, knocking her flat on her face until she ate dust again. A moment later, a bullet pierced her arm. He'd shot her, twice.

Move!

She rolled sideways just as another round hit the ground where she'd fallen. Part of her thought about playing dead, but she tossed that idea out right away, as any assassin worth his weight would keep loading his target with rounds until he felt sure she was dead meat. There was only one solution. Keep going.

Somehow, Quinn managed to scramble to her feet and she began to sprint with the desperation of someone who had nothing to lose. She kept zigzagging, knowing it was only a matter of time until he got her again, and thankful for the fact that he carried only a semi-automatic weapon and not a full auto.

Two more shots whizzed past her, one ricocheting off a nearby rock. She finally reached the hill and ran behind it, enshrouding her in darkness. She stopped to catch her breath. Safe for the moment, she realized she was hyperventilating, dizziness turning everything too bright. She forced herself to slow her breathing and take a deep breath, and she coughed from all the dust and the raspy dryness of her throat.

Deep breaths, Quinn.

She staggered, the pain of her wounds making themselves known in her leg and arm. How long would it be until she collapsed? She didn't know, and didn't have the luxury of waiting to find out. She had no choice but to keep to the hills, running until she couldn't.

Quinn continued west. It would take her farther and farther away from the dune buggy, but it was her best option in case the guard pursued. Out here, he was less likely to find her, and she would see him coming if he approached. She could survive long enough to buy herself time to assess her options.

If she didn't bleed to death first.

After limping west for what seemed like forever, she finally stopped to rest, the pain in her leg and arm screaming at her. She sat down, took off her jacket, and took stock of her situation.

Her leg was gashed from calf to ankle, oozing and coated in dust, probably getting more infected by the moment. Her arm bled, but the round had only sliced through some muscle tissue. She searched elsewhere, patting herself everywhere, knowing there was another wound somewhere, the one that had knocked her down.

She looked for something to stem the bleeding in her arm, and had only one option. She unzipped her pants, yanking them down to her knees but no further, not wanting to pull the fabric from her leg wound. She undid her fake hips and pulled them off, and she tore at the fabric and padding. And that's when she saw it. A chunk of the padding was missing. The guard had shot her in the fake hip. That's what had sent her to the ground.

Quinn tied off her arm wound, then took another look around as she held her breath and listened closely. Nothing. Not yet.

She left all her padding there and continued west-southwest, estimating her distance as best she could in order to eventually circle around and wind up back at her buggy. She just hoped it was still there and not staked out by her enemies, that she'd parked far enough away. But the more time that passed, the more likely the remaining guard would call for backup. She needed to get to that buggy and get the hell back to the city.

As she limped in the darkness, only the crescent moon to guide her, she thought of Jones. She missed him more than anything right now, his strength and know-how, but also just having him there, beside her. Out there in the desert, shot up and pursued by a deadly crew, she felt alone. Before, alone felt okay, even preferable, as it meant not getting into complicated entanglements, not endangering others. Now, it felt like shit.

She shook off that thought, telling herself it was better this way. That if she didn't make it out of this alive, nobody got hurt. Sure, they might shed a tear at her funeral, but they'd go on with their lives. They wouldn't suffer like she had when her mom died, or when she lost Wyatt.

Then, in her pained and exhausted stupor, she saw the truth.

That was why she didn't get close to people. She'd always thought that being a mindjacker made relationships difficult, that her job prevented her from settling down. But it was the other way around. She used the job as an excuse to avoid the pain and loss that came with forming attachments.

She trudged on, adrenaline wearing off and more pain setting in. And thirst, too. Intense thirst, with no water for miles. She tried to process everything that had happened—her lost job, what she found at Olmos's place—but her mind kept wandering to more pressing thoughts. That she longed for water, for salty chips and a salt-rimmed glass filled with a premium diablo... for her friends.

Keep moving. Stay alive. Then find that buggy and scram.

A while later, upon approaching yet another hill, Quinn realized she was lost. She had no service in the open desert... only people with money could afford that. Which meant only one choice: climb one of the hills to get oriented. Even if it meant exposing herself.

Quinn staggered her way up a hill, her leg throbbing the whole way. The higher she got, the more exposed she felt, like a bullet would find its way into her real hip at any moment. She began to slip on the steep hill, the soil eroded from its lack of plant life. She sank to her knees as she got close to the top, then peeked her head over the summit.

There it was, El Diablo in the distance, its lights illuminating the sky with a dull glow. Then she spotted the road ahead, where it curved to the west. She knew where she was.

Suddenly, she saw something else in the distance. Movement. A human, walking at a brisk pace.

Quinn cursed. The guard, tracking her footprints. Because the desert decided that would be the day it would produce no wind to erase them.

She had two options. She could retrace her tracks back toward him and ambush him, hoping her wounded self and her energy weapon could win. Or, she could circumvent him, get to the buggy, and drive away. In her weakened state, she had to avoid confrontation, if possible. It could work, if she hurried.

She climbed down quickly and limped her way in the direction of the buggy, increasing her pace and using the stars to keep her on track. After what seemed like forever, she still hadn't found it. Then, finally, she saw something glimmering in the moonlight.

The buggy.

After taking a good look around, she jumped in, started it up, and took off as fast as she could.

She sped though the dirt, kicking up a pile of dust, taking the corners like Wyatt had taught her, skidding but staying on course. Then she heard it again. A loud crack. Then another. But no whizzing. She had too much lead on him now.

Quinn drove like a madwoman, headed to town. She couldn't return to the place where she'd rented the buggy. They might look for her there, or even be waiting for her. No, she would have to drive as close as she could to the city and ditch the buggy.

Finally, she arrived at the warehouse district on the outskirts of town, miles from the underground and the buggy rental joint. She drove as close to the city as she could before she pulled over on a quiet street, not wanting to get busted by a cop for driving a buggy within city limits. The last thing she needed right now was the cops questioning her.

As she parked, she realized she needed to call Yolanda, to

warn her not to send another set of agents after Hector Olmos, to avoid the power players completely until Quinn could produce the evidence she'd gathered.

The evidence. Halstead's purse, filled with goodies, including Quinn's phone that was loaded with pictures. Quinn patted herself, then looked around the buggy.

A shroud of dread descended upon her.

It was gone.

CHAPTER 32

Quinn stood at the front desk of the Midtown medical clinic she'd stumbled to, waiting as the sleek-haired woman with the bright pink fingernails checked her computer.

"Our records show that your insurance is no longer valid," the woman said, her tone almost disapproving. "As of today."

Quinn cursed. God damn the Protectorate. "Well, as you can see..." Quinn pointed at her shoulder wound, then lifted her shredded leg. "I need treatment."

The woman's lip curled ever so slightly, as if her shiny Midtown clinic had never seen such carnage. "You'll have to pay out of pocket. We'll need a deposit right now, in the amount of—"

"Look at me!" Quinn snapped. "Do I look like I have cash on me right now, lady?"

She pursed her lips. "There's no need to raise your voice. It isn't my fault you let your insurance lapse."

Quinn stared at her, wanting to grab the woman's sleek hair and yank it as hard as she could. Just to wipe that sneering, judgmental look off her face. Instead, she took a deep breath and leaned forward. "You can't refuse treatment because I can't pay up front. I need treatment, and I'm going to stand here until you get off your ass and get me a fucking doctor."

The woman let out an angry sigh. "Fine. Have a seat and someone will call you."

Fortunately, it was a slow night in Midtown, so Quinn got in quickly and got patched up. They gave her just enough painkillers to get her through the next twenty-four hours, probably assuming that someone who looked like her would abuse them or resell them underground.

After they released her, she cleaned herself up in the bathroom, scrubbing the dirt from her face and teeth. She kept her pants rolled up to avoid dirtying her bandaged leg, and cleaned off her jacket and put it on again.

Inside one of the stalls, Quinn sat down and heaved a giant sigh. She was grateful for her meds. For being alive. But she cursed herself for the lost evidence.

She'd had it when she scaled the wall at Olmos's house. She'd had it when she dropped to the other side and some of the contents had fallen out. She'd stuffed them back inside... and that's when the guard attacked her. In her desperation to get away, she'd left it behind.

How could she have made such an error? She'd risked her ass, gambled it all on that night—and almost died—for nothing.

Quinn shook her head. It felt like the night the Borelli job blew up in her face, when she'd also ruined her favorite red dress, found out Noah was jacker police, and went home to find she'd been robbed. Except worse.

And whatever nagging feeling she'd had about pursuing this, what she'd found was even worse. The unholy alliance between the city's powers and the Black Jays put their entire city in jeopardy, ensuring that important resources, resources that were limited in their post-drought world, would never be distributed in an equitable way. Ensuring that her city would become an even darker place than she'd ever known, a place run by tyrants. She didn't know if the Jays had manipulated the CEOs or if the

CEOs had helped form the Jay crew from the start. She didn't know what their endgame was.

But then again, she did. Because the goal was always the same with these kinds of people: power, and more power.

Then Quinn remembered the names on Olmos's screen. Hers, Jones's, Perry's. She couldn't prove it, but she'd bet all her weaponry that everything that had happened since the Linden job had been a trap, designed to bring down the Protectorate. The CEOs seeking out the Protectorate, their intense mind invasion training, even Quinn and Jones being miraculously absent in the memories of the Jay they caught and delivered to the EDPD. Even the CEOs' memories—the encounters with the Jays—were probably planted, not real. That's why they'd seemed so suspect. It wasn't that the Jays hadn't been able to isolate the CEOs in order to steal their memories; they'd used the Jay threat to lure the Protectorate right into their lair. And they would succeed if Quinn didn't do something.

But what?

Who would believe her? Without hard evidence, and thanks to Quinn's "collaborating" with the police, the Protectorate wouldn't trust a word she said. Even if they did, the Protectorate wouldn't get far without that evidence. And she couldn't go to Noah and the EDPD with this; it would expose the Protectorate. Quinn couldn't allow that to happen.

She would call Yolanda. Tell her what she could. Which meant she needed a phone. And there was only one place to find one at that hour.

An hour later, Quinn hid in a Downtown alley, burner in hand. She tried to call Yolanda again. She'd tried earlier and gotten no answer. Not surprising that late at night, especially when Quinn was calling from an unfamiliar phone. She'd then sent a text with her emergency code, hoping Yolanda would call her back. But she hadn't.

This time, there was no ring. Quinn took a look at the phone, hoping the damned thing hadn't already crapped out on her. But the screen showed no service. The towers were down again.

She cursed. Every moment that slipped by, Olmos and his crooked band of mind thieves could cover their tracks. And if the Protectorate had sent Jones and Perry out to Olmos's place, they would walk into a den of rattlesnakes. She had no choice; she would have to risk going to headquarters, and pound on the damned door until they let her in. She took off north again.

About halfway there, she rounded the corner... and came face to face with Noah, a determined look on his face.

Her heart sank. The last person she needed to deal with right now.

"I've been looking for you," he began, frowning at her bandaged leg and disheveled appearance.

"This isn't a good time," she said, trying to pass him.

He blocked her. "It never is."

"I'm serious, Noah," Quinn said, growing agitated. "I have to go."

"You need to come with me. Right now." He reached for her arm.

She yanked it away and tried to leave again, but he blocked her. "Let me go, damn it!"

"Not this time. We've got a lot to talk about."

Her temper flared. "I don't owe you shit, sergeant! I've already given you plenty of information, and it's cost me everything, you asshole!"

His eyes narrowed. "What do you mean?"

She wanted to tell him. But she couldn't risk it.

"I don't have time to explain. I've got a bad situation I need to take care of—"

"So let me help."

She shook her head, ignoring the look of genuine concern on Noah's face. She tried again to leave, only to have him grab her injured arm. Pain stabbed at her, surpassing the effect of the drugs that were already wearing off. Quinn winced and Noah let go.

"Quinn, listen to me. I know what happened at Hector Olmos's house. The whole department knows. And I know you were involved. Plus, there's something important you need to know. So either come with me, or I'll arrest you and interrogate you at the station."

Quinn's agitation grew, and she felt the walls close in on her. There was no way out this time. But she couldn't let Noah take her in. Even if she avoided charges and getting dimed by half the police department, by the time Noah got what he wanted it would be too late. She couldn't let that happen.

She took a deep breath and looked up at Noah. "I apologize, Noah."

"For what?" he said, his expression making it clear he hadn't expected that.

"For this." She punched him right between the legs.

Noah let out a surprised grunt before he doubled over in pain. Quinn bolted, running as fast as she could.

Many blocks later, breathless and her leg throbbing and beginning to ooze, she tried to call Yolanda again. Still no service.

She let herself catch her breath, trying to block out the memory of Noah doubling over, his cry of pain. But it played on repeat, making her feel even worse. She did what she had to do, but she hated doing it. She hated hurting him.

She ran until she arrived at the entrance to headquarters. She entered the code, but it remained locked. They'd already blocked her access too. So she pounded on the door. She waited, looking around, hoping Noah or some other enemy didn't appear. Eventually someone had to let her in, right?

She pounded some more, as hard as she could. Several minutes and two sore fists later, Quinn stopped trying. An empty feeling passed over her. Yolanda wouldn't return her call. And now the Protectorate wouldn't acknowledge her.

Quinn checked her phone again. Service! She dialed Yolanda's number, and it went to straight to voicemail.

"Yolanda, it's Quinn. It's a trap! Say away from Olmos and all the CEOs—"

Upon hearing a strange sound, Quinn pulled the phone from her ear and checked the display.

Call failed.

There'd been a brief moment of service, just enough to let a call through, but no more. Quinn knew from experience that Yolanda might see another missed call, but would never get that message.

"Damn it," Quinn cried, desperation mounting. She was tempted to throw her phone onto the asphalt and smash it under her boot.

Leave. It's too risky here.

She had only one option left. It was a terrible one, but it was her only chance. She would go home. Not to rest or hide, but to wait. Wait for the Protectorate to respond... or for the enemy to find her.

Either way, she would be ready.

In the darkness, Quinn slipped into the alley behind her building. She entered through the rear door and began climbing the stairs in the stifling heat. Her injured leg disliked the effort, and the rest of her exhausted body didn't find it especially pleasant either. But when she arrived at her floor and opened the door, she saw something she hadn't expected.

Merritt. Fiddling with the security console on her door.

Quinn, eager to seize her first good opportunity in what felt like ages, sprinted toward Merritt and grabbed her, immediately locking one arm around her neck and the other around her arms.

"Funny seeing you again," she sneered at Merritt as the redhead tried to wriggle free, to no avail. "I got you, girl."

Quinn went to enter her security code and drag Merritt into the privacy of her place, where she could take the next step. She knew releasing one arm freed Merritt from waging what would be a powerful attack.

"What's going on?"

Quinn craned her head around. Devin emerged from the elevator, a concerned look on his face. Suddenly, Quinn felt a sharp pain in her injured leg, enough to cause her to loosen her grip on Merritt. Merritt broke free and sprinted down the hall.

Quinn began to give chase, stumbling due to the intense pain in her leg. She got back up and sped after Merritt, following her into the stairwell. But she'd lost too much time. By the time she got inside, she heard a door slam. Merritt had already escaped to some unknown floor, and Quinn had no way of catching up.

She cursed as she left the stairwell. Yet another missed opportunity.

"What the hell's going on?" Devin said, his eyes searching her dirty, injured body and her torn-up clothing.

"She was trying to get into my place. I think you were right about her."

He stared at her for a moment. "I knew it. You okay? What happened to you?"

"It's a long story. I just... I need a shower and sleep." She waited for argument, but Devin gave none.

He nodded. "I understand."

She entered her security code and her door opened. She turned to say goodbye to Devin and tell him she'd call him soon. But next thing she knew, he'd shoved her inside and followed her, slamming the door shut. Quinn blinked in surprise, wondering if Merritt had returned and Devin was trying to protect her. But when he looked at her, something curdled in her stomach.

His expression had changed. Gone was the concern, the protectiveness. Now, his eyes glittered with something dark and dangerous as they stared at her. They seemed to swim with malice.

"Well, Quinn. Looks like I finally got you alone."

CHAPTER 33

QUINN STOOD THERE, staring into Devin's almost-black eyes, too many thoughts settling into place.

It was him. Her tormentor. And here she was, alone with him, with no one to help her.

No Protectorate, who still knew nothing of the truth about the Jays.

No Jones, with his muscle, his wits, and his dogged determination.

No Noah, who she'd punched in the nuts and escaped from not even an hour ago.

Nobody.

She was alone. And it was the worst fucking feeling in the world.

As Devin's gaze pierced her, as if contemplating all the ways he would hurt her now that he had unfettered opportunity to do so, she thought about asking him why. Why such hatred for her, for merely having the audacity to want to survive that night at the Lindens' home? For striking against an enemy she didn't expect, who'd attacked her first?

But she remained silent. There was little point in conversing with someone of his kind. Instead, she began planning her defense.

Devin approached her with that same deadly gaze, and she realized something else. He was no longer limping.

It happened fast. She went for her weapon, ready to cook Devin from skull to feet. But before she could even think to aim, Devin's left hand swung around and swatted hers, knocking it out of her hand and sending it flying until it landed with a clatter.

He came for her, his right fist quickly soaring toward her. She instinctively blocked it, turning her body to absorb the second punch she saw coming almost before he executed it. The blow slammed into her ribs and she let out a grunt as pain spread through her, but it bought her time to shove her palm upward into his nose, then plant her foot as she aimed at his knee with the other, putting her entire body into the move. Her boot jammed into the joint, forcing it in the wrong direction, hopefully tearing the fascia into shreds. If executed correctly, the move could hobble him and give her a distinct advantage in what would still be a fight to the death.

But Devin's knee proved impervious to the assault, too strong to fold under the force. A grimace of fury on his face, he grabbed her and took her to the floor. She hit the tile with a hard thud, hard enough to knock the wind right out of her. Nevertheless, she went on autopilot and elbowed Devin in the ribs twice, then reared her head back, hoping to smash his face into oblivion.

Devin was prepared for both assaults and compensated, and the attacks did little more than stall him before he got her in his grasp again. She began to scream, as loud as she could. It felt strange, and went against every instinct. Anytime she'd fought like this, she'd been on the job, where the goal had always been to avoid attracting attention.

Now, she prayed for attention. That someone, anyone, would hear her screams and call someone.

But her high-pitched wails didn't last long before Devin silenced her by covering her mouth with his arm. Her screams muffled now, his legs attempted to entrap hers and force her into submission. She quit shouting and bit him in the arm, sinking her teeth so far into flesh that she tasted warm, tangy blood and ropey muscle. When tooth met bone, she pulled her head back, ignoring Devin's hiss of pain and taking a chunk of flesh with her that she spit out.

Burning pain exploded through her face when Devin's fist met her cheek, then her nose. She tasted more blood in her mouth, hers this time.

She managed to free one hand and reached back with it, hoping to find purchase in a nostril or eye or any orifice she could, determined to tear it permanently from his face. She grabbed something—she wasn't sure what—and pulled with all her might as Devin let out another hiss of pain.

He was like a snake. Silent, hissing, poisonous.

Quinn kept at it, knowing that if Devin wanted the carnage to stop, he would have to release part of his hold on her in order to grab her arm. He did, grabbing her free hand with his punching arm, breaking one of her fingers with a snap that made her scream with pain and rage.

And with every punch, every broken finger, every thing he did to her, her rage grew and began to radiate out like black asphalt on a 130-degree afternoon. Then, she only wanted one thing—to end Devin, to tear him apart from limb to limb until he never exhaled again.

Quinn capitalized on her moment of freedom and she shifted her weight and rolled away, then reared her leg back and smashed her boot right into his face. Before he had much time to react, she threw herself against his upper body, pinning him down momentarily. Then she grabbed his head, lifted it, and smashed it onto the tile.

There was a dull, sickening thump as Devin's skull met with the unforgiving tile. Blood seeped out from behind his head.

Then again, another thump.

His face screwed up in pain, but his eyes still glimmered with hate as he lay there in a daze.

She grabbed his head again, her only thought to keep pounding until those eyes saw no more. Then she could sedate him—

The sedative. In her pocket!

She began rooting through pockets until she found the injector. She grabbed it, but when she pulled it out of her pocket, it slipped out of her hands, which were covered in Devin's blood. The injector slid across the tile and Quinn scrambled for it. Then she was suddenly knocked backward onto the floor.

Devin had punched her. For a moment, she saw nothing but dark spots. She still brought up her legs and kicked, hoping to keeping him away from her until her vision cleared. She reached for her last hope, her knucks.

But the spots remained. And it was then that the fatigue overwhelmed her. She'd been up all night, fighting with the enemy, getting shot and fried, running for her life. It was all she seemed to do in life... fight, run, fight some more.

Everything slowed down, like she moved underwater. Everything seemed harder, more labored, her lungs crying for oxygen and her muscles burning and shaking.

You're not done yet, girl. One more round and you got this motherfucker.

Then Devin was coming at her again. She readied herself with her brass-knuckled fist, adjusting her body as she prepared to launch forward and left-hook him right in the jawbone. She made her move, landing the punch on his cheek as he shifted just enough, causing him to grunt loudly. But his jaw remained intact.

Next move. Build on that momentum and strike again.

She did, lobbing another blow. But her arm felt like it weighed a hundred pounds and he easily dodged the punch as the spots in her eyes got darker. Fatigue overcame her, until she couldn't even lift her brass-knuckled hand or gain her full balance, like someone had drained the rest of her energy. Then her eyes began to blur a little.

Devin suddenly ceased his assault and drew back, giving Quinn just a moment of relief and recovery. And that's when she saw it. Her injector in his hand.

The blur grew denser, and then everything faded to nothing.

CHAPTER 34

The pain was gone.

Her leg didn't hurt. Her shoulder didn't hurt, nor did her face or finger. Fatigue still haunted her, but she had no need for energy in this carefree place, where she rested in her comfortable bed with the air conditioning on a comfortable setting. She was finally safe.

But she couldn't see anything. It was dark, except for one corner of her vision, where she saw the desert outside of El Diablo. It was a sunny day, and she spotted shrubs with silvery leaves, plants with green spines that were three feet long, and cacti as tall as trees towering over everything, their arm-like branches waving hello to her. A spiny iguana with blue streaks scuttled past, and she smiled at the creature. It was the desert of her early childhood, before the worst of the drought. The iguana turned to her, running her way, almost in desperation to get to her. Then he disappeared.

The desert scene faded, and the sun turned to black sky, day into night, and the plants withered to dust. Suddenly she felt cold, and a strange darkness seemed to descend upon her, almost like a shroud of death, a vile force that sent fear to her most protected places.

She wanted to cry out, to shout it away, but she had no voice. When she tried to move, she found she couldn't. She was stuck there, wherever *there* was.

But there was someone with her, someone she couldn't see or hear. But she could feel him.

Dark, evil, unseen.

Devin.

He'd mindjacked her.

Quinn let her mind go blank, preserving her thoughts and mind, still out of his reach. She focused on the darkness instead.

"What's wrong, Quinn? Not happy to see me?"

She looked around in the darkness. No sign of Devin, or anyone. But it was his voice. What the hell was this?

Then she saw it. The jay. A bird perched on a thin post, big and black and shiny, red eyes staring right at her. He was there, but not there. On the outskirts of her mind, blocked by her training.

She spoke, finding that her voice did work after all. "Why are you doing this?"

"You know why," the bird said.

"Tell me."

"I just want to be close to you, Quinn. It's all I've ever wanted."

"Fuck you."

He tsked. "That's no way to treat a guest."

"So which one was it, Devin? Of the two men I fried that night at Linden's place, which one made your heart go pitter-patter?"

Silence as the bird's eyes locked onto hers with a sinister gaze.

"The one you killed first. He was my brother."

His brother.

Quinn recalled that awful night, two men on the floor, dead by her hand. Elliot Carlson, whose father they'd pursued down the wrong path, and the other one. The one she'd fought, smaller and skilled and dark-eyed. Like Devin.

The bird went on. "That was his first real assignment, one that should've been simple and straightforward."

Quinn said nothing. He sounded tired now. Like the memory of his loss had drained the fury right out of him.

"He was a good kid. He wanted no part in the kind of danger you and I live by, but I brought him in because I couldn't stand to watch him toil away in some greasy, hot restaurant Downtown, working six days a week to barely get by."

Quinn recalled Pablo's words to her and Jones, that the man in the second image wasn't "a player." Devin's brother was a newbie.

"If you want someone to blame," Quinn said, "blame yourself."

The bird flapped its wings, and a cold wind blew past her, making her shiver.

"It's not his fault," he hissed, fury returned once more. "I sent him on a straightforward snatch-and-grab, a job run by two low-level Protectorate agents who were forbidden to use weapons. Who were taught to use force only when necessary, and even then only to hobble the enemy. Who *supposedly* live by some garbage holier-than-thou, piece-of-shit 'code' that I learned is as fucking empty and devoid of life as you're going to be soon. You stupid Protectorate fucks are so full of shit, just trying to grab power like everybody else, trying to get the biggest slice of an ever-shrinking pie."

They'd underestimated her and Jones. Everyone had. Little did the Jays know that Quinn and Jones weren't your average thrill-seeking agents. It seemed everyone had been surprised by them that night. Including Noah—

Don't think about Noah. Don't give him anything.

"You can try and block me all you want, Quinn. But I will get the information I came for. Just like you used to. That's what we mindjackers do, right?"

"You're no mindjacker. You're a goddamned mind thief. A hack."

"And here I am, hacking into you right now!"

"How do you even know what happened that night?" she argued. "You weren't there! You don't even know what happened—"

The wings flapped again as the bird squawked loudly. "I know exactly what happened. I was nearby, to look after my brother, just in case. I got the distress signal and got there as soon as I could, but it was too late. They wore micro-cameras, Quinn. I saw it all. You killed them both! You killed my brother."

And you killed Gary Linden and his wife.

Suddenly, Quinn felt the darkness descend, the cold black fear. He was getting closer.

Multiplication tables. Two times two is four. Two times three is six. Two times four is eight...

Quinn kept going, occupying her mind, making her memories and thoughts less accessible. She wouldn't let him steal Protectorate secrets, find weaknesses in the Protectorate's armor. She wouldn't let him thieve her mind, what made her *her.*

The bird flapped its wings once more. Then, its red eyes shut, leaving only blackness, until the bird disappeared. Devin appeared in its place. He stood there in all black, the mark of the jay on his wrist, injuries healed and the blood gone from his face.

He offered a grim smile. "Guess who?"

No. No!

"Yes, Quinn. I'm going to drain your mind of every fucking memory you've ever stored in that blonde little head of yours. Then I'm going to hurt you. I'm going to hurt you every way imaginable, then I'm going to kill you and take your dead corpse with its empty brain and dump it at Jacker Cop Central, where your handsome little fuck buddy Sergeant Martinez will find you."

Fear shot through Quinn's body, and she felt like she could no longer breathe.

Three times three is nine. Three times four is twelve.

He stepped closer to her. "When that's done, we will take every thought, every memory, every secret you have and do what this devil town needs more than anything. We're going to bring order."

And with that, Devin swung his fist and hit her square in the jaw, knocking her flat on her back. When she opened her eyes, she was no longer in that dark place. She was somewhere else.

An alleyway, between two concrete buildings. It had an over-flowing dumpster on one side, surrounded by broken bottles and rotting food covered in maggots. Suddenly, it felt hot, like El Diablo record-hot, and it hit her like a blast from an oven turned to its hottest setting.

Then, a cat. A black and white cat nearby. Quinn's heart leaped and she followed it. Then she halted, remembering herself again. There were no more outdoor cats and hadn't been in ages. She had a strange feeling, like a nagging in her belly... like something was wrong.

It was a trap.

She turned around, and there they were. Three familiar boys, covered in tattoos, leering at her and blocking her path to leave the alley. They stepped closer, smelling of sweat and smoke. Fear pulsed through her like rounds from a military weapon, one after the next, thunk thunk thunk.

She tried to leave. She tried to fight. She tried it all. But it was no good. They were so strong, and there were too many of them, one sweaty hand grabbing her arm, his fingers callused. Another hand at the zipper of her shorts, tugging at it. And yet another pressed over her mouth, silencing her.

Terror flooded her and she forgot everything but survival, everything but scratching and screaming and fighting to get away.

And then the one nearest her was no longer the shaven-headed thug. He was Devin.

CHAPTER 35

QUINN SCREAMED until her throat ached. But her screams were dampened, almost like someone held a pillow over her mouth. She screamed and screamed as she felt her clothing being stripped from her and panic overtaking her.

This was it. She was going to live her biggest fear, the one that had haunted her since she was fifteen, and then she was going to have her mind drained. Then she was going to die... and lose everything that mattered to her.

The city she loved. The mission for justice she loved. And, most of all, the people she loved: her dad. Jones. Daria.

Noah.

No. She couldn't let it happen!

She fought some more, thrashing and punching and kicking and screaming. But no matter what she did or how hard she fought, she felt herself losing not only the battle against Devin, but also losing a battle against herself.

And then, a tiny seed of recognition hit her, a wisp of light and truth.

The mind is nothing but neurons conducting electrical impulses. It's your slave, not your master.

At this level, it's about control over your own mind.

You can choose to stop fighting, if you want to.

She heard the words in her mind, like a distant memory. They were Remi's words, from her training at headquarters.

You can stop fighting. You can stop succumbing to fear. You can fight this... by not fighting it. By not giving it your emotions and attention.

This time, it wasn't Remi's voice. It was hers.

Trust yourself. Trust the strength of your own mind. You've endured so much. You can handle this, Quinn Hartley. You can handle anything.

Quinn stopped fighting. Stopped screaming.

Stopped struggling.

A moment of fear, of terror, of the dark unknown. And then... Devin was gone. The boys were gone. The alley was gone. It was just her and the desert again. The green desert plants, a few clouds, the smell of a fresh afternoon thunderstorm...

A real rainstorm! It was magical, the fragrance of damp sage and clean air, a coolness washing over her as the sun peeked out again to dry everything off. The blue-streaked iguana came out again, running up to her and climbing up her leg until she reached down and picked it up, holding it close to her.

Then Merritt appeared, red-haired and grinning, looking not the least bit threatening. She came up to Quinn so she could pet the iguana. Quinn cooed to the animal for a moment before she handed him off to Merritt, who held him like a treasured companion.

Daria appeared after that, smiling and at ease, like it was another one of her good days. She wore a nurse's uniform and chewed on a red licorice rope. Jones appeared and smiled at her, and it was as if his hard edge had softened, like he'd relaxed for the first time in years.

They faded off, and then Quinn saw her father. His hair had no gray and his face fewer lines, and he sipped a soda while he kept his arm slung around the shoulders of a woman. Her mother. Her mom smiled and brushed Quinn's hair back and kissed her on the cheek.

Finally, in the distance, she saw Noah. He stood aside in slacks, a t-shirt, and a ball cap, looking at her like he wanted to talk to her but was unsure if he should. She went over and threw her arms around his middle. He pulled her close to him.

Then... it was his skin on hers, his familiar, masculine smell permeating her nose as her hand lightly stroked his back. They were in his bedroom, sprawled on his bed, woven together, laughing and drinking one another in, talking and solving the world's problems. It was like she'd finally found the peace she'd always sought but could never quite get, not with Wyatt or the Protectorate or her apartment on Hillcrest Avenue in Midtown. It was everything that could make her forget all that was wrong in the world.

Thoughts coalesced, like puzzle pieces finally coming together to help her see the truth. Noah cared about her. He'd cared about her when she'd assumed she was nothing but a fun time to him, when she'd believed he could do better, when she was briefly convinced he'd been using her to nail mindjackers. It was why he'd let her go that night at the Lindens'. Why he hadn't arrested her since that night. Why he kept tracking her, inquiring about Carlson.

He wanted to see her safe.

He'd shown darker behaviors. Leaning on her, threatening her with prison. But she could hardly pass judgment. Not when she'd insisted on assuming the worst about him, despite ample evidence he wasn't that sort of man... when she'd insisted on pushing him away when he'd wanted to help. Like she did with everyone.

Soon, the idyllic scene disappeared like the rest, fading away along with the desert light. Dusk encroached, only a strip of orangey light along the horizon remaining. She followed it.

She'd found her way out. She'd found an island of calm in the cyclone of her invaded mind, a shield against the forces that tried to use her own mind against her, to end her.

But while she was safe in the cocoon of her mind, out in the material world Devin still had her under his control. She'd avoided drowning in the mental siege Devin had thrown at her, blocked him from accessing her memories, but she'd only bought herself time. Eventually, he would find his way in, and then her thoughts and memories would be his for the taking. Not to mention what he might do to her physical form.

She studied that strip of orange on the horizon as it faded to apricot, then blue. And that's when she saw it. The bird. The black bird. But its eyes weren't red now. They were black. It watched her, then flapped its wings, hovering in the air for a moment before swooping toward her, then past her.

She turned and watched it, and the bird hovered once more, again eyeing her. A light appeared nearby, a soft, shimmering light, almost like... water. The bird headed toward it.

Quinn followed, approaching what appeared to be a small lake. The bird hovered over it and looked at her one last time, before taking a nosedive into the lake and disappearing. Quinn stood there a moment, pulled by the image of the water. She stepped into it... and submerged herself completely.

She was underwater. But somehow, she could breathe, and see. There were images. Some flitting here and there, others lingering, strange odd feelings washing over her like a soft breeze on a desert night. The images weren't entirely clear, but she could make out figures.

Figures dressed in black, their faces uncovered and right there for her to see. Five males, one female with red hair like Merritt's... but not Merritt's face. Flashes and scenes...

Them meeting with the CEOs.

Them jacking someone in a tailored suit, then another.

Then a train whizzing past in the background, the red letter A on it, noise in the streets and the stench of exhaust, like they were Downtown. A flash of fine bedding and a white fluffy rug, two sleeping bodies on the bed and two familiar dead men on the rug. Gary Linden's place.

These were Devin's memories.

Then a man in a navy suit, middle-aged and distinguished-looking, with kind brown eyes but posture that demonstrated power. Devin accosted him, and the man didn't stand a chance. Quinn stared at the face, seeing something familiar about it, like she knew him. Yet, she was good with faces and would remember if he was an acquaintance or a former target. Then, when the brown eyes flashed with anger, she gasped.

He looked like Noah. It was Noah's father.

A flash of the jacking as Noah's father lay slumbering, the redheaded Jay taking a three-inch sleek black device and slotting it into her pocket.

Then a new scene, a beautiful home, brick and large and grand, with a privacy fence. Inside it, wood floors and crown moldings and the smell of plants, like there were lots of them, and then a room with cabinets lining the wall from floor to ceiling, black and businesslike.

Finally, a hand, a male hand, opening one of the cabinets. He held up the sleek black device; its label read *Angel Martinez* along with the date. The hand placed the device carefully behind several identical devices, the shut the cabinet.

The data. The Jays kept the data they stole! It was stored in some Uptown home!

The images began to fade.

All of a sudden, the darkness seemed to suck her in, and she sank into its depths. Fear consumed her and she felt evil all around her.

Quinn fought it, focusing with all her mental power on conjuring up images of those she cared about most. Dad, Jones, Daria, Noah, various memories offering her shelter from the storm. But no matter how hard she tried, the evil force attacked her with all its might. Then, one of the images vanished. Then another.

Devin. He'd found his way in. And he was wiping her memories, the ones he'd already downloaded into another sleek black device.

One that would be labeled *Quinn Hartley.*

CHAPTER 36

Noise. Violent noise.

Cursing, grunting, then a loud bang, like a large object had collided with the floor.

Her eyes fluttered open. Two men were fighting near a toppled desk. One was covered in tattoos, including his shaven head, his considerable size giving him some advantage over the smaller but skilled one with the dark hair and intense scowl. They lunged and clawed at one another, neither getting the upper fist over the other, crashing into things and laying waste to what was once a decent Midtown apartment. Both had blood streaming from their faces, and veins popped in their necks as they fought.

It was a death match, and a terrifying one. She had no idea who the men were or why she was here. Or why they didn't seem to notice her.

Another loud bang made her jump. She tried to sit up, but found she couldn't. She was too tired, and everything hurt. Someone had thrown open the door, sending it slamming into the wall. A third man walked in, handsome and dark-eyed, a gun in his hand. He moved like someone who was used to breaking through doors and wielding firearms.

Like a cop.

What the hell was going on? Who were these people? And why did she feel like she should get up and join the maelstrom? But she couldn't. She couldn't move at all. An awful feeling shot through her, one she somehow understood at a gut level.

Fear.

The two fighting men kept at it, oblivious to the third.

"Hammond! Get out of the way!" the cop shouted.

The tattooed thug, Hammond, upon finally noticing the cop and the gun pointing at them, ceased his attack. But the smaller one, face torn up and haggard, ignored everything and went for Hammond again, clobbering him in the cheek with a fist. There was a popping sound, then another, and the smaller fighter stumbled backward.

"Don't shoot him!" Hammond shouted.

But it was too late. The smaller fighter flagged as blood began spilling from his shoulder and arm. But, relentless, he came for Hammond yet again. Hammond right-hooked him hard, knocking him back again, then got him into a chokehold while the cop cuffed him. They sat him down on the floor and leaned him against the wall.

"You'll fucking regret this," he seethed at his oppressors. "I know who you are."

She finally got a good look at the sitting man. She didn't know him, but there was something about his face—his eyes—that sent a bolt of terror through her. Before long, Hammond reached for something in his pocket and stuck it into the angry guy's arm. He tried to dodge the injection, face contorted in half fury, half pain. Then, he turned and looked right at her, eyes glittering with hate.

"This isn't over," he said, before his eyes closed and his head slumped to the side.

Next thing she knew, tattooed Hammond stood facing the

cop, a weapon in his hand. Not a gun. Something shiny. Danger-ous. Each aimed his weapon at the other.

"You have no fucken right to be here, man," Hammond growled, oblivious to the blood on his face or his own heavy breathing.

"Look, Hammond—" the cop began, his tone level.

"Get the fuck out. This ain't your business. And don't bother with them threats I know you're good at, 'cause that shit won't work with me. I got a superior weapon here, and we both know it."

The cop's jaw clenched, and he looked torn between wanting to shoot Hammond and wanting to reason with him.

She watched the two men maintain their standoff, each unwilling to yield to the other. What the hell was happening? None of it made sense, but somehow felt like it should. Famil-iarity tickled at the back of her mind, but nothing coalesced.

She only felt lost.

The fatigue overwhelmed her suddenly. Everything began to fade, growing blurry and dim, shrinking until it was only a tiny pinprick surrounded by darkness.

Then the darkness took over.

Her eyes opened. She was still so tired.

She was in a bed, in a Midtown apartment. This was familiar. She'd seen this before.

Then she saw the two men again. The cop and the tattooed one... Hammond? Yes, Hammond. He didn't look like a Hammond. He sat at a desk, his back toward her, hunched over a computer. The other, the cop, sat on the floor nearby, fidgeting restlessly with his gun. She didn't see the third one, the angry one they'd put to sleep.

"Did you find anything?" the cop said, sounding impatient.

"Not yet. I told you not to shoot him, man. You can't get data on a fucken dead guy."

"You can't get data if he's kicking the shit out of you, either," the cop argued.

"I had it under control until you came around, waving your gun like some fucken hero."

"Didn't look like it to me."

Hammond ignored him, focusing on the computer. He resumed typing away on the keyboard.

"So this is it, huh?" the cop said. "This is what you guys do for money, go fishing in people's minds for information that doesn't belong to you, then analyze their private selves on a computer like you're calculating census data?"

"I ain't gonna get shit if you don't stop talkin'."

She tried to speak then, but all that came out was a rasp.

The cop turned and looked at her. He'd heard it.

His eyes widened and he stood up quickly. "She's awake."

Hammond turned around, eyes trained on her. She didn't like how they looked at her. Like something was wrong. Like she looked no better than she felt. He stood up.

When the cop approached the bed, a series of conflicting emotions ran through her. Part of her wanted to trust him, believed she could. But another part of her rebelled at that. Trusting him could be a mistake. Trusting anyone could be a mistake.

With her hand, she felt for a pocket. Something told her it would contain something useful. Like a weapon. But her pocket was empty.

She tried to sit up, and found that she had the strength to. The cop drew closer, dark eyes studying her, filled with things she didn't understand.

Then, she saw him. On the floor. The angry guy who'd given

her that menacing look. He lay there, blood on his smashed-up face, unmoving and pale. Like he was dead.

Fear overwhelmed her, and before she knew it she was out of bed and on its other side. Away from all of them.

"It's okay, Quinn," the cop said in a soothing tone. "Everything's okay."

No, it wasn't. She didn't know what the fuck was happening. There was a dead guy on the floor, someone who scared her. Now they all scared her. They might do to her what they'd done to that guy.

"Stay away from me," she growled at them, her voice hoarse and her throat dry.

The cop turned to the tattooed guy. "What's wrong with her?" he cried.

"I'm trying to find out. Just... grab her."

The cop didn't move. "No fucking way. Last time I did that she racked me."

Hammond approached now, reaching into his pocket. For a weapon.

Soon, the two men loomed over her, Hammond getting closer. Fear coursed through her like poison, shooting adrenaline through her veins as she poised to fight. She knew she couldn't beat them, but she wouldn't go down easy.

Once Hammond reached for her, she took aim. But he blocked the punch, and it was only a matter of a moment before the two men had her pinned on the bed and something stuffed into her mouth to muffle her screams.

She felt a sharp pinch in her arm, and soon she struggled no more.

CHAPTER 37

A VOICE. A male voice. Definitely a Downtownie, talking but receiving no answers.

"I don't know, man. I ain't ever had to restore memories before." Pause. "Dunno. Only time'll tell." Pause. "Yeah, I'll be here." Pause. "Alright, see ya."

The phone. Someone was talking on the phone.

Quinn opened her eyes.

It was dark. Everything was dark. But then she noticed light coming from the window, the glow of city lights. She was on her bed, in her apartment. She sat up, trying to figure out how she got here.

In the soft light from the window, she spotted a man in cargoes and a tank top lying on a portable cot.

"Jones."

Jones started, then sat straight up. He stared at her for a moment. "Hey, girl." He stood up and turned on a lamp. "You know where you are?"

"My apartment. In Midtown."

He nodded, looking hopeful. But suddenly she felt scared. Like so much had happened... and she couldn't recall any of it.

"What's going on?" she cried.

Jones sat on the corner of her bed. "It's alright. You're safe. You've been mindjacked."

"What happened?"

"You remember anything?"

Quinn ran through her thoughts. "No," she replied, a fresh wave of fear gripping her.

"What's the last thing you remember?"

As if on cue, flashes ran through her mind. "Yolanda and the spec ops guys taking my equipment. Arguing with Noah and..." She grimaced. "Punching him in the nuts because he wouldn't let me go. I had something important to do..." She paused, trying to sort through too many thoughts. "I got away. Then I was at headquarters. I knocked and knocked and those assholes wouldn't open the goddamned door." More thoughts came at her in random order. Olmos's house. Getting fired. Fighting in the desert. Running, escaping...

"You remember callin' Yolanda?"

The burner. The messages. "Yeah, but I couldn't get through. The service was out again." Jones nodded eagerly, as if he liked what he heard. "But I don't remember why I was calling her."

"To tell her what you found. At Olmos's house in the desert."

Olmos. More images came. Olmos on the floor, out cold. Others, familiar faces. Hatch, Halstead, the mayor...

"It's so jumbled," she said, worry returning. "That's not like me."

Jones shook his head. "Don't be worryin' now. After what you been through, be glad you remember anything. You remember the important stuff, and I suspect some more'll come back to you later."

Quinn nodded, calming a little. At that moment, for the first time in her life, she understood the cops' desire to nail mindjackers as well as the harsh punishments for those who got pinched. They wanted to prevent anyone from feeling like she did at that moment, or worse.

She also understood Noah's hatred of mindjackers now. His anger at her.

"Tell me what happened," she said. "Every detail."

Jones told her everything. The aborted Olmos job. Her getting fired. Her going rogue and heading back to Olmos's place with black market equipment. Finding out Olmos and Halstead and the rest were collaborating with the Jays. Her narrow escape, her calls to Yolanda. Running into Noah, heading home. Some of the memories she already had, others resurfaced when Jones mentioned them.

"Wait," she said. "How do you know all this? You weren't there."

"I got some of it from right there." He pointed at her head. "The rest I got from Yolanda and—"

Quinn closed her eyes, remembering more. "Fuck. Please tell me Yolanda doesn't know about this. I already violated their rules by removing my tracking device and going back to Olmos's. If she knows everything else, I'll have an enemy for life, especially since I lost the evidence..."

Jones shook his head. "She ain't your enemy, Quinn. She called after you tried callin' her. Guess one of them messages got through, or part of one anyway, 'cause she said you warned her about some trap. She didn't know what you meant—the line cut— but she had me and Perry goin' after Olmos and she pulled us, told us to go to the safe house. And from what I saw in that head of yours, thank the fucken devil she did. That woulda been a disaster of huge proportions."

Quinn nodded, trying to process it all. "But... how did we wind up here?"

Jones let out a sigh, eyeing her. "You weren't returnin' my calls. I knew you were up to no good, so after Yolanda called I headed here to find you myself." He paused. "And that's when shit got interesting."

Quinn waited, knowing in this case interesting wasn't a good thing.

"I broke into your place, and found some guy jackin' you. You were both beat to hell, like you'd given him a good fight."

Devin.

Fragments of their fight returned, making her shudder. Jones continued, telling her about his brawl with Devin, then Noah showing up.

"When that cop walked in the door, I thought... fuck. I'm done, goin' to the clink. I figured you'd pissed him off so much he decided to raid your place for evidence, and would find plenty of it. Well, shit got off to a rough start... he shot the guy who was jackin' you, the guy who I figured had some answers, you know? Anyway, he finally said some shit that made me listen. He knew you were in trouble and he knew you were bein' stalked, and he figured out that the stalker was your neighbor. Turns out the fucker's a Black Jay. Had a tattoo and everything."

She nodded. Devin always wore a watch to cover his tattoo, faked that limp... and she didn't see it. A cold wave ran through Quinn at remembering him, at all of it. The black butterfly. The notes in Noah's writing, copied from when he'd stolen her original art. The messages. His befriending her. And his strange intensity that had never seemed quite right. He'd been her tormentor the whole time, waiting to make his move until his odds of success were maximized.

"Did he rape me?"

Jones hesitated. "No."

"Don't lie. I need to know the truth, no matter how bad."

"He didn't. I don't know if he didn't get the chance, or maybe he just threatened it to scare you. Fucker knew which button to push."

An uncomfortable silence ensued. Jones had seen things. Too much. Again, she understood what victims of mind thieves must feel like.

Finally, Quinn said, "Where's Devin now?"

"Dead. Beyond that, dunno. Noah took care of it." He shook his head. "That little fucker could fight."

"Tell me about it." She sighed. "So Noah shot him, which means you got no data. After all that."

"I got some before we lost him. I had to go in myself, and put Noah in charge of pullin' me out..." He shook his head. "I tell you what, I got a whole new respect for you. The Devin guy had training, and that was some messed-up shit I had to deal with in there. Good thing is, after takin' a beating from you and then me, then gettin' shot, his defenses were down. Didn't have much time to look at what I got from him before you woke up that first time."

"First time?"

"Yeah. You didn't remember any of us. I spent all yesterday and last night restoring the memories Devin thieved from you."

Quinn stared at Jones. "Restoring the memories? You can do that?"

He shrugged. "Guess so."

Quinn sat there in disbelief. She'd downloaded memories, wiped memories... but to take them and then give them back? It was unheard of. And Jones had not only decided to try it, he had managed to make it work. And then acted like it was nothing.

That was Jones. He looked like a big dumb thug, but he was turning out to be the smartest person she knew.

"Anyway," he went on, "after that—"

Before he could even finish his sentence, Quinn went over and threw her arms around Jones. She was so overwhelmed by all of it, but at that moment all she could think about was the hundred reasons she had to be grateful for Jones. He'd saved her life again. He'd gone out of his way for her... again.

Jones hesitated for a moment, unprepared for the assault, but then put his arms around her. Quinn blinked a couple of tears away as she pulled back.

"I'm sorry, Jones."

"For what?"

"For not trusting you. For not letting you help me. I just... I've learned to rely only on myself. It's a hard habit to break."

"Trust don't come easy to people like us. I'd be the same way if I didn't have my family. They remind me of what's important." He paused. "But it ain't me you should be apologizin' to."

"What do you mean?"

"That cop boyfriend of yours has a bruised set of nuts, thanks to you. Turns out he was tryin' to help you too."

Quinn closed her eyes as that memory resurfaced, shame spreading through her. Then she thought of another question. "There's one thing I don't understand. You said Noah figured out Devin had been stalking me. How is that possible?"

"That's between you and him." He eyed her. "And by the way, I told you so."

"Told me what?"

"He's still into you."

A strange feeling seeped through her. For once, she didn't feel the need to argue with Jones. She didn't recall when, or how, but somehow she came to see the truth about how Noah felt about her... and how she felt about him.

Jones spoke again. "Now that we've gone over the whole thing, you remember anything else now? Like what happened when you linked with Devin?"

A tiny light seemed to go on in some dark recess of her mind. "Only fragments. At best. I saw faces... and Devin was talking to me." She lit up. "The guy I fought at Linden's place... he was Devin's little brother, on his first job."

"Explains why he was after you. And Pablo said that guy wasn't a player."

"Oh, and I think Devin killed the Lindens." Then, another memory. "I saw Noah's father."

"What's he got to do with anything?"

"He was jacked once, by mind thieves. Ruined his career. And—" Quinn concentrated as hard as she could, her mind reaching for something like a hand reached for curtains, waiting to yank them open and see the world outside. But she couldn't get there, and slapped her bed with both hands. "God damn it! It was something important, but I can't remember!"

"It's alright. We got enough."

Quinn shook her head in frustration. She was glad to have her memory restored, but it drove her nuts knowing that key pieces of a puzzle were missing, especially when that puzzle had so much riding on it.

Before Quinn could say anything more, she heard beeping. There was a click, and she realized someone was opening her door. Quinn looked around frantically for a weapon, hoping Jones had one on him.

When the door opened, Quinn stared.

It was Noah.

CHAPTER 38

NOAH'S EYES landed on Quinn immediately, and her stomach swirled with a perplexing mixture of nervousness and relief. He wore slacks with a light jacket, under which Quinn knew was a holster with weapons. He was on duty. Noah glanced at Jones and offered a brief nod before shutting the door.

Jones took his cue and left Quinn's bedside. The two men exchanged a longer look, and Jones nodded at him, as if to say she was in better shape than last time Noah had seen her.

"I'll be next door," Jones said.

Once Jones closed the door, she turned back to Noah. He sat down in the chair Jones had occupied, pulling it just a little closer to her. Now, she didn't see a jacker cop or the man she'd fought with for weeks. She only saw the man she'd fallen ass over cactus for and never quite recovered... and who'd helped protect her.

"Hi." She hoped she didn't look too terrible, after everything.

"How are you?" Noah asked, brown eyes watching her closely, briefly scanning the rest of her, as if to ensure she was okay.

"Tired."

"I guess a few knock-down drag-outs and a mindjacking from

an angry psychopath will take it out of you. Not to mention assaulting an officer of the law." He smiled a little.

But Quinn didn't laugh. "I'm so sorry, Noah. For hurting you like that. I—"

"It's alright. I know now what was at stake that night."

"How did you know? About Devin? About all of it?"

"It's what I do, Quinn. It's called police work."

She shook her head. "Tell me the truth."

Noah took a deep breath, then leaned forward and rested his elbows on his knees. "I've seen some bad stuff in my time, but that night at Linden's place... something about that seemed really off, the same way Tony Borelli's death and those violent jackings were off. These weren't your everyday mindfuckers. Anyway, between you tracking Carlson and the information you fed me— including what you wouldn't say—I knew you were being hunted, in addition to facing some enemy organization. And when I saw you at the ballgame, with..." He motioned with his head toward the floor, where Devin had probably been. "Call it cop's sense, but I knew there was something wrong with that guy the moment I laid eyes on him. So I watched you guys, waited for him to throw out his drink cup, and scraped it for DNA. I ran it and didn't get any matches, so I let it go. But once I started to see the big picture, I ran it against the samples we took from those stiffs at Linden's and found a sibling match. Then I knew what kind of trouble you were in."

He paused, a wrinkle forming between his brows. "I went looking for him, but couldn't find him. Then we got the alert from Hector Olmos's place. I suspected you were involved, and talking to you only confirmed it."

"How'd you wind up here?"

"You wouldn't listen, so I needed to find someone who would."

"Jones."

He shook his head. "Too risky."

Quinn frowned, trying to figure out who else Noah could get key information from. Then, her jaw dropped. "You leaned on my dad?"

"Didn't have to. He gave it up pretty easily."

She shook her head. "That's impossible. My dad doesn't trust anybody. Especially not cops."

"I made a convincing case."

She arched an eyebrow. "I'm sure you did."

Noah chuckled at that. But then the brow wrinkle returned, worse this time. "I saw those images, Quinn. The ones he sent you. You should have said something."

"I know."

He looked surprised at that. "You're agreeing with me? Jesus, you are in bad shape."

Quinn reached over and slapped his knee, and Noah laughed.

"Look, Quinn. I know I can be pushy. But the more I know—about what you saw, what happened—the more I can put the department's resources behind nailing these assholes to the wall—"

"I saw your father."

He stared at her, eyes hardening. "What?"

"I saw him, when Devin jacked me. Which means Devin was one of the mind thieves who attacked your dad. And it makes sense, given that they seem to be targeting powerful people—"

Noah blinked a couple of times. "What do you remember?"

"Not much. Just them attacking him and jacking in."

He stood up and began pacing, pain on his face. "How'd you know it was him?"

Quinn hesitated. "I... he looked like you." She paused, realizing how dumb that sounded.

Noah dug out his phone and tapped a few times, then showed her an image.

She nodded. "That's who I saw."

"What else do you remember?" he said, sitting down again. "Think hard."

She tried, but still recalled nothing. "I'm sorry. My memories from the jacking are spotty, especially that part."

Noah muttered a curse and closed his eyes for a moment.

"I'm sorry, Noah."

He shook his head. He sat there for some time, deep in thought. Finally, "We've got traction now. Thanks to you. And Jones."

"We're not the enemy, Noah. We never were."

"I know that now."

Quinn grabbed his hand, and it felt warm and strong in hers. "I'm sorry. That I hurt you."

He smiled a little. "Which time?"

Quinn gave a rueful smile back. "And I'm sorry I didn't trust you—"

He shook his head. "Don't apologize. I acted like an asshole, leaning on you like that, trying to... to..."

"To win."

He gave a bitter laugh. "We were doomed from the start, weren't we?"

She squeezed his hand. "Maybe. Or maybe we're perfect for each other."

It was out of her mouth before she could stop it, before her mind could even consider what she'd said, and its ramifications. Noah's eyes darted back to hers, surprise and a whole host of other emotions roiling in them. She suddenly felt exposed, and almost wished she could hide under her blanket. But she didn't. She couldn't hide from the truth anymore.

But when Noah looked down, another crease between his

brows, she knew. He didn't feel the same, and the realization made her gut clench.

"Look, Quinn..."

She gave his hand one last squeeze and let go. "It's okay. You don't owe me anything. What you did here is enough."

Noah gave a faint nod, like he wanted to say more but didn't have the words. He glanced at his watch. "I'm sorry, but I have to go. Okay if I send Jones back up?"

She nodded, suddenly feeling dead tired.

After Noah left, Quinn closed her eyes and fell right to sleep.

A couple days later, when she heard the knock at her door, Quinn smiled, taking a quick glance in the mirror. She looked even worse, her face bruised from her recent battles. But as grisly as she looked, she felt better. And at least her place was cleaned up.

When she opened the door, Daria stood there in a striped sundress, her smile growing as Quinn's did too. Next to her stood Jones, his tats covered by a jacket and a hat on his head. Quinn let them inside and hugged them both. Daria then studied Quinn's face, her happy smile giving way to anxious disapproval.

"Look at you," she said. "Abrasions, second-degree contusions..."

"Look who's a nurse now," Quinn joked, glad she wore pants to cover her leg wound.

Daria shook her head. "I can't believe I associate with you people and your illegal activities. Hammond wouldn't tell me what happened." She glanced at him, patting him on the chest. "It's probably better that way."

Quinn glanced at Jones, who only smiled, then back at Daria. And that's when she noticed Daria's necklace. It was obviously genuine gold, a chain with an elegant heart pendant hanging from it, a small topaz along one side. Daria's birthstone.

"Where did you get this?" Quinn gushed, touching it with her finger. "It's gorgeous." But before Daria even answered, she knew.

"Hammond gave it to me." She smiled up at him. "A little extravagant, I think, but he insisted on thanking me for helping him."

Quinn nodded. She felt so happy for them, and glad that her advice to Jones had started to pay dividends. But she also felt a little sad, knowing that the only gift she would receive from Noah in the future was a stay-out-of-jail card.

Daria frowned again. "And don't change the subject, Miss Thug Face."

Quinn shrugged. "You know how it is with bruises. They always look worse than what caused them," she said, continuing her and Jones's unspoken agreement that they would spare Daria the details that would only scare her.

Quinn got them cold water and they sat down.

"Good news!" Daria said. "Guess who got admitted to the Solera Clinic?"

Quinn's eyes widened. "Really?" She glanced at Jones. "They admitted Jeffrey? That's fantastic!"

"I never thought it would happen," Jones said. He glanced at Daria. "But this girl... she got a way with people."

"That she does," Quinn said. "But you know what this means, right, Mr. I Don't Wanna Change? Time to pack up and move to Sunnyside."

Jones heaved a sigh. "Don't remind me."

Daria patted him again. "The move will do you good. You can't live in White Sands, not with all those shootings. And it's Sunnyside, not Midtown."

Before Quinn could reply, her burner phone rang. She froze for a moment, having learned to dread the phone. She grabbed it off her bed.

Yolanda.

CHAPTER 39

When Quinn arrived at headquarters, she hesitated, memories of the night she'd been locked out returning vividly. She pressed a button. Soon, she heard the latch release and the door opened for her. Relief washed over her like a cool shower on a hot day.

Yolanda waited in a gray printed dress, her dark hair blown out straight and shiny. Quinn took a seat.

"Well, if it isn't my most rebellious agent," Yolanda said coolly. "Former agent, that is."

Quinn pressed her lips together but said nothing. She sensed that, for once, she should be cautious with her words.

"You have quite a bit of explaining to do," Yolanda said.

Quinn nodded. She knew Yolanda would have questions, and she knew the answers to those questions would determine her fate.

"Why did you neglect to tell the Protectorate about this Black Jay who threatened you personally?" Yolanda began.

"At first, I thought it was Noah... I mean Sergeant Martinez."

"You knew telling us would mean revealing not only that you'd had relations with an EDPD jacker unit officer but also that he'd identified you as a mindjacker."

"Yes."

"And you preferred to deceive us in order to protect yourself, rather than share crucial information that could have manifold impacts on this organization."

Quinn cringed. This wasn't going well. "I preferred to keep a job I loved and needed, knowing that I had as much dirt on Sergeant Martinez as he had on me, if not more."

"Did you know Sergeant Martinez was jacker police when you were involved with him?"

Quinn shook her head. "No. I knew he was into something different, but so was I... and it seemed like... we were a good match." She looked down for a moment. "You know how lonely life can be in our line of work. When I discovered the truth, I ended things. But then he showed up at the Lindens' that night—"

"So he ID'd Jones too."

"No. Jones was disguised, and Noah didn't know him like he knew me. And he let us go."

Yolanda sat back, crossing her legs and eyeing Quinn before she finally spoke again. "We gave you a place here. We trained you, promoted you, gave you the premium jobs. To say the least, being lied to felt like a betrayal of all we've done for you. Jones made a very strong case for my reinstating you, but I don't know if I want to. I can't trust you, because you don't trust us."

Quinn closed her eyes for a moment. "I know."

"You know?"

"Yes. I don't trust anyone. And it almost cost me my life." Quinn sighed. "Look, Yolanda. I have no doubt I'm the most problematic of your agents. Or was. I know I'm a pain in the ass. I take risks, I do questionable shit... but I do it because I believe in what we do and why we do it. And I'm willing to risk my ass—risk everything—to do it. I proved that at Linden's place and I proved it again at Olmos's. And both times something good came out of it." Quinn took a deep breath. "And Noah... he could have arrested me, then and anytime after, but he didn't. And he won't. He won't because I know him. His father was jacked once, his career damaged by mind thieves... by *Devin himself.* Noah cares about nailing bad guys more than anything, and now he's found his enemy. It's not us—"

"Not yet."

Quinn shook her head. "I'm telling you, this guy cares about justice more than anyone I know. And he's smart. If you guys want to win this war, find a way to work with him—"

Yolanda stared at her like she was nuts. "You want to work with the police."

"Why not?" Quinn cried. "It's not just us breaking the law to jack crooked people for cash and a side of do-gooding anymore. There's a terrifying enemy out there and they're in bed with the powers that run this city. They've killed one of ours and almost killed me, and God only knows what they have planned. And 'we' don't have to work with the police. I," she pointed at herself, "can work with Noah, if you're willing to give me another chance. I know how to deal with him. And keeping it tied off and isolated like that... if it goes malignant, it's easy to cut it out before it infects the system."

Yolanda watched her, pondering. "You've broken rules. Iron-clad rules. You've broken trust."

"I know, but—"

"There is no *but,*" Yolanda said sharply. "Yes, your rule-bending paid off this time, but what about next time? We have rules for a reason, and they apply to all."

Quinn wanted to say more, but decided to keep quiet.

Yolanda stood up, signaling the end of their meeting. "I will talk to the others, and we will consider what you've said."

Quinn, surprised and relieved, stood up as well. "Thank you." After an awkward pause, Quinn turned to leave.

"And Quinn?"

She turned back around.

"You're correct. You were my most difficult agent, by a fair margin. But you were also my best."

Quinn smiled, then left.

"Well, look who decided to pay her old man a visit."

Joe Hartley gave Quinn a hard look before he opened a can of cheap soda and reclined his chair.

"Why the cheap soda?" she said, feeling indignant. "After I bought you the good stuff?"

"I ran out." He took a big swig. "I've been worried as shit about you, after you comin' here and givin' me all your secrets and your money."

"It was necessary." She sat down on the couch, glaring at him. "And did I not tell you that if anyone came looking for you because of me, don't tell them *anything*?"

He shrugged.

"Dad!" she cried. "Why would you give it up, and to the cops of all people? What happened to the Joe Hartley I know, who would never fold to police manipulation?"

"You're alive, aren't ya?"

"That's not the point."

"Then what is?" he griped. "The fucken guy said you were in danger—"

"Dad! You're a Downtownie! Since when do you believe what people tell you? Since when do you trust cops? Yes, it worked out this time. But what if it wouldn't have?"

He slammed his soda down and leaned toward her, finger pointed. "You listen to me, girl. Who do you think you're talking to? You think I'm just some old Downtownie who deals sand and watches baseball? 'Cause I learned a thing or two in my day. Yeah, he was a cop. He said so. He told me you were in danger and it didn't take much convincin', what with you over here in that ridiculous getup, givin' me the 'if something happens to me' speech and handin' me all your valuables. He told me what he wanted and why he wanted it... and I knew right away that boy woulda given up his badge if it meant savin' you from whatever shit you got yourself into."

Quinn went silent for a moment, her indignation fading away. "Loud and clear, Dad. Glad you're still a Downtownie."

"You're the one who moved, not me."

She grabbed a soda and opened it, the low-quality beverage bringing back pleasant memories. "Midtown sucks. And it's not safer. Not for me, anyway."

He nodded, looking slightly pleased, then sat back and put his feet up. "Looks like you picked a good one for a change."

"What do you mean?"

"The cop."

Quinn hesitated, fiddling with a stray fiber from the couch cushion. "Turns out I did pick a good one. He didn't, though."

Her dad scowled. "How do you figure?"

"He can do better."

He looked back at the game, turning up the volume. "Doubt that."

Quinn sat there for a moment, then went over and threw her arms around her dad. "I love you, Dad."

He cleared his throat as he patted her on the back. "Love you too," he said quietly.

Quinn sat back down and they watched the baseball game. It wasn't the Demons—they were out of the playoffs. When it was time for commercials, there was an ad for beer that featured a talking iguana. He looked a lot like Lucifer.

Lucifer. Where was Lucifer?

She stood up. "Dad, I have to go. I just remembered something."

Before he could even respond, she was gone.

When she arrived at Devin's apartment, it took her a while to break in. The place was nearly empty, with only a foldable mattress, a few clothing items, and a lamp. The place stank like animal smells, and not in a good way. There were small dark lumps on the floor from Lucifer. She looked around frantically, spotting a terrarium in the corner and running over to it. It was empty.

"Lucifer?" she called out.

Nothing.

Fear descended upon her. At best, he was in the hands of another Jay. At worst, he was hidden in some corner, dead from neglect. And that thought made her want to cry.

But then she heard it. Swishing, then the sound of reptilian feet padding on the tile. A head appeared from the bathroom, and when Lucifer saw her he scurried over and climbed up her leg.

Quinn grabbed him and pulled him into her arms, tears coming to her eyes. "There you are! I'm so glad to see you!" Lucifer clung to her, his tail whipping a little but then calming down as she petted him and cooed reassuring things.

"What's going on?" said a voice.

Quinn froze and turned around. Merritt stood there, her face in a frown as she looked around the bare apartment.

"Merritt. Hi," Quinn said awkwardly. "Devin... hasn't been around. I had a bad feeling, so I let myself in. And poor Lucifer was in here all alone."

"How'd you get in?"

Shit.

"I... I tried the lazy person's code and it worked," she lied.

"You mean one-two-three-four-five-six?"

"That's the one." She paused, more memories returning. "Merritt, I'm so sorry I attacked you like that—"

Merritt shook her head. "You thought I was trying to break into your place. It must've looked suspicious." She looked at the floor for a moment. "I was just there to say hello, to see if you wanted to get a drink... and I got curious about your fancy security system..." She smiled sheepishly. "You know me, always curious..."

Quinn smiled. Merritt was a little eccentric, but in the end she was nothing more than a lonely woman, a Downtownie lost in Midtown and looking for a friend. And a convenient tool for Devin to draw suspicion away from himself. "It's okay. I overreacted. It's my Downtown roots."

Merritt looked around the room. "This makes sense. I always suspected Devin was into something illegal, and seeing his place only confirms it." She paused. "Maybe he's dead," she added matter-of-factly.

"Huh. Maybe you're right."

Merritt approached her, eyeing Quinn's face for a moment, noticing her healing injuries before she focused on petting Lucifer. "It smells like he's been here for days without any care. You poor guy, abandoned by that weirdo. But you're a tough one, aren't you? You're made of tough desert stock, able to go without attention or water for a while, aren't you?"

Quinn, seeing the look in Merritt's eyes, handed Lucifer over so she could hold him. He took to her and nestled into her neck. She went over to his bowl, picked it up, and filled it with water, then brought it to his mouth so he could drink.

"I love animals," Merritt said. "They're nicer than people."

"Agreed."

"Especially in Midtown."

"Also true." She paused. "What do you say we go get that drink sometime? My treat. For the assault." She smiled.

Merritt's face lit up. "Tonight?"

"Tonight isn't good, but I can go the day after tomorrow." Then she had another idea. "Lucifer will need a new home. Can you afford to care for him?"

Merritt's eyes grew wide. "Can we do that? Shouldn't we ask someone?"

"Who?" When Merritt appeared to contemplate that, Quinn added, "I won't tell if you don't."

Merritt grinned. "Deal."

They left Devin's apartment after clearing out Lucifer's terrarium and supplies. Quinn returned to her place and took stock of her things. It was time to relocate, to somewhere safer. She laughed at the absurdity of that. How long had she dreamed of moving to Midtown, into this very building, hoping for a better, safer life? She'd gotten neither.

If she'd learned anything, it was that safety and happiness, at least the kind she sought, couldn't be found in an apartment or a neighborhood.

And with that thought, she began to pack.

Hours later, everything ready to be transported to storage, Quinn picked up her phone to call a truck. She was stopped by a news alert.

"Man dead, identified as member of underground mind-jacking organization known as the Black Jays."

Quinn got on her computer to investigate. When she found the announcement, it had an image of Devin's face along with another image featuring the tattoo, the blackbird with red eyes. So that's what Noah did with the body. Turned it in, told his fellow cops what he knew. And the EDPD was showing its hand now, essentially waging war on the Jays.

Quinn jumped when she heard a knock at her door.

She frowned. Was it Merritt, coming to visit? Or someone else with less friendly intentions? She tiptoed to the door and looked through the peephole.

It was Noah.

Surprise flooded her. After everything that happened, and after her unreturned gesture, she hadn't expected to hear from him for a while, if ever. She opened the door.

Noah stood there in slacks and a jacket, like he was coming from work. It pained her to see how handsome he was, to see those intelligent eyes. He must have something important to tell her, and he had no way to contact her now that her old phone was gone.

She wanted to make a quip about him stalking her, but something in Noah's eyes told her not to.

"Hey," she said, stepping aside to let him in.

Noah entered and she shut the door behind him.

"I just saw the news alert," she said. "I assume that's why you're here..."

He shook his head. Quinn watched him, his gaze glimmering with something unsaid, something that sent a tingle through her.

Noah grabbed her and kissed her.

CHAPTER 40

QUINN LAY on her bare bed, the air conditioning cooling her perspiration as she fought off sleepiness. Noah lay next to her, fast asleep. She got up and quietly put a t-shirt on, and headed over to pour herself some chilled water.

"You don't have to leave this time," came a sleepy voice. "This is your place."

Quinn glanced back at Noah, whose eyes gleamed with humor. How she'd missed that.

"Not for long," she said.

He looked around at her packed belongings. "Where to now?"

"Where the cops can't find me." She grinned and poured a second glass of water.

"Sure about that?" he said in that confident tone of his.

She stuck her tongue out at him. "With all due respect, Sergeant Martinez, you're the least of my worries."

Noah shook his head. "We've got the department on this now, and it's top priority. It's only a matter of time until we catch those motherfuckers."

Quinn couldn't argue with that. She only hoped "we" included her, that the Protectorate would focus on the larger problem instead of its anger at her for defying the rules. When she handed Noah his glass, his smile faded.

"You aren't going to make me hunt you down again, are you?" he said.

She sat down next to him on the bed. "No."

"Where will you go?"

"Don't know yet. Depends on what I can afford. I kind of pissed some people off by working with you."

"They'll come around, if they're smart. So, are you ever going to tell me about this band of do-gooder mindjackers you work for?"

She smiled. "One thing at a time, sergeant."

Noah drank from his glass before setting it down. "That partner of yours looks out for you. He's loyal."

"I know. I don't deserve him."

He frowned. "Don't say that."

"Why not?"

Noah sat up and faced her. "You asked me once why I let you two go that night. Well, I know something about how people like you work. I know that once you get that proximity alert, you drop and go, and the only thing you protect is that data. If you'd left Jones there like the rest of them would have, you'd have been gone by the time I entered that alley. And he'd be in the clink, or dead."

Quinn nodded. It was true. But she would never have left Jones there. It wasn't who she was.

"Instead, you risked yourself to save him," Noah said. "That's why I did what I did."

She smiled. "Not because you didn't want me to go to prison?"

Noah grabbed her and pulled her down next to him. "Maybe that too."

Quinn kissed him, basking in the warmth of his skin, how good he felt.

When she heard a faint noise, she pulled away. A strange feeling nagged her.

She couldn't put her finger on it, but the noise seemed almost too quiet, too unnatural. She sat up and looked around, wondering if some creature had found its way into her apartment. Then she realized Noah was looking around too, his expression completely changed. He was in cop mode now.

He stood up quietly and put on his briefs, retrieving his gun from its holster. Quinn got up to find her own weapons, but before she could do anything, a loud explosion erupted near her door, tearing a gaping hole in it.

"Get down!" Noah shouted at her.

It all happened so fast.

A man in all black at the door. Then others. Black Jays.

Gunfire rang out like a deafening staccato. Quinn ducked behind the bed as she heard bullets pierce her mattress. She immediately went for her weapons cache and pulled out her latest and greatest. Her Udi 99, already loaded.

Devin's words echoed in her head: *This isn't over.*

We'll see about that, asshole.

Crouched down, Quinn peeked around the edge of the mattress just as a Jay found her. She was ready for him and began unloading the automatic weapon, spraying rounds into him and then the rest of them, immune to the noise and power of her weapon and how badly it rattled her hands and arms.

By the time they knew what hit them, it was too late.

She'd riddled them all with holes until her magazine was spent, and the three men fell like aluminum cans knocked over by a BB gun in the desert. Then it was silent.

She waited there, crouched down... ears ringing, arms shaking, heart pounding.

She waited for one of them to get a second wind and try his luck again, or for another to appear in her doorway. But no one moved.

Quinn stood up slowly, eyes darting all around her. Three Jays down, blood seeping from their skulls. The hallway was empty.

Then she realized. Noah. He was nowhere to be found.

Maybe he'd hidden in her bathroom. She looked around, and found him on the floor on the other side of her bed.

He lay there on his back, eyes closed, his gun still in his limp hand.

Blood ran from his chest.

Thank you for reading *Mind Thief* and for supporting my work. If you want to find out about my story and book releases, get access to special deals on good sci-fi books, and receive occasional sci-fi-related news, sign up for my email list on my homepage (cahartmanfiction.com). I only email once a month for the most part, because we're all busy people.

Looking for more dystopian sci-fi with badass women doing questionable deeds? Check out my Daughters of Anarchy series, which is all that and more.

You probably already know that book reviews and ratings are like bread and butter to authors, especially indies. As unfair as it may seem, the more ratings I have, the more people recognize my work. Which means more time to write stories for you. Even one or two lines ("I loved this book! I can't wait for the next one...") is awesome. Thanks so much!

I enjoyed writing this second installment of the Mindjacker series, BUT it wasn't easy to write. It required keeping track of a LOT of details from the first book—what happened with the Jays, how the mindjacking sequences should go, everything that happened between Quinn and Noah, including the fact that she was wrong about him a lot of the time—while trying to take all of it to the next level. It was complicated and took multiple passes to get it right.

But it was worth it. And... I like complicated.

Anyway, happy reading to you...

Christie

ALSO BY C.A. HARTMAN

Korvali Chronicles series

(Space Opera)

The Refugee

The Operative

The Forbidden Planet

The Escape (series prequel)

Daughters of Anarchy series

(Dystopian Sci-Fi Thriller)

Book 1

Book 2

Book 3

Book 4

Mindjacker series

(Dystopian Sci-Fi Thriller)

Mindjacker

Mind Thief

ABOUT THE AUTHOR

C.A. Hartman specializes in writing science fiction with badass female leads. An academic scientist gone rogue, Hartman's books have been praised for their great characters, intricate worlds, and their intriguing but understandable science.

A graduate of the University of Colorado, Hartman earned her PhD in Behavioral Genetics and worked as a scientist for 11 years. She lives in Denver with her husband, and has a special fondness for good TV, the desert, aviator sunglasses, and dark roast coffee (decaf, of course, because you DON'T want to be around her when she's caffeinated).

www.ingramcontent.com/pod-product-compliance
Lightning Source LLC
Chambersburg PA
CBHW021230250626

47155CB00008B/2945

* 9 7 8 0 9 9 8 9 4 4 5 7 9 *